W9-BJZ-197

THE WAY LIFE

SHOULD BE

ALSO BY CHRISTINA BAKER KLINE

FICTION

Sweet Water
Desire Lines

NONFICTION

*Room to Grow: Twenty-two Writers Encounter
the Pleasures and Paradoxes of Raising Young Children*

Child of Mine: Original Essays on Becoming a Mother

*The Conversation Begins:
Mothers and Daughters Talk About Living Feminism*
(coauthored with Christina Looper Baker)

THE WAY LIFE
SHOULD BE

CHRISTINA
BAKER KLINE

WILLIAM MORROW
An Imprint of HarperCollinsPublishers

This book is a work of fiction. The characters, incidents, and dialogue are drawn from the author's imagination and are not to be construed as real. Any resemblance to actual events or persons, living or dead, is entirely coincidental.

HarperCollins books may be purchased for educational, business, or sales promotional use. For information please write: Special Markets Department, HarperCollins Publishers, 10 East 53rd Street, New York, NY 10022.

FIRST EDITION

Designed by Susan Walsh

Library of Congress Cataloging-in-Publication Data has been applied for.

ISBN: 978-0-06-079891-8
ISBN-10: 0-06-079891-2

07 08 09 10 11 ID/RRD 10 9 8 7 6 5 4 3

To the memory of my own grandmothers,
Ethel Seay Baker and Christina Curtis Looper,
who knew all the secrets

Invariable repetition causes the excessive prolongation
of a settled condition: therefore, says the poet,
change is in all things sweet.

—Aristotle's *Rhetoric*, book 1, chapter 11

THE WAY LIFE

SHOULD BE

PROLOGUE

My grandmother is stirring the soup. "It's almost ready," she says without turning around. "You want some?"

It's a Thursday night and I'm in New Jersey visiting my father and stepmother and grandmother. I usually take the half-hour bus ride from New York City to Nutley every week, but I haven't been here once in the past month. I call on Sundays, but none of them is much for the telephone. My father and stepmother don't like to chat, and Nonna frets about my phone bill, no matter how many times I tell her my cell phone is free all weekend.

"Sure," I say. "What are you making?"

"*Stracciatella alla Romana,*" she says. "But this is only stock. I haven't added the rest yet."

When I was young, my father used to take the family out to dinner once a week. After my grandfather died and my mother ran off with her gynecologist—the same year, when I was nine— my grandmother moved in with us, and she scoffed at this habit. Mediocre restaurant food, she declared, was soul destroying. "In the same amount of time it takes to go to a *ristorante* I could mash nice plum tomatoes with a little garlic in some good olive oil and have a fine, simple meal. Why waste time and money on food that is no good? *Non lo gradisco.* I will not do it!"

In Nonna's kitchen, life was pared down to its simplest elements: flour, yeast in water, an egg. I loved coming home to a warm kitchen, the windows steamed from baking, the presence of a woman who didn't seem to wish she was elsewhere. I was grateful to her for taking care of us. She sewed buttons on my father's shirts; grew herbs in the yard; baked *taralli*, spicy cookies, in the afternoons. I'd stand by the stove and watch her make tiny meatballs, the size of large marbles, and plump gnocchi from scratch. As soon as I was old enough to wield a knife, I began to help her—as I'd never helped my mother, who didn't teach me anything about food, who equated cooking with indentured servitude—by chopping vegetables. "*Taglilo sottile.* Slice it thin," Nonna would say, handing me a garlic clove. "Like a fingernail."

I learned the importance of the *soffritto,* the first step in many Italian dishes, a foundation of flavor: Put olive oil or butter in the bottom of the pan and add finely chopped onion. Cook it slowly, stirring often, then add a sprinkle of fresh garlic, which will turn a pale gold. The next step, *insaporire,* or "to bestow taste," involves adding parsley, celery, carrots, possibly some ground meat. If the *soffritto* is not cooked precisely, the flavor of the dish will be compromised. The onions must be sautéed until they are translucent. The garlic must not be allowed to burn.

"You have *il regalo,*" Nonna told me one steamy August evening before I left for college. The gift. A light touch, an instinctive ability to substitute and improvise. I knew I had it—it was one of the few things I was certain I did well. Though hopeless at chemistry in the classroom, I intuitively understood the alchemy of cooking. Once I learned the basics, the *soffritto* and the *insaporire,* I was on my way.

Nonna is eighty-eight now, and she moves slowly. Yet despite all the changes of the past fifteen years—I moved to New York; my brother settled in Westchester; my mother died and my father remarried—Nonna continues to rule the kitchen. More often than not, my father goes to the store to pick up ingredients for her after she dictates a list. She stands at the counter making dinner and listening to the radio, her hands trembling as she minces the onions and the garlic. When she has finished everything she needs to do, she sits at the table staring out the kitchen window at the driveway, her hands in her lap.

"So how do you make *stracciatella*?" I ask. I know how to make it; she has told me before. But I want her to tell me again. Nonna doesn't use recipes; she cooks by feel, by touch and taste and sight. She takes out the spinach, the eggs, the pecorino romano cheese, and instructs me to add a handful, a sprinkle, *una punta piccola,* a little pinch, just enough.

In my other life, in New York City, I am Angela Russo, Italian-Irish-American, not too much of any one thing. I don't conceal my Italian heritage, but I don't make a lot of it, either. It is hidden in plain sight. But in Nonna's kitchen I am an Italian girl, just as she used to be, learning to cook from her grandmother, who knows all the secrets.

CHAPTER 1

After college I wanted to apply to culinary school, but my father, who is an accountant, objected. "Cooking isn't a real job," he said.

"Too much hard work," my stepmother chimed in. "Terrible hours. Take my advice, Angela: Get a normal job where you can leave at five. You'll thank me when you have children."

"Nonsense. Carpe diem!" my mother exclaimed long-distance, but I wasn't inclined to take her advice. When she ran off with Murray Singer, she didn't just leave my father, she abandoned my brother and me. I overheard the arguments before she left— she needed a clean break, she wasn't emotionally equipped to deal with needy children, my father had always been the better parent anyway. She and Murray moved across the country to Portland, Oregon, and I only saw her three times before, in my midtwenties, she was killed in a car accident. My brother and I flew out to the funeral, but it was hard to feel much for a woman who had written us out of her life fifteen years earlier, when we needed her most.

So after college I moved to New York City with Lindsay, my best friend from high school. We rented an apartment near the river on the Upper East Side and did temp work at consulting firms while looking for normal jobs where we could leave at five.

I cast a wide net for positions available to liberal arts majors with no discernible skills except the ability to make lists, follow directions, and look fairly presentable. As in a game of musical chairs, the music stopped at event planning, and I sat down.

For the past five years I've been planning events at the Huntsworth Museum, a modish showcase for contemporary art in lower Manhattan. While I like some things about my job—the long-term planning combined with last-minute urgencies, the immediate gratification of momentary accomplishment, the blinking red light on my phone and the jaunty sherbet pop-up Post-its in a little box on my desk—I also have to admit that it's no longer much of a challenge. For the first few years the learning curve was steep, but now my days are spent gliding across a smooth plateau of predictability. I can't erase the nagging sense that there's something else out there for me, if only I knew which direction to take.

It's midmorning and I'm sitting at my desk sipping my second cup of coffee, researching novelty circus acts online. My big project at the moment is a black-tie gala four weeks from now, a benefit for a new wing of avant-garde art featuring the works of the French artist Zoë Devereux. Mary Quince, the curator and my boss, has said only that she wants "color, pizzazz, an element of the outrageous." My idea is to stage an evening that animates figures from Zoë Devereux's paintings—circus and carnival performers, acrobats and fire-eaters and jugglers.

Mimes, jesters, clowns, you name it, apparently they're all for hire, à la carte or as a group. I print out a selection of options to discuss with Mary and start e-mailing several of the acts to see if they're available to perform on September 19. As I'm tapping out an e-mail, my glance strays to the small ad at the bottom right of the screen:

Looking for Your Love Match:
DO SOUL MATES EXIST?

My finger hesitates for a moment over the mouse, and then I click on the tiny blue typeface.

I have found that the biggest moments in life, the ones that change everything, usually catch you by surprise. You might not even recognize them as they happen. Your finger is straying over the mouse and you click on the icon and suddenly you find yourself at the portal of a website—an embarrassingly named website, one that makes you wince: kissandtell.com.

Now why would you ever be drawn to such a place? More important, why would you linger?

A few days ago, during our usual Monday morning check-in, I told Lindsay about the abysmal blind date I'd been on the Saturday night before, and then waited to hear the details of hers.

"Well," Lindsay said, "it wasn't, actually."

"Wasn't what?"

"Abysmal. Believe it or not."

Riffling through the cluttered filing cabinet of my brain, I retrieved a scrap of memory: Lindsay joined an online dating service about a month ago. An amateur photographer took her picture. The resulting image, an off-the-shoulder embarrassment in soft focus, provoked a deluge of responses, mostly from shady guys on Long Island. "Don't tell me—it's Hot4U," I joked.

Lindsay laughed uncomfortably. It was clear she regretted sharing this detail. "Actually, it is," she said. "But the name is tongue-in-cheek. You know, an ironic commentary on the whole online-dating thing."

"I see," I said dubiously.

She sighed. "This guy is so great, Ange. So cute, so nice. So smart. I don't know. This is going to sound crazy, but I think maybe I've found my soul mate."

"Are you kidding? It's—pretty soon to be talking soul mates, isn't it, Linz?"

"I know!" she said. "Aren't you happy for me?"

That night, after a dinner of four warm Krispy Kremes straight from the bag, I climbed into a sudsy bath and closed my eyes. How many people, I wondered, can actually claim to have found their soul mate, the one person in the world destiny has set aside for them? Not many, I'd bet. I'm skeptical that there is such a thing. I'm inclined to believe that the whole concept of a soul mate is like Sasquatch, the giant hairy ape-man of legend who turned out to be nothing more than a guy in a monkey suit running through a forest.

But now, sitting at my desk, I think—if Lindsay believes she's actually found her soul mate, who am I to scoff and ridicule?

When you read the Sunday wedding section—the women's sports page, as Lindsay calls it—to see how people met, you discover that it's often in the most accidental of ways, in the unlikeliest of places. At a funeral. In the park. In the back of an airplane. At the grocery store. Which makes those of us who haven't found the right one edgy. *Are you my life partner? Are you?* If I don't go to this party, or if I stay in my apartment on a sunny Saturday instead of heading over to Central Park with a picnic blanket and the *Times,* will I miss meeting the man of my dreams? You could drive yourself crazy with the what-ifs and why-nots.

After a while you start appraising fire hydrants and telephone poles—hmm, tall, sturdy, good posture, could be the one.

The other day on TV a so-called relationship expert said that it's when you aren't looking for love that you find it. But what does that mean, exactly? The truth is, even if you make a pact with yourself that you're not looking and don't care, a piece of you is always waiting for love to happen. Especially if you're a woman who might someday want to give birth to a kid or two, and you're thirty-three.

The problem with your best friend putting an idea in your head, even if it's an idea you loathe (or perhaps especially if it's an idea you loathe) is that then it's in there, gestating, like the larvae of a nasty insect that burrows under your skin.

So . . . given the myriad ways in which people can and do meet, and the frank reality that I have managed to live for more than three decades without meeting my "soul mate," perhaps I should give it a try.

And so it is that I find myself at kissandtell's buoyantly graphic home page. "Never go on a bad date again!" promises the slogan at the top, and while that strikes me as unrealistic, I find myself caught up in the madcap hopefulness of it all. Pricking up my ears for the click-click of Mary Quince's heels, I fill out the free entry form. I compile a shopping list of my requirements with the zeal of an early-bird shopper on the day of a big sale: male, between the ages of thirty-five—scratch that, twenty-nine—and forty; no kids; college educated. I specify my geographical locale as "New York region" and click "Done."

A little human icon on the screen crosses its arms and cocks its head, as if considering my request. After a moment a database of postage-stamp-size photos and screen names pops up. I scroll down the seemingly endless list, most with suggestive or boastful screen names and subtle-as-a-mallet opening lines, only the first eight words of which are visible, followed by a trail of ellipses. The screen names generally contain a vanity-license-plate combo of numbers and letters, upper- and lowercase, puns and double entendres. Look4Love, Bod4U, SINgledad. (That one's just creepy.) Though most photos are clearly intended to show off the subject's best features, the men tend to look either menacing, intense, meek, too pumped, or downright dweeby.

I click on a photo, and the profile is revealed. Chuck, thirty-four, is an actuary who knows how to have a good time. He has been burned before but remains confident that the woman of his dreams is out there. Robert, thirty-one, wants a mutually satisfying relationship with a fellow bodybuilding enthusiast from the tristate area. Colin, a thirty-nine-year-old firefighter, is looking for a red-haired beauty who is ready to start a family and would be happy living on Staten Island. It doesn't take much reading between the lines to spot the guys who live in the same house with or next door to their parents.

As I consider these options, my gaze strays from the computer screen to the bulletin board on my wall. Tacked to the gray synthetic fabric is a photo, torn from a magazine, of a weathered elfin cottage on the Maine coast. Several times a day my glance strays to this photo; the image has become totemic, as unreal a place as Middle Earth. Just looking at it soothes me, the way sound machines of waves or rain can calm your nerves. I have never been to Maine, but in my imagination life there isn't so complicated. I picture a lump of dough rising under a tea towel on a kitchen counter; pansies spilling from a window box; seagulls the size of small dogs, circling in slow motion overhead.

Impulsively—perhaps recklessly—I widen my search, inching up the East Coast. Near Boston I find fewer Italians and bankers, more Irish Catholics and lawyers. Curiously, my qualms about serial rapists and ax murderers diminish the farther north I go, as if all the miscreants and deviants in the northeastern U.S. have confined themselves to the New York area, and the rest is safe.

Moving up the coastline, the pickings get slimmer. Maybe there's a dating website specifically for Mainers, or perhaps Internet dating hasn't really caught on there yet. There is a grand total of six profiles. Most of the head shots feature guys wearing baseball hats with obscure local slogans. Then, all at once—hey! I am gazing into the ice blue eyes of a thirty-five-year-old with the screen name "MaineCatch." His opening teaser is "Sail away with me . . ." No baseball cap, a nice tan, a full head of slightly tousled blond hair, navy blue tennis shirt. I sit up straight in my desk chair and click on his picture.

". . . in the night, and all day, too," the teaser ends. As I read the profile I have to remind myself to breathe. It turns out that Rich, thirty-five, runs a sailing school in a coastal town on Mount Desert Island (*Where?* I must Google it immediately). Five eleven and 180 pounds, he has never been married, is a nonpracticing Protestant, loves Italian food and shellfish. Besides sailing, his interests include curling up with a good book, "my dog Sam (short for Samantha)," hiking, and . . . cooking.

My heart thumps.

I click a button that says "Register for free!" I can post my profile and picture, and receive and respond to inquires, but if I want to contact someone, I'll have to pay the monthly charge of $29. There's a feature called "tagging" that allows you to comment on someone's profile without joining by using one of ten canned lines they provide ("You're hot! Check me out—maybe we can start a fire together").

I fill in the blanks:

Name: Angela (no last name).

Age? Am tempted to lie, then realize that it might lead to a potentially unpleasant spurning scenario. 33.

Religion: Nonpracticing Catholic.

Profession: Event Planner.

Hometown: New York City.

Vital statistics: Hmm. Tempted to ignore or minimize, but

realize that this is risky. How is it that most people on this website describe themselves as "slim" when most Americans are overweight? I check "medium height, medium build." Then, reconsidering, change it to "slim."

Hobbies/activities: Watching old *Lifetime* movies in bed, drinking vodka tonics, going out with friends, reading the Styles section, trolling the Chelsea flea market, eating out. Going to the gym every four or five days and trotting on the treadmill for the duration of *Access Hollywood*.

My fingers hover over the keyboard.

Had I the kind of lifestyle wherein one might actually cultivate interesting hobbies, what would they be? Not that I have ever actually done it, but if I did exercise in a nongym way, I think I might enjoy hiking.

So—"Hiking."

The one time I went sailing, with friends at a time share in the Hamptons, I threw up over the side of the boat, but I'm sure I could grow to love it. I like everything except the water part. The beautiful wooden vessels, the salt-crisp nautical wear, picnics on deck with a glass of wine. The shiny, curving wood in the cabin and the rounded windows belowdecks.

"Sailing."

When I was little I wanted a dog. I begged for years, and finally got a mutt named Rusty. He didn't take well to housetraining and tended to snap, and when he was almost a year old he met an unfortunate end after ingesting rat poison left in the garage by my dad. But I have no doubt that I could grow to love someone else's adored dog, particularly a Lab named Sam.

"Dogs."

And then there's cooking. For this one I don't have to lie or fudge. I write, "Enjoys cooking Italian food and shellfish with friends, al fresco dining under a clear, star-filled sky." The lyrics of that oldies song about piña coladas and getting caught in the rain waft through my head.

So call it coincidence, call it kismet, call it what you will, but my interests dovetail quite nicely with those of MaineCatch.

Several months ago the publications director of the museum took a picture of me for the annual report. It's like a yearbook photo—stiff smile, white blouse—but it's all I've got. I fish it out of a drawer and hurry down the hall to the industrial-strength printer/scanner, scanning it through before I have time to second-guess myself. On the computer screen, I am cheered to see, I look a little better than in real life.

I finish filling out my profile and hesitate over the screen name. It should convey cool nonchalance as opposed to sluttish desperation. What would appeal to Mr. Catch? I try out a few. "Ready2Sail"? Too obvious. "NewYorkCatch"? Erk. I flash through a few possibilities—SpicyGirl, LemonLover (like my grandfather, I do love lemons, but—no)—before trying out NewYorkGirl.

NewYork . . . Girl. I think about it for a moment. It's a stretch, but anyone can see my age on the form. It's breezy. I'm going with it.

Since I am disinclined to pay for this, I scroll through the short list of generic options and fix on the one that seems most neutral: "I'm intrigued! Check me out."

I send my profile and the canned tagline to MaineCatch and get a confirmation notice from the website. I feel a flash of regret, and then a tingle of hope. It's the same feeling I had when I was ten and stuffed a message in a bottle and tossed it off a pier into the ocean. Now that I remember it, the bottle kept washing up onshore with the tide and I finally gave up—but still. My message is out there, and now all I can do is wait and see.

CHAPTER 2

Mimes and jesters, it turns out, are a dime a dozen, but a good fire-eater is hard to find. After half an hour of following leads, I am finally on the phone with one of them, a cranky, demanding guy named Frank. I'm doing my best to get him to give me some references, but he doesn't want to cooperate.

"Yeah, yeah," he says, sighing dramatically. "I've got references, but I gotta dig 'em out from god-knows-where, and frankly, right now I don't need the work that bad. Fire-eating's big these days, Cirque du Soleil or I don't know what. . . ."

"Sure, I understand," I say. "It's just that it's a formality. I can't hire you unless I talk to someone. Anyone. Your dog, even, if your dog could talk."

His laugh sounds vaguely evil. "Well, that can be arranged."

As we're talking I click idly onto kissandtell again. *Oh my God!* MaineCatch has written back. Now Frank wants to know which other carnies I've been talking to—"It's a small world, kid, believe me, and I can't stand the half of 'em"—but I can't resist peeking at what I've reeled in.

You intrigue me, too. But why is a city gal like you interested in a country boy like me?

Frank is going on and on, and it's all I can do to stop myself from hanging up on him.

"Well, you're my number one choice," I tell him. "I'm not signing anybody else until I get you."

Runs a sailing school. Lives on an island. Dog named Sam.

Maybe opposites attract, I write. And send.

"Let's talk about your fee," I say to Frank, settling down to business. The price seems exorbitant to me, even given the fact that he shoves fire down his esophagus for a living.

I click back to kissandtell. *So maybe we should find out,* Maine-Catch has written. Already! My heart pitter-pats, then thumps, like the tail of a friendly dog as you get closer to petting it. *Let's take this conversation off-road. Call me, 207-555-2814.*

I sit back in my chair, flummoxed. A number! Isn't Internet dating supposed to be anonymous, at least for a while? Doesn't this break the rules? (And isn't the guy supposed to call first?)

For advice on these and other questions, I do what any sane woman would do: I call my best friend.

"He gave you his number? He wants you to call *him*?" Lindsay repeats.

"Uh-huh."

"That seems a little—fast."

"He's from Maine. He lives on an island."

"Maybe that explains it," she says. "He clearly has no idea what he's doing. There's an etiquette to this, for God's sake!" She pauses for a moment, then says, "What are you doing hooking up with a guy from Maine, anyway?"

"Oh, he says he wants to move," I lie. "So—what should I do?"

"Just ignore him and he'll go away. Something's not right about this guy."

I hang up the phone and brood. What's so wrong with talking to him? Hearing his voice? You can tell a lot about a guy by his voice.

There's a sharp rap on my door—instantly identifiable as

Mary Quince's knuckle—and I click quickly to another screen. She pops in, all business, frameless glasses perched on her head and lavender cardigan buttoned at the throat. "Big Apple Circus," she says, click-clicking over to my desk and looking over my shoulder at the screen. "Are we having any luck?"

"Just got off the phone with a bona fide fire-eater," I report. "I'm about to call his references."

Mary looks at her watch. "We're cutting this close," she says, as if the party is minutes away. Her watch has no calendar; it's a symbolic gesture. Also, she doesn't mean "we," she means me. I've never actually missed a deadline or botched an event, but that doesn't stop Mary from obsessing. It's what she does best.

"Everything's coming together just fine," I say in my most competent voice.

The big secret of event planning is that hundreds of things always go wrong. The planner's skill comes in knowing how to minimize the problems. After you've organized half a dozen events, you realize that you don't have to invent the form each time; some things universally work, and some don't. You must send invitations by mail. Important people must feel pampered. Nobody eats crudités unless the vegetables are fancy. Speeches should never last more than seven minutes.

What truly matters can be counted on one hand: the invitation, the food, the entertainment, the drinks, and the little details people have time to dwell on—gift bags, table centerpieces. Having a theme that's carried out from the invitation through the party favors also impresses people. You learn to focus 90 percent of your attention on these things.

"You know, Angela, this event is *very* important to the identity of the museum. It's imperative that we get it absolutely right." Mary taps her pen against her teeth. "I'm thinking of sending you to Boston to meet with several of our key benefactors, the

Charles Byemores and the Langley Biddle-Smyths. I think it's not a bad idea to explain our vision for the gala, get their input. We want to make them happy."

Tapping her teeth again, she turns and heads for the door. Then she turns back and says, "When I say 'send' I mean we'll do what we can—the train, at least. Do you have an old college roommate up there you can stay with?"

I do not, in fact, have an old college roommate up there I can stay with. But this is the first time Mary Quince has proposed that I travel for work, and I'm as thrilled as a monkey would be about escaping from the zoo. "I can rustle somebody up," I say, and Mary says, "Good. Then let's make this happen. I will call the Byemores and the Biddle-Smyths to set up a meeting." She beams at me. "I am so pleased—*really*, Angela—at how this is working out. This event could be a career-maker for you, you know."

To call or not to call? While I'm ostensibly working—okay, I am working; my job is not so difficult that I can't obsess about my personal life at the same time—I am weighing pros and cons in my head.

CONS

1. Calling looks overeager, even desperate.
2. He might be a dud, a freak, or worse.
3. The whole point of this Internet thing is to get to know someone slowly and safely.
4. I've been Internet dating for less than a day! Maybe somebody better is out there. Isn't it too early to focus on one random connection when there are so many other possibilities?

PROS

1. What if this is The One? It would be a story to tell our grandchildren: "There I was, in New York City, and there your grandfather was, on the coast of Maine—and now here we are, happy as honeymooners forty years later, running an international sailing school from our cozy waterfront cottage. . . ."
2. What do I have to lose?

I pick up the phone. Clear my throat. Take a breath. Put down the phone. Pick it up again and punch in the numbers.

"Hello?" a male voice answers.

"Hello?" I say idiotically, as if I'm not the one calling.

"New York City?" His voice, a little gravelly with a slight Boston accent, sounds far away, and he seems to be shouting. I realize that he's probably outside somewhere, and the area code came up on his cell phone window.

"Yes. This is, um—Angela. New York—" I'm about to say "Girl," but it feels too dumb to say, so I just leave it hanging.

After a moment he says, "How are ya, Angela." It's not a question, simply a greeting.

"I'm fine," I answer anyway. I feel like I'm in a foreign country, trying out an unfamiliar language.

How are you?

Fine, thank you. And you?

Fine, thank you.

Can you tell me where I can find

. . . a toilet?

. . . a nice restaurant?

. . . some cheap souvenirs?

I hear a flapping sound. Wind? "Are you on the water?" I ask.

"Just about," he shouts. "I'm on the dock. It's a beautiful day for sailing, Angela. Guess you can hear the sail."

"Yep," I say.

"So you called," he says.

"Are you surprised?"

"Nah, not really," he says. "But I wouldn't have been surprised if you hadn't, either."

"That's—philosophical of you."

He laughs. "You can't waste your time worrying about shit, right? *Que sera,* as they say."

This is not, it must be said, a viewpoint I share. Which isn't to say that I don't find it immensely appealing. "Well, *I'm* surprised I called," I say. "It's very unlike me."

"Oh, really. How's that?"

"I'm not usually so—bold."

"Well, I like it. It's working for you."

In the background I hear the caw-caw of a seagull. The sail is flapping and the wind is blowing and I'm sitting here in my basement office staring at an in-box filled with 114 e-mails, most of which are subject-headed things like "Mail Merge Lists" and "Head Count for Gala."

"Look, I'm getting ready to head out," he says. "Though I'd rather keep talking to you." That husky voice. Those seagulls. "Can I call you later this afternoon?"

Oh, jeez, I don't know. "Okay," I say, trying to sound nonchalant.

"I've got your number," he says, and I'm thinking, yes, indeed you do.

The rest of the day is a blur. E-mail, e-mail, e-mail, phone call, phone call, down the hall (within earshot of my phone) to talk to Audrey Gruber, who is coordinating the lists. Lunch at my desk. Finally, sometime around four o'clock, the phone rings and it's him. The next thing I know it's five fifteen and people are starting to leave and I'm still talking to MaineCatch—aka Richard Saunders—about everything and nothing. The members of my family have become characters in a sitcom—the old-country Italian grandmother, the accountant father and his cat-loving wife, the free-spirited mother, the estranged yuppie brother. In this TV-Land universe I'm a spunky career gal who had a revelation one day that she was working too darn hard and maybe it was time to wake up and smell the sea salt.

Of course, it turns out that Rich isn't exactly a country boy. From our conversation I glean details, like silverfish caught in a net: He grew up in a wealthy Portland family and went to boarding school before attending a small, leafy New England college. After a couple of restless years, mostly spent sailing instead of studying, he dropped out and invested some family money in the sailing school he owns in Spruce Harbor. It's been ten years now, and the business is doing fine, but something, he confides, is missing.

The more he talks, the more convinced I become that that something is me. I'm keeping my cool, keeping the conversation going, but my mind, as usual, is racing ahead. The wind is blowing, the air smells of pine and the sea, and Rich and I are living in that white cottage with the wood-shingled roof, apricot roses blooming on a trellis by the front door. A fire glows in the fireplace, a dog drinks water in the back hall. I stand in the kitchen baking bread, and the cottage is warm and yeasty.

Rationally I know that these tepid Hallmark images have nothing to do with reality. But it's too late for reason. In my heart I'm halfway to Maine.

CHAPTER 3

I try to keep my mind on my job, but it's a struggle. Mimes and jesters are no match for a husky-voiced sailor who might just be the man of my dreams.

Dating—well, okay, online flirting—gives your life a whole new perspective. Describing myself and my habits, I'm struck by how cramped and rote my existence has become. I work underground and live in a box. My social life has dwindled as one friend after another has paired up, married, gotten pregnant, and moved out of town. I've been to so many wedding and baby showers in the past few years that I buy vases and crib quilts in bulk. I love to cook, but my airplane-galley kitchen has room for only one, so if I invite people over for dinner they have to huddle in the hall. Lately I've taken to storing sweaters in my oven.

Communication between us is as straightforward as a children's book. We talk about sailing and the weather and what the weather was like out sailing. We talk about our favorite childhood memories (his—going to Disneyland; mine—wearing down my feminist mother enough to get a Malibu Barbie town house for Christmas when I was seven). It doesn't matter what we talk about. I just like to hear him talk. And I like feeling wanted. I lie on my bed chatting on the phone as if I'm in high school. It's *all* very high school—the love notes (now e-mail), the heart-melting sound of his voice when I pick up the phone, the breathtaking high of a crush.

He doesn't hide his feelings. "I'm lonely," he says.

He is refreshingly direct. "You're too far away. I want to see you."

I want to see you.

He tells me about the slap of salty air on his face at six in the morning, the sharp waves and slick surface of the boat. He describes being out in deep water when the only boats in sight belong to hardy lobstermen, or when there aren't any other boats. He talks about building a fire at home at night, collapsing in a big chair, exhausted and sunburned, watching the flames.

The stories he tells reinforce all my fantasies. Little cottage, rocky coast, solitude. I want to fall through the phone and into his arms.

He laughs about our long-distance romance. "What the hell are we doing?" he says. "I haven't dated anybody south of Augusta in ten years." Augusta, I find out through MapQuest, is way up there.

When he learns I was an English major in college, he starts sending me haikus:

> *She lives in New York*
> *I'm on an island in Maine*
> *Who? What? Where? When? Why?*

Okay, not exactly lyrical, but who needs a tortured poet when you can have a man of the sea?

As it happens, the when and where present themselves sooner than I expect. Mary Quince sets a date for me to meet in Boston with the Byemores and the Biddle-Smyths, and even offers to put me up in a hotel—not a hotel I've ever heard of,

mind you, but surely a step above my nonexistent college roommate's couch. When I happen to mention to Rich—that is, plant
the idea—that I'm coming to Boston, he muses that maybe he'll
journey down the coast to meet me.

Sailing to Boston
Angela will check me out
I'll check her out, too!

Early on a Thursday morning, I board the train from Penn
Station to South Station. My stomach is fluttery; I've barely
eaten for three days. Once again, in my head I am narrating my
experience as if to grandchildren: "And then Grandma got on
the train for the ride to meet your grandpa for the first time. She
was nervous, but also excited. She went to the hotel and sat in
the lobby reading *Metropolitan Home*. Then she looked up, and
through the revolving door . . ."

There he is. He has an athlete's confident movements, and he
is—cute. Really cute. He's wearing faded Levi's, a white T-shirt,
and a heather green wool V-neck sweater, with a small duffel
bag slung over one shoulder. When he sees me he grins boyishly
and saunters over, leaning down to kiss me on the cheek.

"How are ya, Angela."

"I can't believe you came," I say.

"I can't either," he says. He swings the duffel off his shoulder
and onto the floor. The sheer animal fact of him shocks me; he
is a cartoon character come to life, Pinocchio transformed into a
real boy. Part of me truly believed that he existed only in cyber-
space, in the disembodied blink of a cursor.

Now that I have a chance to look at him, I try to put the
pieces together. How to reconcile the gravelly voice, the goofy

haikus, the Buddha-like serenity of his screen persona with this lanky, slightly preppy guy in front of me?

"So, are you checking me out?" he asks.

"Yes," I say.

He sits down beside me on the couch and smiles. His front-right tooth is slightly chipped, and he has fine lines around his eyes, the kind I imagine you get from squinting into the sun out on the open sea. "What do you think?"

He doesn't need confirmation of his looks; he must be plenty aware. So I say, "What do *you* think?"

He looks me up and down—flirtatiously, easily, as if just by looking he's telling me what he thinks. "You're prettier than your picture. A lot."

"Thanks." I didn't realize my picture was *that* bad, but good to know.

"I like your hair." He reaches out and lifts a strand. "It's so shiny and dark."

What a strange thing to say! But kind of endearing. "Thanks," I say. "I like yours, too."

"Thanks." He laughs. Chuckles, actually. "You don't really like my hair."

"No, I do. It's all—blond and windswept."

"That's true. At least I have some, right?"

"Yeah." Then I hasten to add, "Not that I have anything against bald guys."

He laughs again. "Well, that's good. Not that I care, really. Not being bald."

"Well, how do you feel about bald women?"

"You're telling me that's a wig?"

"No. I just mean—in general."

"Oh. Well, I guess when I see a bald woman, I think she's probably sick."

"Oh. Yeah," I say.

Shaking his head, he says, "This is a weird conversation."

"I know. How did we start talking about bald women?"

"I don't know."

"Should we start again?"

"Yeah. Let's start again."

Now it's a little awkward. I'm not worried, though; I'm so high on adrenaline and nerves that I'm hovering on a cloud. We're sitting side by side and in the silence I'm wondering if there's anything stuck between my front teeth. It's a warm fall day—warmer than I expected—and I wonder if he can tell that I'm sweating. I also wonder if he thinks he's staying with me here, in this hotel, or what. Then I remember that he sailed here—sailed here!—and it occurs to me that a sailboat that's big enough to make the trip from halfway up the state of Maine must have a sleeping cabin.

"So how was your trip?" he asks, and I say, at the same time, "God, I've been so rude! You *sailed* here. How was it?"

He raises his eyebrows, seemingly amused. He tells me about his voyage, using words like knots and wind velocity and aft, the basic gist being that the trip was fine, if bumpy, and getting into the harbor was a little complicated, maneuvering around all the big boats, and that he'd never actually sailed such a distance alone before, but it was a good thing to do and now he could really use a drink. Should we go somewhere for a beer?

I'm listening closely but only catching every other word. Instead I'm noticing how his jeans are slightly worn on the front of his thighs and his forearms are evenly tanned, like a perfectly toasted marshmallow. I look into his eyes, piercing and blue. He's chewing gum, spearmint, I think, and I listen for the hard snaps between words, inhale the waft of mint in the air between us. It's a manly way to chew gum, a Heath Ledger way.

A man like this does not, I think, exist in New York.

We go for a drink at a pub called the Irish Nickel and sit in a corner booth and I tell him about the mimes and jesters and the planning for this overblown, silly event and the crazy French artist whose canvases are startling and fresh. He wants to know all about living in the city—the dirt, the crime, the congestion—and I find, as I always do when encountering people who've never been to New York, that I am caught off guard by both the truths and mistruths in the stereotypes. Yes, New York is dirty, and crime occurs, and apartments are small, and restaurants are crowded. But I also tell him about what it's like to walk along West End Avenue at dusk when no one else is on the street, and the surprising wilderness of the Ramble in Central Park, and the quiet civility of most New Yorkers, who simply want to exist in peace. I can't figure out whether he is genuinely curious or nodding along out of politeness. Or something else.

After several beers—he convinces me to try Bar Harbor ale, a beer on tap, which has a tangy, earthy flavor I could get used to—I'm more interested in the "something else" than in what I'm saying. We've been talking for two hours, and now all I can think about is how nice it would be to kiss him, to feel his rough stubble on my cheek, his wind-chapped lips on mine. Our conversation slows. I sense his hand on my thigh.

His hand. On my thigh.

The beer, his hand, no dinner . . . somehow I end up on his boat, clutching the wooden banister as I sway behind him down the narrow stairs to the cabin. I pull my shirt over my head in the moonlight. He slips a finger under the low waistband of my skirt, runs his hand up my side, traces the underwire of my bra, slips the clasp, bends down and runs his lips lightly along my hardened nipple. His breath is warm and dry. His touch is tender; he knows just how fast to move. When I stretch out alongside his warm mammal self, I press the bottoms of my toes against the tops of his, standing prone on his feet, the parts of us joining like a puzzle.

My eyes open. It's dark, and for a moment I think I'm in a hotel room with the shades drawn. Then I feel beneath me the pull of the water, the slight turn of the hull, the vertiginous sensation of rocking in darkness. I see the disheveled head on the pillow beside me, a slope of shoulder. I lift my wrist and turn it slightly to squint at my watch: 6:25.

I'm supposed to meet the Byemores and the Biddle-Smyths at the Fogbottom Gallery downtown at nine o'clock sharp.

Rich doesn't move, doesn't open his eyes as I extract myself from the bed, shimmying around him to creep to the floor. The bed is flat against the curve of the boat, so snug that you can barely sit up. It would be the perfect bed to stay in all day, emerging up the stairs into twilight and cocktails.

Now that I see the cabin in the daylight—or as much daylight as you can get through narrow, foot-tall windows with blackout curtains—it's a little dingy. A bachelor pad. There's a row of empty amber beer bottles lined up along the window near the sink, which is full of Hot Pocket and American cheese wrappers.

I have to pee really badly, but don't want to. The toilet, behind a flimsy door, is right beside his sleeping head. Last night after peeing I couldn't figure out how to flush, whether to push or pull or pump, and he had to do it for me. I'll say one thing—I thought I'd experience a living space less private than a New York studio apartment.

Quietly I pull out my clothes, my crumpled green skirt and smoke-smelling black top, both as unappealing the day after as a hangover. I step into my slingbacks, and they flap on the floor.

Rich stirs—a slumbering giant; I'm the damsel trying to escape before he awakens. I've already started up the stairs when he says, "Hey."

"Hey," I say, frozen halfway up the ladder.

He props himself on an elbow. "Where you going?"

"My meeting's at nine," I say.

He squints at the clock and falls back on the bed as if exhausted by the effort. "It's six thirty. Come back here."

"I can't," I say. "I've got to get to the hotel and take a shower."

"No you don't."

I laugh. What?

"Come here," he says.

And I do.

A few days ago I went to a fortune-teller on West Fourth during my lunch hour. She examined my wrist for a moment, then raised her eyebrows and shook her head. "Big change coming," she said. "I don't know when exactly, but I predict soon." That evening in my apartment I ordered moo shu from the Chinese take-out place downstairs. My fortune read "Of all forms of caution, caution in love is the most fatal."

These messages, taken together, seem too significant to dismiss.

For several years in my midtwenties, I went out with a cellist named Lewis who eventually broke my heart. We'd met in a normal, old-world way: at a dinner party hosted by mutual friends. Lewis was slight and intense, with dark wiry hair and mud-puddle eyes. I appreciated his long musician fingers and martini-dry wit; he appreciated my rent-controlled sublet and homemade marinara. And maybe a few other things. But he left me for a violist even slighter and paler than he.

It took a while to get over him. I dated a succession of lawyers and bond traders who had in common an unapologetic cal-

lowness, an adolescent charm. For a while I found these quali-
ties hard to resist, but as the years passed and the charm was
revealed, more often than not, to be little more than arrogant
self-regard, it became decidedly less appealing.

I have always been an optimist, teased by my friends for my
tendency to look on the bright side, but in the past few years
I've begun to feel the insidious embrace of cynicism, to seek
comfort in the warmth of that cloak. I fear that my capacity
for joy is dimming, that my standards have become impossibly high, that I am peremptorily dismissive, inventing facts to
build a case against someone, like a corrupt prosecutor. And for
what? Sometimes I wake up on a Saturday morning appalled
by my own sovereignty in my life, at the authority I have to do
whatever I want with my hours, my furniture, my Netflix queue.
Every decision I make is determined solely by the spark and the
limitations of my own perspective.

I wonder if it's my own fault—it must be, at least partially—
that I have not found the man whose mysteries I want to unlock.
I have not found a man who can unlock mine.

Until—perhaps—

Gasp.

This man, right at this moment, is unlocking my mysteries,
and, as it turns out, he is quite adept at it.

So it's 8:14 and I'm still on the boat, naked again, with a hickey
on my neck, behind my ear (a hickey! I'd never let a guy from
New York give me a hickey), and sticky thighs, and if I'm going to make it to this meeting (he's whispering in my ear, "Tell
them you're sick, tell them you got lost") I have to leave right
this instant.

For a moment, lulled in the berth, I'm swaying along with
the boat, Rich's arm behind my head, thinking, what the hell,

I'll tell them I'm sick, when the specter of Mary Quince, like the Wicked Witch in the crystal ball, flashes through my brain. I sit upright.

"I have to go," I say, and as the words come out of my mouth I know that this time I mean it. I climb on top of Rich and kiss him, run my tongue over his chapped lips, and he slaps my butt and says, "Go."

As soon as I leave, I know he'll be sailing back up to Maine. Later today I'll get on a train to New York, and by nightfall there will be five hundred miles between us. This boat will seem like a distant mirage, conjured out of dreams.

As I walk along the dock to the stone steps to the street, the harbor is fresh and wet and beautiful. Large white sailboats rise magnificently from the dark water; gulls caw and men call to each other, and all I can think is how different from my life this is. As I often do when I see people living lives no New Yorker would dream of, I'm struck by the freedom of their choices. Are these people happy living like this, so far away from the center of everything? Could I be?

Thinking about all of this, I feel a sudden rush of anticipation, an abstract yearning. Unfamiliar as it is, I do remember it. I experienced this feeling as a little girl the night before Christmas, and later when I was applying to college, and even later when I moved to New York. It's a longing for things to come, possibilities unfolding before me, the charged expectation of change.

CHAPTER 4

Mary Quince is standing in the middle of my office with her hands clasped together, beaming. "Susie Biddle-Smyth just called," she says. "Apparently they were quite impressed with you."

Indeed, the Byemores and Biddle-Smyths seemed not to notice my unkempt hair and generally less-than-fresh appearance, my crumpled skirt and the faint odor—mostly expunged by sea air—of bar smoke and god-knows-what-else. Ordinarily I might have been intimidated by their patrician New England formality, interpreting their aloofness as condescension. But because I wasn't nervous—in fact, barely cared—about what they thought of me, I felt relaxed and comfortable. I listened intently and nodded thoughtfully and asked the right questions (every now and then, for a little private frisson, replaying highlights from the evening before in my mind). I sold them on our plans for the gala, stressing the gaiety of it, the sense of excitement building around Zoë Devereux's exhibition. I knew that these were the kind of people who go to gala after gala; they wanted to be wowed, and that morning I was just the person to wow them.

"They said you were—what were Susie's words?—'an absolute pleasure to work with.' And just now the Biddle-Smyths have agreed to underwrite twenty-five thousand dollars of our cost for the event up-front. I can't tell you how long that pro-posal has been on the table. We might need to move you to Development!" She laughs; that part is clearly a joke.

"That's great," I say, taking a sip of coffee. What joy, to be so effective and yet care so little.

For the next few hours I work on details of the gala—the catering menu, the centerpieces—but I'm keeping one eye on my e-mail in-box. Nothing from Maine. Finally, I can't stand it anymore, and I send one line:

Hope you made it home in one piece.

And then I wait. Jim Metcalf, who works in Acquisitions, stops in to discuss a memo, and for once I welcome the intru-sion. But when I ask him to have a seat, and then inquire about his weekend, he acts flustered. In all the time we've worked together, we've never actually had a personal conversation, and it dawns on me that he may interpret my sudden interest in him as romantic.

So I begin a sentence with "My boyfriend," which, I soon see, is a mistake.

"*You* have a *boyfriend*?" he asks, as if I've just said I have a pet shark.

"Umm-hmm."

"Here? In New York?"

"Uh, no. He lives in Boston." (Maine being too specific, too far, too inviting of questions.)

"Well. Huh. So were you visiting him up there just now?"

Oh dear. That wasn't very smart. "No. He was on a—business trip."

"What does he do?"

"Uh—er—he . . . runs his own business." God. Must get out of this.

"Really? Interesting. What kind of business?"

All right, enough. I flap my hand. "Oh, you know. Business. Money—whatever." Just at that moment I hear a faint click on my screen and there he is, MaineCatch, ensnared in my in-box. "Oh," I say, in my best I'm-a-busy-woman-with-work-to-do voice, "I'm sorry, Jim. I actually need to get this."

"Yes, by all means," he says, stumbling backward out my door. "Well, 'bye," he mutters, ducking down the hall.

I close my door, open my e-mail, and find this:

> *Life was smooth sailing*
> *Till Angela came along.*
> *Her port is real far.*

I feel a surge of happiness.

It sure is, I write back. *When are you coming down here to visit me?*

When are you moving to Maine? he blips seconds later.

My hands are frozen over the keyboard. Then I type, *Is that an invitation?*

Though I'm sitting at my desk for three more hours, he doesn't write back before I leave for the day. It doesn't matter. I don't really mind. Maybe it's the kind of question best left hanging.

He never does answer the question, but he sends roses. Twelve thawed roses swathed in baby's breath that wilt and die within three days, but roses nonetheless. He writes five more haikus, fills my in-box with flirty messages. As the date of the gala approaches, I am deep in a romantic fog, just barely managing to hold it together enough to keep Mary Quince happy. Since my triumph in Boston she has cut me some slack, as if she thinks I am actually an adult capable of making intelligent decisions. Predictably, I have taken full advantage of this.

Now it's the day of the gala and, like a straying boyfriend, I'm doing my best to look passionately committed. It's eight thirty in the morning, and the museum is quiet. I'm the only one here except the security guard. The museum is closed to the public today; Mary Quince and her small army of worker bees will show up soon, but at the moment I have the place to myself.

When it's quiet like this, I can pick up the faint mildewy smell that is somehow disguised by workaday clatter. And it's dark—I haven't turned on the overhead halogen spots that dot the basement hallway like an orderly lineup of stars, fostering the illusion that all of us down here don't spend our days like moles.

Entering my office, I shake out my soggy umbrella and prop it against the wall. Rain fell as I left my apartment this morning, the kind of thin, relentless spray that makes you look twice when you're checking out the window—perhaps it's only mist?—until you look down at the street and see the peppered puddles, hear the *shussh* of taxis. Rainy days remind me of Nonna, and I am guiltily aware that lately I have been out of touch.

Tomorrow, I tell myself. Tomorrow I'll go out and see her.

I haven't spoken to Lindsay lately, either. In the past couple of weeks, since I got back from Boston, we've only talked on the phone twice. She knows I've been swamped with planning the gala. "Call me when you have time; I'll be here," she said. The truth is, I've been kind of avoiding her. Ever since our conversation about MaineCatch I've been reluctant to talk about him, maybe afraid to jinx it, maybe not wanting to invite her opinion.

I haven't even told her about our rendezvous in Boston.

Well, when this event is over, we'll go out to dinner, and I'll tell her everything.

I turn on the overhead light and my desk lamp and touch my keyboard to wake up the computer. Then I check the answering machine. There's a barely intelligible message from Frank, the fire-eater—something about how he hasn't spoken to the juggler, his second cousin, in three years, and doesn't want to be anywhere near him at the gig. Frank says he won't show up unless I can guarantee he won't have to, as he intones dramatically, "set eyes on that fuck for as long as I live."

I play the message twice to get the gist of it, then try to think for a moment. I had a feeling this guy Frank was going to be a problem. The first time I spoke with him he sounded a bit unstable—the demands, the flash of his pride. Perhaps I should have spent more time trying to find someone else. But really, what kind of person is attracted to fire-eating in the first place? Maybe the personality is a prerequisite for the job.

I call the number he left on the message. "Frank the fire-eater," his recorded voice barks. "State your need." I tell the machine I had not been aware that the juggler was Frank's cousin, but I'll do what I can to keep them apart; they're scheduled to perform at staggered intervals, so it shouldn't be a problem. "I look forward to seeing you tonight," I say. "You're going to be the highlight of the show."

There's a vast checklist to go over. Five hundred different things could go wrong today, and any one of them would be a mess. As I go online to confirm flower delivery at twelve thirty and catering at four, I see that I have two messages from Maine-Catch, each a haiku:

The big day is here
Circus guys are everywhere
But where's the sailboat?

Who else writes haiku
It's pretty unique I guess
You won't forget me!

Okay, they are really dumb. But they make me smile. Suddenly I understand how a mother can love a child who is, objectively, ugly. The impulse is not logical. It is driven by something more powerful than reason.

Since Boston, I have been in an altered state. I replay scenes from our brief time together in my mind. Like a forensic pathologist reconstructing a face from a disintegrating skull, I have extrapolated enough from our few hours together to construct a real relationship. I am like those women in wartime who become pen pals with random servicemen and end up falling head over heels with the slant of a pen, the fantasy of a soul mate, the glamorous thrill of the unknown.

At five o'clock I am overseeing the placement of tables in the main gallery, seating chart in hand. My dress for tonight—a floor-length black sheath, appropriate but unassuming, hangs on the back of my office door in a dry-cleaning bag, along with pearls and pumps. Mary Quince and most of the others have gone home to get ready, but I'm here for the duration.

When the tables are set up, I walk around the room distributing centerpieces. These centerpieces, twenty different topiaries, miniature ivy sculpted onto two-foot-tall wire forms, represent hours of planning. Each one is an astonishingly accurate repro-

duction of one or two of Zoë Devereux's fantastical figures from
the paintings that hang on the walls around the gallery.

The performers begin to trickle in around six. Marcus and
Milo, the floor acrobats, arrive first. Ten minutes later, Domingo,
the juggler, shows up. "Just so you know," I say, trying to keep
my tone casual, "your cousin Frank is performing tonight."

"What?" he says sharply in a nasal lilt. "Here?"

I nod, unsure of how much to reveal. Does Domingo know
that Frank hates his guts?

"Never told me," he says. "Motherfucker."

Apparently he knows. "Look, you won't be performing together," I tell him. "You're scheduled to go on at different times,
so you don't even have to see each other if you don't want to."

As I'm talking to Domingo, Mary Quince arrives, bangled and
baubled and swathed in a musky scent. She exclaims, "Off now!
Get beautiful and get back here soon. Are we under control?"

Looking around, I do a last-minute check: topiaries, table
settings, Tanqueray Ten. The musicians are setting up near one
of the bars. All the performers are here except the fire-eater.
Where is he?

Relax. Deep breath.

"All set," I inform Mary Quince, and skitter off to change.

CHAPTER 5

From my office I hear the blare of trumpets. My watch says 7:18 P.M., twelve minutes before the gala officially starts, and I'm in my bra and Spanx, trying to fasten my necklace. The clasp secured, I throw on my dress, yanking the zipper up and tugging the hem down as I race through the hall. On my way up the stairs, I frantically apply lipstick, like a bank robber trying to change identity mid-escape. When I reach the main gallery, the horns are quiet and the band has segued into precisely the whimsical, vaguely sinister music I requested.

White-haired ladies in sequins and hunched gentlemen in tuxes are tottering to their seats—old old money tends to come early and leave early. In another hour the younger set will begin to arrive. Marrieds-with-children inevitably underestimate how long it will take to get out the door, and twentysomethings don't really care; they come with their friends and could be anywhere. They'll go to a club afterward anyway.

With a practiced eye, I survey the scene. The magician and juggler are already at work, having started early so patrons would feel they were entering an ongoing act. In a far corner of the room, Domingo, the juggler, balances a paintbrush on his nose while keeping aloft a spinning array of paint tubes, either as an homage to the artist or a nice coincidence. A few feet away, a jester-magician performs a pantomime number with a dove. Her exaggerated clown emotions—happy! sad! puzzled! confused!—are freaking people out a little. One man practically falls backward over a chair in response to her wink.

As the evening unfolds, the guests greet each other and point to the performers, enjoying the spectacle. The juggler juggles champagne flutes; the magician pulls a black rabbit out of a top hat. A waiter glides by with a tray of sliver-thin crepes filled with duck and green onion, and I pop one in my mouth. It melts on my tongue. The music is festive without being obtrusive. The tables are elegant. I glance over at Mary Quince and catch her eye. She gives me a covert thumbs-up.

Mary Quince doesn't give thumbs-ups.

My shoulders drop with relief. It appears that I have pulled it off.

Suddenly, I'm aware of a small commotion at the entrance. Turning toward the raised voices, I see security guards with their hands up, pushing someone back. And then I see him: a curly-haired man dressed in black tights and a red-and-black-striped shirt, gesticulating wildly. With a start I realize that he must be the fire-eater.

As I hurry closer, I hear him insisting, "Let me through!"

"What is happening here?" I ask calmly.

"Do you know this man?" asks one of the guards.

"Are you Frank?"

The fire-eater sighs dramatically. "Obviously, I am Frank," he retorts.

I look at my watch. "You're an hour late." The guards eye him suspiciously. "This is one of the performers. He's supposed to go on in five minutes."

Grudgingly, the security guards step aside. One says, "Let us know if there's a problem."

Frank follows me toward the dressing room, muttering under his breath. As we reach the corridor leading out of the main gallery, he stops abruptly and looks back. I follow his gaze. He is watching Domingo, the juggler, now executing an intricate maneuver involving ice-cream scoops and somehow, impossibly, what appear to be balls of real ice cream.

Before I can say anything, the fire-eater strides out into the room. Weaving between tables, he unzips the bag on his shoulder and reaches inside. I have a horrible, momentary vision of a machine gun, then remember that Frank was patted down at the front door like everybody else. No, it's not a gun—instead, it appears to be a long stick with a slightly bulbous end. Holding the stick aloft in one hand, he fumbles in his pocket and pulls out a lighter.

I sense that something unpleasant is about to happen, yet I don't want to make a scene. Things have been going so well. The room is full of exquisitely dressed people sipping cocktails and nibbling on canapés. No one seems to be paying attention to Frank as he makes his purposeful way through the crowd. Out of the corner of my eye I see Mary Quince talking to Mr. and Mrs. Charles Byemore, her head tilted back in a laugh, the Kenneth Jay Lane pearls around her neck, as large as jawbreakers, gleaming in the candlelight.

Closing in on Domingo, Frank ignites the end of the stick with the lighter. It bursts into flame, a glowing orange corona. People standing nearby murmur an appreciative "Ooh!"

Domingo, wisely, has stopped juggling. He is cradling six ice-cream scoops in his hands, balancing the ice-cream balls (cleverly constructed out of Styrofoam, I see now) in a pyramid on top.

"This man is a liar and a thief," Frank declares, holding the flame aloft like a torch.

"*You* are the liar," Domingo hisses. Sensing his tactical disadvantage, he sidles over to his black prop suitcase, keeping an eye on Frank, and kicks it open. He drops the Styrofoam balls and plastic scoops into the suitcase, then kicks the suitcase shut. Domingo stands defiantly, his arms folded in front of him like a Turkish dancer.

A small crowd gathers. They still think this could be part of the act.

Frank points the flame toward Domingo for a long moment. Lifting the stick and tilting his head back, he opens his mouth, like a reticulated python, and slides the stick down his throat. Then, slowly, he pulls the stick out of his mouth and blows a stream of fire into the topiary on the nearest table. The ivy smolders briefly before the entire centerpiece bursts into flames.

For a beautiful moment the guests are willing to believe the flaming topiary is part of the show. Only when the dry moss inside the wire frame begins to emit a dense, dark smoke is it clear that something is dreadfully wrong.

"You fool!" cries Domingo, clutching his head with his hands.

A thin black cloud rises, drawn toward the air vents above, and a lump of burning topiary falls onto the table. People on the other side of the room stop what they're doing and turn to look. In the background, a haunting Edith Piaf song serves as an unintentionally appropriate score for the unfolding drama.

The stream of smoke rising above our heads now resembles a malevolent wraith. Suddenly, from the flaming centerpiece comes a loud pop, a sound like gunfire. Shrieking guests dive under tables; the music stops. In the ensuing pandemonium, Frank steps back and slips the wand in his pocket. Out of the corner of my eye, I see him weaving through the crowd, sinuous as a ferret, until he disappears.

Without thinking, I yank the tablecloth from a nearby table—china, wineglasses, and the topiary crashing to the floor—and throw it over the burning table to contain the flames. But the fire, unabated, eats through the fabric, searing a hole in the cloth and releasing even more noxious fumes and smoke. A security guard runs toward me brandishing a fire extinguisher and pulls the pin, spraying foam in every direction.

Within seconds, the fire is out. A loud bleeping noise starts up, and a recorded voice booms over the loudspeaker: "PLEASE EVACUATE THE BUILDING. PLEASE E-VAC-U-ATE THE BUILDING."

I hear the wail of sirens, far away and coming closer.

Many, many sirens.

Guests leave in the Christmas-light brightness of the train of fire engines lined up outside. The head of museum security asks to see the supplemental fire-insurance policy.

My stomach lurches.

Any event planner knows that if an entertainment involves a live flame, you take out a supplemental fire-insurance policy. As soon as the museum official opens his mouth, I realize that I completely forgot to do it.

I forgot.

I thought I had planned for any contingency—I made sure we were covered for injury to the acrobats; I devised a backup plan should the catering fall through; I ordered a hundred burgundy umbrellas with the Huntsworth logo in the event of rain. But I did not take out fire insurance.

The head of security raises his eyebrows and looks at me for a long moment. "That's a real problem," he says, and in that moment I know that my career as an event planner is over.

Despite a sleeping pill, I drift miserably in and out of lurid dreams all night. Circus figures loom toward me; a topiary springs to life with writhing figures. The sound of a fire alarm winds through my dreams. Gradually I realize that the high-pitched noise is coming from outside my head.

Without opening my eyes I feel around for the telephone. "Hello?"

"I saw the news," my father says. "I think you'd better come home."

"Okay."

"I'll be there in an hour to pick you up."

The thought of going back to New Jersey with my father fills me with dread. What I'd like to do is hide in my apartment for the next month or so, but apparently that isn't an option.

My father hands me the newspapers when I get in the car. The cover of the *Daily News* is "FIRE-EATER'S FURY." The *New York Post* says "FIERY GRUDGE MATCH!" The front page of the *New York Times* Metro section declares "Museum Fiasco: Fire-Eater's Revenge Damages the Huntsworth."

The *Times* article ends, "Because the museum neglected to take out supplemental fire insurance for the event, officials say, the final cost of damage to the Huntsworth could run into the mid six figures. This does not include the incalculable cost of losing a piece of art as important as Zoë Devereux's 'The Pantomime Artist,' which appears to have been severely damaged and possibly ruined."

For the next twenty-four hours, I talk to no one but my family. When I turn on my cell phone, I find thirty-one messages— mostly once urgent invitations from news organizations large and small to tell my side.

My brother, Paul, calls to commiserate. In his way. "Jesus, what a mess," he says. "Isn't fire insurance Event Planning 101?" Paul, who is six years older, has never had much to do with me. I was twelve when he went off to Rutgers and double-majored in economics and political science, determined not to spend his life, like our father, toiling at a tedious job and bringing home a modest paycheck. Later Paul went to business school, and now he works as a consultant, putting in hundred-hour work-weeks and raking in lots of cash. He married an associate at a rival firm who promptly got pregnant, quit her job, and started house hunting in White Plains. Kim stays home with their two kids while Paul commutes by train to Manhattan, arriving back home after dark.

"If you need advice or anything, give me a call," Paul says. "But if my secretary answers, don't leave your name. I don't want anybody to know I'm related to you. Hah—kidding."

On Monday I call the office, and Mary Quince tells me to stay home. Take a few vacation days, she says.

My father and stepmother leave for work. I climb back into bed.

What was once my bedroom has been converted into my stepmother's dressing room with a pull-out sofa. When I try to sleep, my skull thrums; the ache behind my eye sockets is re-lieved only by finger pressure. I curl under the covers on the foldout, massaging the sides of my head, every rib of the couch mechanism poking against my spine. One of my stepmother's three cats is draped, beanbaglike, across my legs.

I am allergic to cats.

There's no question in my mind that as soon as I summon the courage to slink back into work, I'm going to be out of work. I'll be surprised if my stuff isn't already packed when I arrive. I have managed to screw up the single most important event of my ca-reer, effectively ruining my chances of ever working in the field again. My reputation as the planner responsible for the biggest debacle in Huntsworth history will precede me wherever I go.

As I lie under the covers in a state of near catatonia, a recovered memory bubbles to the surface of my brain, a casual exchange in the hallway with Mary Quince several weeks ago as I was leaving the office for the day:

"Angela. You're hiring a fire-eater, right?"

"Yes. In fact, I just checked his references."

"We need supplemental insurance for his act, of course."

"Of course," I said, and went merrily on my way, stopping on the way home at Vicky Slut (Lindsay's affectionate name for Victoria's Secret) in anticipation of another MaineCatch encounter in the near future. I bought something silky and pink.

What was I thinking?

If I am honest with myself—and as the hours progress, drugged up on Benadryl to avoid a full-blown allergy attack from the cats, sleeping in my stepmother's dressing room, watching daytime TV in the den she recently redecorated with Thomas Kinkade reproduction prints, I am driven close enough to despair that honesty is unavoidable—I have to admit that I probably wasn't thinking at all. Despite the fact that "fire insurance'" was on several of my many lists, as soon as I was out the door that day, Mary Quince's words melted in the air and I never thought of the insurance again. My brain was distracted by sailboats and sea air. In my blissed-out state, it seemed inconceivable that anything could go wrong anywhere.

CHAPTER 6

My grandmother shuffles around silently, trying not to disturb me, except when she joins me in the den to watch TV. Joy Behar, I learn, is Nonna's favorite host on *The View*. Kelly really knows how to put Regis in his place, and Ellen, well, you'd never know she was a lesbian if she hadn't felt the need to announce it to everybody.

"It wasn't your fault," Nonna tells me, and when I say, "Unfortunately, it was," she sighs, "Who doesn't make a mistake?"

Tuesday is gloomy and rainy, the kind of day when Nonna likes to make food my stepmother disapproves of, slow-cooked soups and stews and bread from scratch. I watch her assemble ingredients for a loaf, flour and yeast and an egg, as I sit at the table drinking coffee. "Nobody makes bread anymore, Annalisa," Sharon clucks, bustling through as she's leaving for work. "It's pennies at the A and P." Nonna shakes her head and pushes her daughter-in-law out of the kitchen. "I don't tell you how to do your job, don't tell me how to do mine. I'm busy. Now shoo." When Sharon is gone, she mutters, "*Quella donna è un'idiota.*"

I feel sorry for Nonna, living here with my dad and Sharon, whom he met through a lunchtime dating service—Sharon, who is constantly patting her stomach and saying, "None for me, thanks, I'm watching my weight." Who hates to cook, hates everything about the kitchen. Who calls homemade cavatelli "carbs" and won't touch it. Sharon wishes that she and my dad lived alone. She is jealous of his time and wants him to herself. She is cold and stiff around Nonna, always acting as if she's in the way.

Sharon loathes having Nonna in her clean kitchen, filling it with the simmering reek of strange food. Unrecognizable things in the refrigerator—pieces of chicken she'd never cook with; wet, lumpy cheeses. She hates the work this kind of cooking generates, splatters of marinara on the stove top, endless dishes in the sink. Foreign smells, pungent and pervasive, wafting through even her bedroom. Nonna openly disapproves of the low-fat convenience foods Sharon prizes, disapproves, too, of her poor cooking skills. The two of them have been engaged in a long-running, passive-aggressive battle ever since Sharon moved in.

I sit in my pajamas chopping tomatoes and *cucuzzielli*, baby zucchini, and I feel as if I'm in high school again, home sick, hanging with Nonna while she makes dinner.

"Die," Nonna says. Her voice is hoarse.

"What?" I ask, startled.

She makes a chopping motion with her hand, first one way and then the other. "Dice." She lifts her apron to her mouth and coughs into it. "*Scusilo*," excuse me, she says.

"Oh. All right. Are you okay, Nonna?"

"Fine," she says, flapping her hand. "Just a cold. I get one every fall."

"You do? I can't remember your being sick."

"Kids don't notice such things."

"I'm hardly a kid, Nonna."

"Really?" she says, arching an eyebrow. "Then what are you doing in your pajamas in my kitchen, in the middle of a week-day?"

"Good point."

"You know," she says, "when I was your age, your *father* was a teenager."

Nonna's hands are ropy with veins but stronger than mine. Her thumbs are like mallets. When I stand beside her at the stove, I inhale her Jean Naté scent, notice the yeasty rise of her bosom beneath the red gingham apron, her glasses fogging as she checks the sauce. Like a magic trick, her eyes disappear behind frosted glass.

There is red sauce on the stove, bubbling like a lava pit; dough rising under damp tea towels on the Formica countertop; onions and garlic minced on a worn cutting board. The radio (a sleek white Bose that hovers on the counter like a miniature spaceship, a Christmas gift from my stepmother, who complained after giving it that Nonna didn't seem to know or care how expensive it was) hums low, Top 40 hits that Nonna sometimes, incongruously, hums along to. She mouths offhand snatches—"I got you, girl" or "You're as cold as ice"—words that, in her Italian accent, sound like sentences from a phrase book. She is in constant, sharklike motion, chopping, stirring, rinsing vegetables in the sink. Shaping veal meatballs in her hands, holding her fingers away from the meat as if she doesn't want to get them dirty, palms only. Wiping the counter once, twice, again. And with each turn she makes she is teaching. *Here is how you cut a potato, slicing it just so and slipping it into a pot of cold water to stop it from turning brown. You carve a tomato perpendicular to the stem. Sprinkle sea salt over cut eggplant in a sieve to drain the bitterness out.*

Chicken stock, marinara, the *soffritto*—these are the essential elements of Nonna's cooking. Each requires long, slow preparation, but once done, the rest of the work is relatively easy. Flavor, she says, builds up from the bottom. Nonna is a good cook because she has patience and because she can sense proportion. She has an uncanny ability to pinpoint what is missing—a pinch of sugar in the marinara, another bay leaf in the stock.

When Sharon comes home from work, she peers at the dinner in the white casserole dish and frowns. "Too much olive oil, Annalisa. I thought I told you."

"Not so much." Nonna smiles and shrugs. "One tablespoon. Two at the most."

"I got you cooking spray, remember? You said you'd try it."

"I tried it. Terrible. Nothing but chemicals." Nonna makes a face.

"You know, olive oil is actually good for you, Sharon," I interject.

"Well, we don't need the calories. Any of us," she says, clearly irritated that I'm taking my grandmother's side.

"Calories, pah," Nonna says.

"I just want to live a long and healthy life. I want Louis to live a long time, too."

"I lived a long and healthy life already, and I never ate cooking spray. You want skinny, not healthy," Nonna says.

"I want both," Sharon says.

Nonna turns back to the sink and starts noisily washing dishes. "Tell your father we're having *fave e cicoria*." Fava beans and chicory. "His favorite. Unless that woman has forced him to change his mind."

Sharon snorts. "That woman, Annalisa, is still standing right here."

"I know she is. *Purtroppo ha uno cervello come uno cetriolo*."

Unfortunately, her brain is as fleshy and watery as a cucumber.

Sharon doesn't speak Italian, but Nonna's message isn't hard to figure out.

Later that night, when Nonna and my father and stepmother have gone to bed, I wander into the kitchen and plug in my laptop. Dial up. It takes forever. But there, in my inbox, is exactly what I am hoping to find.

> *No message from you*
> *What's going on, I wonder?*
> *Run off with a dwarf?*

I click "Reply," then think for a moment, staring at the empty screen. Then I write *Lost my job. Weighing my options.*

I log off and go to bed, the rest of my life hanging in the balance.

It's Wednesday, midmorning. My cell phone is ringing somewhere in the house. I spring from the couch and scramble around trying to find it, like a dog on the scent, cocking my head and listening. The ring tone is the theme song from *The Partridge Family,* which I downloaded from the Internet as a cultural in-joke, and it's really annoying. Now it's repeating the entire song. *"Hello, world, hear the song that we're singin'—C'mon, get happy! A whole lot of lovin' is what we'll be bringin'—We'll make you happy!"*

Yes, it's upstairs. I bound up two steps at a time, swinging on the railing around the corner, and skid into Sharon's dressing room. There I fall on my knees, tossing clothes and shoes into the air before glimpsing the silver phone on the narrow arm of the sofa. The little window reveals a now-familiar 207 number.

"Hey," Rich says when I pick up. "That sucks about your job. Are you okay?"

I appreciate that he asks how I am before going after the gory details. "That's nice," I say. "I'm all right."

"You had that big party."

"Yeah. It didn't go so well."

"Really?" I was afraid he might have read about it, but evidently he hasn't. Or he's being polite.

"There was a fire-eater. A centerpiece went up in flames. Not good."

"Oh, man," he says. "And it was your thing, and they think you're responsible."

I feel tears well up in my eyes. His empathetic summation casts me rather nicely as victim, and I wallow for a moment in the feeling of having been egregiously wronged.

"That New York grind, man," he says. "It can wear you down."

So right! I think fiercely. He is *so right*!

"I think you need a vacation."

"What do you pro"—I start to say "propose," but my brain catches up to my mouth halfway through—"suggest?" It's a coquettish question, one I might ordinarily have considered beneath me, but nothing is beneath me now.

He sighs into the phone and doesn't answer right away. "Maybe you could, ahh—take a little trip up here," he says finally.

My heart pit-pats. Did I hear that right? Did he just invite me up there? He did, didn't he? "Do you think that would be—smart?" I ask.

He laughs. "Nobody ever died trying something new."

For a moment my analytical brain switches into gear. What a ridiculous thing to say. Of course people have died trying new things; they do it every day. Think of all those novices on Everest! Or driving cars, for that matter! But this is not the time or place for my analytical brain. It is not the time for thinking at all.

I flash through my options. I could go back to school or, god forbid, stay in Nutley and try to find a job in New Jersey. I could start temping again, I suppose, though what seemed insouciant at twenty-three isn't quite as attractive at thirty-three. What else can I do?

As I see it, there's only one thing. Escape. Isn't this what you call serendipity, when you meet the man of your dreams just as your life is falling apart? I have never done one truly impulsive thing in my life. *Follow your bliss. Listen to your heart.* All of those slogans that once seemed so sappy suddenly resonate. *Seize the day. Reach for the stars.* If I don't grab this moment, it will pass by me like so many others.

When I look at it this way, I feel I've been handed an incredible opportunity, one that most people my age are too settled or focused or successful to take. It's a risk, perhaps, but what is life if not a series of risks? It's when you start avoiding risk that your life becomes calcified, codified, boring.

That is not what I want!

What I want is a good man who loves me, a sense of unfolding possibility, and that little cottage on the Maine coast with roses climbing artfully around the door frame. So maybe this was meant to be. Not, I mean, the thousands of dollars of damage to the museum—that was unfortunate. But the series of events that have led me to this moment.

One day, perhaps, this will be the pivotal moment in the story that Richard and I tell our grandchildren. And when we get to the part about the fire-eater, we'll all laugh and laugh.

CHAPTER 7

By the time I actually hear the words "Mary Quince would like to see you in her office," I am already packing books and three-ring binders from my shelves into a box.

"Sure," I tell Mary's secretary as casually as if she's invited me to lunch. "I'll be right there."

Mary's face is even whiter than usual. "The fire insurance was an egregious mistake. And, unfortunately, grounds for dismissal."

"I know," I say.

"I hope you'll find something that you really want to do. I don't think event planning is it, do you?"

Over the next few days, I call my landlord and talk him into letting me sublet the apartment, find a sublettor on craigslist.com, crate up my stuff, and haul it to my dad's garage. When I finally tell him and Sharon about MaineCatch—select details, anyway—they think I'm a little out of my mind, and more than a little desperate. "You met him *how*? You're moving *where*?"

"I'm not moving there. I'm just" —I remember Rich's wording—"taking a little trip."

"Trip? You mean vacation?"

"Yeah." The truth is, I have no idea how long I'm staying. I haven't thought much about the particulars beyond arriving on

Rich's doorstep, falling into his arms, and living happily ever after.

"You're not thinking clearly," Dad snaps, silhouetted in the door of the garage like a killer in a horror flick. "You met this guy on the Internet, for Christ's sake. Who knows what kind of deviant—?"

Kneeling on the cement floor, I am writing "ANGELA RUSSO—BOOKS," "ANGELA RUSSO—KITCHEN," "ANGELA RUSSO—BEDDING" in permanent black marker on the front panels of a stack of boxes. "Don't you trust my judgment?" I ask.

"It's not you I don't trust. It's *him*." My dad jabs the air for emphasis.

"He's a nice guy. He runs a sailing school."

"Never trust a sailor," he says.

My dad is always issuing bombastic declarations like this. About Korean food: "They eat dogs over there." About protesters: "If they don't respect this country, they should leave and never come back." When I was a teenager it made me light-headed with fury, but the years have mellowed me. "Some people say never trust an accountant," I say.

"Very funny," he says. "You're making your grandmother sick with worry. The screwup at the museum. Getting fired. Now this." He shakes his head.

"Nonna wants me to be happy."

"Not exactly," my dad says. "Your grandmother wants you happy—here. She doesn't want you moving six states away. It's like the whatshisname, Wizard of Oz, said. Everything you need is right here in your own backyard. And if you can't find it here, sweetheart, maybe there's something wrong with you."

"Well, maybe there is," I say. "Or maybe I just want to try something else. I'm a grown-up, Dad. I can do that."

"I don't know," he says, frowning. "Frankly, this strikes me as pretty juvenile. What are you going to do up there?"

"I have a little money saved," I say, smiling up at him. "I'm not going to starve; I'll find something."

"Pah. This is the time in your life to be settling down, not traipsing off in search of—I don't know what." He shrugs. "But I suppose it's your life."

"Yep. It's my life."

In the kitchen my grandmother puts her hand, as cold and bony as a chicken wing, over mine. She says, "Stone soup? I made it this morning."

"Thanks, Nonna."

She ladles up a bowl of *minestra,* a soup of winter vegetables. Since I was a child, she has called it stone soup, after the folktale about a village that was going hungry until a stranger, passing through, said he could make soup from a stone. He put a rock in a pot and covered it with water, then began calling for scraps of vegetables that the villagers had lying around—an old turnip, a rubbery carrot, wild herbs. Eventually the pot was full. The villagers thought it was a miracle. I did, too; Nonna would send me outside to choose a small stone, which she would wash carefully and place in the bottom of the Dutch oven before adding the rest of the ingredients.

"It's cold in the north," she says. "You'll need stone soup up there."

"Why don't you come with me, Nonna?" I ask playfully. "We can make it together."

She sets the bowl on the counter and leans closer. "Your father," she says. "His nature is *conservatore.* He settled here, and can't see any other way. To him, this is how life is. And the way it should be. You work hard, you make a decent living, that should be enough."

I nod. I know this is true.

"But you are not your father. You are young—"

"Not that young."

"Young enough. And you want something else. Something more, something less—doesn't matter. Something different." She is silent for a moment. "I was younger than you—much younger—when I left my family and my country."

"I know. Did you regret it?"

"Naturalmente," she says. "But what could I do? Here I was. And you—what is the word?—adapt. You adapt. There are surprises. I learned from my neighbors to cook dishes from all over Italy, things I had never tried before. And there was an Italian-American cookbook someone gave me. Your father's favorites are not from Basilicata at all—chicken marsala and potato-crusted sole and baked ziti, god forbid. And there are other things—the baker in Nutley is better than the baker in Matera, and so on." She turns and cuts into a crunchy ciabatta, hands me a piece. "Taste."

Most Italian immigrants from Basilicata, my father has told me, refused to have anything to do with foods from other regions, let alone countries. But Nonna was different. As a teenager in Matera, she worked with a maiden aunt who cooked for a priest sent to their parish from Rome. Even in times of hardship, when people in the village had little to eat, the priest ate what he liked—cheeses and sausages from other parts of the country, fresh vegetables. So Nonna learned to cook a variety of foods from different parts of Italy.

The bread is chewy and elastic, and as I bite into it the smell of yeast wafts up.

"You need to know how to make a good ciabatta. And my *minestra,*" she says. "Maybe that's all you need." Her face softens into a smile, and she places the bowl in front of me. "So. You cook the onion and the garlic very slowly, in good olive oil. Not extra virgin—too bitter. Regular. Peppers next. Then tomatoes. The pasta you prepare al dente; it will cook more in the soup."

In my stomach I feel a twist of regret. I don't want to leave her. "Tell me the rest of the recipe," I say, though of course I know it by heart.

When I tell my brother Paul I'm going, he says, "Are you out of your mind? You'll freeze your ass off up there! With nine million men in the tristate area, you'd think you could've found someone closer to home."

Lindsay comes out to Nutley Friday evening on the bus from the Port Authority. "Hate that bus," she says when I pick her up at the local stop. She looks over at me, sitting in the driver's seat of the silver Honda Civic my dad bought used for my eighteenth birthday, and says, "It's like we're back in high school. Heading to Willowbrook Mall to check out the sale at Benetton."

"You wanna go?" I say. "It's a Friday night. Like old times."

She laughs. "Sure, why not. When in Jersey . . ."

We take Bloomfield Avenue to Verona and turn right on Pompton Avenue, one of several off-highway options, to the mall. When we get there we drift in and out of shops, lingering in our stodgy old favorites—the Limited, the Gap, Ann Taylor. The mall has had a glitzy makeover for a new generation, and we're a little out of step. Hordes of teenage girls wearing low-slung Seven jeans and cropped, candy-colored tops roam the stores, chomping bubble gum and slicking on glittery lip gloss, collapsing against each other in giggles. After an hour or so of regressing to our teenage selves—"These cords are cute," "This would look so good on you!"—we are overcome with mall fatigue and stagger to California Pizza Kitchen to order our old standard, Thai chicken salad.

I am nervous. I've been waiting for the right time to tell Lindsay about Rich. About Maine. I'm hoping she'll take it well.

The waiter places the salads in front of us, and we aren't disappointed; they're as big as our heads. "Awesome," Lindsay says.

We each order a glass of house white "just because we can," Lindsay tells the waiter, who doesn't say it but is clearly thinking that carding us was the last thing on his mind.

I raise my glass and say, "To you, for coming to visit me in exile."

"What are friends for?" she says. "Besides, this is fun. I love the mall." She takes a sip of wine and makes a face. "Eugh."

I take a sip, too. It's both cloyingly sweet *and* too tart, a seemingly impossible combination.

"Order wine in a mall, what do you expect?" she says.

"And house wine, at that."

As we pick at our salads, all slivered almonds and crispy chow mein noodles, Lindsay tells me about the latest with Mr. Hot. He's staying over a lot these days. They've had sex in all three rooms of her apartment, as well as in Central Park one afternoon and in a stairwell at a restaurant late one night.

"Is it serious?" I ask.

"Seriously good," she says.

Finally I say, "Okay. I have some news."

I tell her about my evolving correspondence with Maine-Catch. "Uh-huh, uh-huh," she says. My tongue is awkward around his name, *Richard,* sticking to the "ch" sound. Mentioning his name seems too intimate, somehow, exposing him to Lindsay's obvious skepticism. When I tell her about our tryst in

Boston and the haikus and the roses and the invitation to Maine she purses her lips.

I can't take her silence anymore. "For god's sake, Lindsay, I thought you might be happy for me."

She shifts in her seat, then utters some trite admonitions I've already heard from Sharon. *You need to be careful. This is moving so fast. I don't want you to get hurt.*

"But you made me do this," I protest.

"I wanted you to be happy. If I'd known you'd find a guy in Alaska—"

"Maine is not Alaska."

"Whatever. It's Siberia, as far as I'm concerned."

"That is so not true," I say, knowing full well that as far as she's concerned, it so is true. "And besides, we're getting way ahead of ourselves. I've only met him once, and we didn't exactly discuss the names of our future children. I'm just going up there to see."

She sighs. "This taps into all of my deepest fears of being in our midthirties—"

"Early to midthirties," I say.

"No," she says so fiercely that I sit back in my chair. "We are not *early* anymore, Ange. And I'm afraid we're just going to grab whatever comes along next because—because it's time, and we think we should be with someone, anyone. Starting a family."

"Not just anyone," I say defensively.

She shrugs.

"You don't really feel that way."

"Yes and no," she says.

"Come on. We are two intelligent, good-looking babes. I don't care if I'm single until my boobs touch my knees. I'm not settling, and neither are you."

"Why would you even start up with someone who's so far away?" she says. "What is the point of that?"

I don't have a good answer. "You know I've always had a thing for Maine," I say lamely.

"You've never even been there." She pushes her half-eaten salad away. "Your 'thing' is a fantasy. It's a state of mind, which for some inexplicable reason you have attached to a particular place."

"And what's wrong with that?"

"There's nothing *wrong* with it, as long as you realize that's what it is—a fantasy that has nothing to do with real life. And now you're hooking up with this guy from nowhere who just happens to fit into the slot of your preconceived dream."

"Hold on." I feel my cheeks getting warm. "Isn't that what it's all about? Isn't that, in fact, the core of the human experience—that the person you end up with is right for you precisely because he fits your idea of what you want, he fills your gaps, fulfills your fantasies? Otherwise, what's the point of love? I want to have an ideal, and I want to find someone who will fit it."

"No, no, no!" Lindsay is violently shaking her head. This may be the strongest disagreement we've ever had, and I'm a little disconcerted by how heated we're both getting. Usually when we disagree we try to defuse things as quickly as possible. But clearly there's enough at stake here that neither of us wants to let go. Lindsay looks at me as if I've just told her I'm a Scientologist. "It is *not* about fitting some ideal, Ange, and that is so wrong it doesn't even sound like you. I have known you since you wore high-waisted pants and leg warmers, and I've never heard you say anything like that." She balls up her napkin and tosses it on the table. "I think it's exactly the opposite. It's when you have preconceived ideas that you get into trouble, when you're trying to fit a person into a mold. For me, love is organic. It's about being open to people and possibilities even when you feel closed—letting go of your fixed ideas and preconceptions and living in the moment."

"For god's sake!" I say. "You don't call finding a sailor in Maine being open to possibilities? Why are you unable to be happy for me? I'm really surprised, to tell you the truth."

She clenches her teeth, which is how I know she's really upset. For a moment she doesn't say anything. Then she reaches across the table for my hand. "I don't know what I'll do without you," she says. "You know that already, and what pisses me off is you think that's the whole explanation for this, which makes it easier for you to dismiss what I'm saying. But I am truly, genuinely concerned about this move, Ange. I think you're vulnerable right now and you're not thinking through the consequences. This guy might be the nicest guy on earth, but you barely know him. And you're moving up to an island off the coast of Maine, where you've never been before, not even to visit. In October."

"If it doesn't work out, I'll leave," I say.

"You've lost your job. Given up your apartment. Packed your stuff away. You have nothing to come back to."

"Except you."

"Yuh," she snorts.

"I have a good feeling about this," I say. "I think things are going to work out just fine for both of us."

"You had a good feeling about that gala, too," she says, "and the whole thing went up in smoke."

"Okay, okay, I'm trying to get some closure here," I say.

As we futz with the bill, each of us ineptly trying to divide and add the tip, I say, "Promise you'll visit."

"Maybe in the summer. If you hold out that long."

"Well, if things with Mr. Hot don't pan out, maybe Rich has a friend up there."

"No thanks," she says. "Moving to Iceland to shack up with a native isn't in the cards for me." She smiles, a clear effort to blunt the sharpness of her words.

CHAPTER 8

I slam the trunk of the old silver Civic. It's seven o'clock on Saturday morning, and I'm set to go. I'm leaving most of my boxes in my dad's garage, taking only warm clothes and shoes and bedding and books. And pots and pans and mixing bowls. Even so, the car is jam-packed. It occurs to me that the car, with its various dents and gouges, rust frilling the wheel caps, frying pans and spatulas poking out of a paper bag on the backseat, looks like some unfortunate person's home.

Maybe, in fact, mine.

My dad comes out of the back door with a plastic travel mug I haven't seen before and hands it to me. The mug is black, with a pattern of grinning white skeletons dancing around the sides. I take a sip. Fresh coffee. "Where'd this come from?" I ask.

"Starbucks," my father says. "I thought you could use it for your trip. Halloween, I guess. It was all they had."

"Wow. Thanks, Dad. Is this the first time you've been to a Starbucks?"

"Not exactly." He looks pained, then confesses, "I kind of have a thing for that caramel macchiato."

"Well, you're full of surprises," I say.

As if on cue, Sharon appears. She is more cheerful than I've seen her for days; I think she was afraid I might sleep on the foldout forever. "Leaving so early?"

"If this old clunker can make it," my father says, patting the hood. "You know this car is seventeen years old. And what's it got—a hundred and fifty thousand miles?"

I look at the mileage. "A hundred and fifty-eight."

"We'll cross our fingers," Sharon says.

"Just remember, the earth is flat," my father tells me, reprising a running joke from my childhood. He said it whenever I set off anywhere new.

"It's round and I'll prove it," I say, sticking to our script.

He puts one arm around my shoulder, a partial hug. "I just don't want you to fall off the edge."

"It's round. There is no edge."

"Oh, there's an edge," he says. "There's always an edge. Promise me you'll keep your eyes open for it."

My dad tends to communicate emotion through metaphor. All you can do is play along.

"I promise," I say.

Sharon has that frozen look she gets when she thinks she's being left out of a joke. "I missed something."

"Never mind," my father says. He smiles at me tenderly. "I think you're making a mistake."

"I know, Dad."

"I just wanted to say it one last time. For the record."

Nonna is standing in the doorway, wiping her hands on a dish towel. When she sees me looking over at her, she holds her arms up and moves her fingers like a crab flexing its pincers. "Come here, *mia figlia*," my child, she says.

When she squeezes me I smell powder and yeast and the oil from her scalp. She holds me out at arms' length, clutching my shoulders, and says, "Do you have a warm coat?"

I nod yes.

"Maybe you need my rabbit fur. The one made in Italy."

Nonna's black rabbit fur coat is part of our family story. My grandfather gave it to her several years after they came to America, proof of what his new money could buy—a coat he never could have afforded back in the country where it was made. In old photos Nonna wears it over an evening dress, in the backseat of a slope-nosed motor car, posing with my grandfather on a snowy street. "I could never," I say. "But you will wear it when you visit me."

"*Va bene.*" All right, then, she says to be polite.

"I'm expecting you, Nonna," I say insistently, and she says, "*Tutto il a destra,*" all right, "we'll see."

When I pull away, the three of them are standing in the driveway. I watch them in my rearview mirror: my father waving, Nonna clasping the dish towel to her bosom, Sharon turning to go back inside.

There's an accident up ahead on the Mass Pike, and for the first time since leaving New Jersey, I'm stuck in traffic. I open my window and breathe. It's a warm early October morning; the sky is cloudless. Orange trees explode against a blue sky, as vivid as Technicolor.

One evening last week my father went to Radio Shack and surprised me with a CD player for my old car, then spent another evening installing it.

"You are a lucky girl to have a father like that," Sharon said. We were watching him out the living room window as he lay on his back fiddling with the controls, his legs sticking out the driver's side. I could tell she disapproved of his indulging me.

"You're a lucky girl to have a husband like that," I said.

"You're both lucky girls. And you can thank me for raising

him," Nonna called from the kitchen. Sharon looked over at me and rolled her eyes.

Now, sitting in traffic, I rummage around in a box of CDs on the passenger seat, find a Van Morrison and slip it in. Van is singing in his velvet voice and the trees whisper as I pass, and I am halfway between two worlds, the known and the unknown. I feel as transparent as the wind, as if my spirit is hovering in the sky, waiting to land. I am driving toward a future I can't see, leaving behind a past that already feels distant. Nothing is clear—and yet the trees are sharp against the sky; I can see the hard outlines of everything. The highway signs, the center line, the eighteen-wheeler in front of me.

A faded green bridge rises out of the earth. From a distance, as the road winds toward it, the bridge looks like a mirage. My spirits soar. This is it—the narrow band of river on my MapQuest printout that separates New Hampshire from Maine. I'm here!

The road is wide, four lanes in each direction, sloping toward the midpoint of the bridge. Halfway across the river a small sign says WELCOME TO MAINE. This is not like the border of any other state I've been to, where you pass a road sign and things stay pretty much the same. When you enter Maine, you are crossing over water into new territory.

On the other side of the bridge, now, I drive past two white water towers with twenty-foot red lobsters painted on the sides, signs for outlet malls, acres of evergreens. After about forty-five minutes I feel like a little kid who has stayed up too late. My high is wearing off. Consulting my directions, it becomes clear that I won't actually be "here" for quite some time. It's more than four hours from the border to where I'm going.

I put in a Lucinda Williams CD, roll my neck, and arch my

back against the seat, like a cat. I need to pee, and the car could use some gas, but I'm determined not to stop until I absolutely have to.

I'm singing along to Lucinda—*I am waiting in my car, I am waiting at this bar, I am waiting on your back steps*—going about seventy in a sixty-five-mile zone, when the car starts losing power. What the hell is going on? I press the gas pedal to the floor and the car goes from 40 to 30 to 20. *Fuck.* As the car rolls to a stop, I steer onto the shoulder.

I check all the warning lights—oil, brakes, battery. (I wouldn't know what to do even if I could identify the problem, but that doesn't stop me from checking the warning lights as if I might be able to solve this.) The gas gauge doesn't work; the needle hasn't moved from Empty in at least a year. But this car has always been fuel efficient; I thought that a tank of gas would get me at least as far as—

Oh.

As far as right about here, I guess.

Where in the world am I? Looking around, I see only trees. About a hundred yards back is an entrance ramp sloping down to the road, but no signs are visible anywhere. Looking at the map, I deduce that I passed Portland a while ago, but I haven't— or at least I think I haven't—passed Augusta.

"*I haven't dated anybody south of Augusta in ten years.*"

Every now and then a car whizzes past.

So, huh, this is why people join Triple A.

The only thing I can think to do—and really, to even call it thinking is an overstatement, it's more like blind panic—is call Rich. I punch his number into my cell phone.

"Hey," he says. "You're here already?"

That "already" gives me pause. I talked to him yesterday. He knew I was coming today. "You knew I was coming today."

"Ah, yeah." He sounds distracted, as if I've interrupted him in the middle of something. "I just didn't know you'd be so fast. How close are you?"

"Not that close," I snap. "That's why I'm calling. I don't know what happened. My car just—stopped."

"What do you mean?"

"I mean . . ." I feel foolish and needy. "I think maybe I ran out of gas."

"No way."

"Yeah, I think so."

"No *way*," he says again.

This is his response? "Yeah."

At first I think he's catching his breath, but then I realize he's laughing. "I don't believe you," he says.

Now that I'm actually talking to him, I'm not sure why I called. For moral support? Practical advice? So far he's giving me neither. "I'm not kidding."

"No—I mean, I *believe* you, I just can't believe you ran out of gas. Who runs out of gas in this day and age?"

Who says "day and age" in this day and age? "Look, I live in New York. I'm not used to driving. And my car is really old and the gas gauge is broken. Anyway—I don't need to make excuses for running out of gas. Whatever. It happened. And now I'm sitting here on the side of the highway in the middle of nowhere, and I only called you because I don't know what else to do."

"Jeez," he says. "That's rough luck, Angela. You got Triple A?"

"No."

He lets out a sigh. "I don't know what to tell ya. You gotta get to a gas station."

"I know. I just—I don't know where I am."

"Have you thought about hitchin'?"

"'Hitchin'?" I repeat dumbly.

"Maybe you can get a ride to the nearest station."

"Where I come from, people who hitchhike end up in gulleys without their heads."

"Aw, c'mon. You're in Maine. Stuff like that doesn't happen up here. Not usually, anyways."

Is it my imagination, or has his Maine accent gotten thicker since I spoke to him yesterday?

As we're talking, there's a knock on my window. I look up to see a Maine state trooper with a shiny gold badge motioning for me to roll down the glass.

The whole time the kindly state trooper is giving me a lift to a Mobil station off the next exit, helping me fill the gas can the owner keeps in the back (apparently I'm not the only one who runs out of gas on these long stretches of road), ferrying me back to my car, waiting to make sure it starts, and giving me his number in case something else happens, I'm replaying the conversation with Rich in my mind.

Like white blood cells, rationalizations rush to the site of my wounded pride to minimize the damage. I did catch him off guard. I wasn't clear; he thought I was on Mount Desert Island already—of course he was surprised. It was childish to call him. I didn't know where I was; how could I expect him to come to the rescue?

Then, I can't help myself, I start scratching the scab. He could have responded better in a dozen different ways. A little empathy, for a start. "That's awful" or "I'm so sorry" or "What can I do to help?" He could've offered some practical advice, like calling

911. The state trooper says I could have pinpointed my location by giving a dispatcher a mile marker.

Tim, the state trooper, is all of twenty-three. He has a blond buzz cut and glasses, and it is his second year on the force. As he drives me around, he tells me about the obstacle course police trainees have to maneuver before they get to drive a cruiser. "Even at a hundred miles an hour, I'm probably the safest car on the road," he says. On his shooting test he got a perfect score from twenty yards, then ten and five and two. "What do you aim at?" I ask, and he spreads his freckled young hand over his chest. "Body mass," he says. "It's unfortunate, but if you aim for the leg and hit a little kid behind the guy instead, there's nobody to blame but yourself."

I can tell he hasn't been on the job long, or doesn't run into many people on the road, because he is so eager to talk. He's the youngest of four kids; he grew up listening to his parents' music, Jackson Browne and Bonnie Raitt, and that kind of soft rock is still his favorite.

After he drives off, it occurs to me that I now know more about Tim than I do about Richard, the man I am on my way to see. My supposed soul mate.

The highway is long and empty, narrowing from four lanes to three and then two, and flanked by trees, only trees. Who has ever seen such colors in nature? Vermilion, brilliant gold, hunting jacket orange, olive green—the colors of L.L. Bean turtlenecks. I feel as if I'm passing through a magical forest.

Just before Bangor I veer off I-95 North to 395 East. The trees fall away and soon I am coasting up and down wide, sloping hills. Cottages that look quaint from a peak are revealed, in the valley, to be modest dwellings with cheap siding and dismantled trucks in the side yards. I pass through Ellsworth, or at least its commercial strip, a gauntlet of strip malls and fast-food restaurants culminating in a Wal-Mart that sits on the edge of town like a fat tick on the back of a dog.

Even without MapQuest I'd know I'm nearing the coast, because after Ellsworth the road is lined with lobster shacks and tourist shops. Garden ornaments, weather vanes, a Cannon towel outlet, boarded-up ice-cream stands. Shabby motels with vacancy signs have "Enjoy leaf season!" spelled out in crazy letters on white rectangular placards facing the road. For a long stretch I'm stuck behind a pickup with a bumper sticker that says, "Hug a logger—you'll never go back to trees."

It's now five o'clock, and the sky is a colorless wash. All at once, I notice a long stretch of mud and seaweed on both sides of the road. Without quite realizing it, I have driven onto the island—a sign on the right confirms it. My heart hops once again. I am here. I am here! Despite my earlier misgivings, I am giddy with excitement. The air is crisp, the water to my right a silky black, the rocks as jaggedly picturesque as the tourist websites promised.

The road forks and I bear right, following Rich's directions. I'm clutching a printout of his e-mail, holding it up to the fading light. I knew the island wasn't small—it has numerous harbors and hamlets and coves—but somehow I'd envisioned the place as one charming fishing village. Here I am, still driving. Why am I still driving?

Then I see it, just as promised in the directions, the turnoff for 102. It seems marvelously unlikely that the places noted in the e-mail really exist—like seeing a celebrity in person, a movie star you feel you know. Back at home I looked at a map and saw the names of these roads, and now here they are. A part of me thought this was all make-believe, especially the preposterous name of Rich's road: Blueberry Cove Lane. It's like something out of *Murder, She Wrote*. But no—here's the street sign, white letters on a green background, illuminated by my headlights in the grainy dusk.

I turn right. The road, crackling under my tires, is evidently unpaved. I look around. If I'm not mistaken, this appears to be a new development of cookie-cutter condos in a rocky lunar landscape. I ponder the directions in my hand as if they might yield fresh insight. This can't be right. Can it?

Fourteen A. Attached to 14B. Beige vinyl siding, white trim, a forlorn shrub under the front window. Across the road is a vast muddy lot with a yellow backhoe listing to one side on the slant of the hill, trailing deep, puddled ruts.

Rich didn't tell me he lives in a town house, or that it's in a brand-new development. But why would he? It's nothing to be ashamed of. I had a picture in my head and . . . I assumed. Blueberry Cove Lane equals cottage of my dreams. (I should have figured out what is instantly apparent now, that "Blueberry Cove Lane" was the shrewd choice of a calculating developer to evoke precisely the image I had in my head.)

I pull into the driveway behind a shiny maroon truck with custom-appliquéd flames licking the rear. It has to be Rich's. Are those factory applied, I wonder, or did he select them himself? The house is dark on the first floor except for one room lit by a single naked bulb.

I am monstrously disappointed. It takes all my will not to put my car in reverse and creep back down the driveway.

Taking a deep breath, I try to be open. Flames on a truck are an interesting style choice. This is not a hovel; it's a nice apartment in what will soon be a lovely subdivision. They'll plant trees and flowers, pave the street, dig a sidewalk. These new homes have sound heating systems and snug windows—what's not to like?

I tell myself that I'm being petty. After all, I'm here for Rich; these small things don't matter. I am sulking like a spoiled child, unhappy with her Christmas present. I hear my father's voice in my head: "Stop pouting! You're lucky to get what you got." Maybe I was—but it didn't change the fact that it wasn't what I wanted.

CHAPTER 9

The man of my dreams, my MaineCatch, is visible through the front window of his town house, talking on a portable phone and drinking a beer. He's pacing around, looking for something. From this distance, with his coat-hanger shoulders and sun-streaked hair, he looks like a dissolute prep-school kid, one of those dangerous boys who possesses all the charming arrogance of privilege but assumes none of its burdens. I didn't see him this way before, or not quite this way. In Boston I was drugged with infatuation, and his skin was so smooth. Now, observing him from a distance, I wonder if we would have been attracted to each other in a bar.

As I sit in the car watching him, his most recent haiku comes to mind:

> *Soon you'll be coming*
> *We'll have lots of sex I hope*
> *My bed is king size.*

I laughed when I got it, assuming that was his point in sending it. A sex poem to ease the awkwardness. But now I'm not so sure it was supposed to be funny.

I turn off the engine and he looks up, startled, like a farm animal. He sees the car in his driveway, half hidden behind the truck. I watch him become self-conscious, click off the phone and set it on top of the TV, put down the beer bottle, tuck in his T-shirt. Then he vanishes from the window.

When the front door opens, I run my hands through my limp hair, up from the roots at the nape of my neck, my fingers like a wide-tooth comb. He's walking toward me with his hands shoved in the pockets of his sweatpants, shoulders hunched forward.

"Hi," I say, getting out of the car.

"Hey, you made it." His words are toneless, a little slurry.

"Yeah, finally." I squint up at him in the gloom.

"Was it gas?"

"What?"

"Your tank was empty?"

"Oh. Yes."

"Sorry I didn't—couldn't—" He shrugs.

"That's okay. A nice state trooper came by and helped me out."

"Well, that's good." He kicks a rut in the dirt. I notice that he's wearing his sneakers with the heels folded down, like mules. "So did he ask for your number?"

"What? No."

He raises his eyebrows suggestively. "I'll bet he wanted to."

"Oh, come on," I say. "Anyway, he was on duty. Isn't that against the law?"

"Relax, I'm joking," he says, with a little edge in his voice.

I don't say anything. In my experience, when somebody says "Relax, I'm joking," they usually aren't.

He leans down to kiss me and I feel his rough stubble, smell the sour aftertaste of beer and the mushroomy odor of dried sweat.

"Did you just go running?" I ask.

"Huh? Oh, what, you mean because of my sneakers?"

"You're—sweating," I say, attempting to be playful but instead sounding pinched and accusatory.

"Maybe you make me nervous."

"I'm sure that's it."

"Maybe I'm thinking of later," he says, snaking his fingers through the belt loops of my jeans.

"Oh," I say. Maybe he is.

Despite everything, I feel myself warming to him—those Siberian husky eyes, the bleached hair on his tanned forearms. He tugs my belt loop on one side, pulling me off center, my left hip bumping into his right. When our bodies touch I feel a shiver. Oh, yes, this—now I remember.

"You want a beer?" he asks. "I could use another."

"Yeah, all right," I say. He releases my loops and I follow him into the house.

He turns on the shower and pulls the T-shirt over his head. His beautiful stomach, almost hairless, skin as thin as a puppy's. The hollowed-out bone at the top of his rib cage. The sunburned back of his neck.

I tilt my face into the spray and he is behind me, water running over his hands, over my breasts and hips, both of us slick as seals. He rubs a bar of soap down my spine and between my legs and I'm not thinking about anything now except his hands and the soap and his dick pressing hard against me, his lips on my neck, in my seaweed hair.

I close my eyes and see Frank, the fire-eater, blowing flame, like Zeus blew wind. The topiary ignites in a brilliant fireball. Such passion—such uncompromising rage! The fire-eater knew. He knew that letting loose this flame would destroy him, ruin his future, wreck all that he had worked to accomplish. He knew, and he went ahead and did it anyway.

When I wake the next morning, Rich isn't there. My bags are still in the car. I am naked under a cotton-poly sheet decorated with sailboats on a mattress on the floor. Striated light filters through a plastic venetian blind on the window.

I get up, find my wadded, damp clothes from yesterday strewn around the bathroom, get dressed, and pad downstairs noiselessly on the wall-to-wall carpeting. The apartment is as featureless as a motel room, with fewer amenities. A black pleather couch, a large-screen TV with gigantic speakers, and some free weights populate an otherwise empty living room. On the kitchen counter are a small microwave, a Mr. Coffee machine, and a take-out pizza menu.

Okay, this isn't the vision I had in my head. But I have decided to be open-minded. This is a real guy living in a real place, not some New York art director's idea of what "real simple" is.

I open the front door, and it makes a vacuum-sealed *swock*. Outside is cold and gray, and I stand back with a shiver. Rich's truck is gone; he must have maneuvered around my car in the driveway. He would have had to drive across the lawn, but there are no tire tracks. The ground is hard-packed. It isn't giving anything away.

I run out to my car and yank a giant wheeled duffel bag full of clothes out of the backseat. Then I steer the duffel up the driveway to the house, bump it up the three stairs to the front door like I'm trying to dispose of a body, haul it inside, and close the door.

In the kitchen I open the fridge. I find several cans of Red Bull, a six-pack of Bar Harbor ale, a box of Pop-Tarts, a small jar of mayo, and a bottle of ketchup. My stomach is rumbling; now that I think about it, we never had dinner. I take a twin, foil-wrapped pack of Pop-Tarts out of the box.

"You just need to relax," he said last night, *relax,* for the second time. At that moment it had seemed sweet, given what else he was doing with his mouth, but as I think about it, I'm not so sure. Where is Rich, anyway? He didn't tell me he was going out; he didn't leave a note. I wonder now if "relax" means don't ask questions.

The cold Pop-Tart tastes like piecrust-flavored cardboard with Elmer's-glue frosting. Mechanically I eat one and then the other, breaking off small pieces and nibbling them like a hamster. I'm not hungry anymore, but it seems somehow impolite to leave one behind.

It occurs to me that Sam, the dog, is nowhere to be seen.

Rich comes home when I'm in the shower. He calls my name and I freeze, nose twitching like a rabbit. Quickly I rinse the shampoo out of my hair and turn off the water, grabbing a towel and wrapping myself up like a sorority girl on TV.

"Hey," he says, coming into the bedroom. "I brought you a coffee."

"Oh. Thanks!"

He sets a paper cup with a white lid on top of his dresser. "Cold out there."

"I know. I got my bag out of the car."

"Oh. I guess I should've—"

"No! I didn't mean—" I break off. There's an awkward pause. "Let me get dressed and I'll be down in a second."

He turns away and I let out a breath, drop my towel, scramble for my clothes.

"Thanks for the coffee," I say again in the kitchen, taking a sip. It's weak and lukewarm, but I'm glad to have a prop.

"I had to get gas anyway," he says.

Flattering. "Right. Well," I say. "So here I am."

"Here you are."

"So . . . what do you think?"

"What do I think about what?"

"About my being here."

He nods, a beat longer than necessary. "I think it's good."

"Really?"

"You look good. You feel good," he says, moving closer. "I'm always happy to have a good-looking girl in my house."

"Gee. That's lovely," I say.

"No, I mean it," he says earnestly, as if to prove that his sentiment is heartfelt.

"'Always happy'?" I say. "Sounds like you entertain a lot."

For a moment he doesn't answer, just looks at me as if he can't figure out what my problem is.

"By the way, where's your dog?"

His face is blank. Then he twitches slightly, as if jolted by memory. "Aah—he, actually, he ran away."

"'She,' you mean."

"What?"

"'Sam-short-for-Samantha'?"

"Right," he says. "She—you know, she acted—like a guy. Roughhousing and all that." He crouches and moves his hand as if he's playing with a big rambunctious dog. Then he stands up straight and sighs. "I miss her."

"Gosh. I'm sorry."

"That's all right. Let's just not talk about her again, okay? It's kind of a sore subject."

"I'm sure it is."

He knows I don't believe him, and clearly wants to close this topic as soon as possible. "Hey," he says, clapping his hands together. "How much have you seen of Mount Desert?"

I'm willing to switch gears—for now, at least. What's my alternative? "Not much. Am I really on an island?"

"A-yuh," he says in an exaggerated Maine accent. "Come on. Let's go for a ride. I'll show you around."

The road rings the interior of Mount Desert, dipping in and out of small villages with scenic harbors, glimpses of the sea. I am riding shotgun in Rich's truck, high above the ground, my finger tracing our route on a free map he picked up for me in the convenience store. On the map, Acadia National Park spreads out from the middle of the island, like an ink stain. Rich tells me about how it was built, how Franklin Roosevelt established a jobs program for World War I veterans and how the vets spent fifteen years cutting and hauling granite and building bridges to carve a park out of these mountains and valleys—carriage roads, bicycle paths, hiking trails. The Rockefellers donated eleven thousand acres, the Vanderbilts gave money, and now this is one of the most scenic national parks in the country. The population of the island swells from fifteen thousand to over a million in the summer. Cadillac Mountain, its heathered purple face visible for miles, is, for many months of the year, the first place in North America to see the sun rise; tourists come up at three thirty or four in the morning, huddled in blankets, to wait it out.

I guess if you live in a place like this you can't help but turn into a tour guide. Still, Rich's enthusiasm for the place catches me off guard.

"You love it here, don't you?" I ask, and he gives me a sidelong glance; he thinks I'm making fun of him. But after a pause he says, "I think it's the most beautiful place on earth."

"All year round?"

"Winter's tough," he says. "But we find things to do."

"Like what?"

He puts on the blinker and turns left into a park entrance. Traffic was sparse before, on the main road, but this road is deserted. Rich points at the granite blocks lining the asphalt, bumpers to keep cars from pitching off the sides as the road winds up into the hills. Touching the windshield with his finger, he identifies various trails whittled into the hillside: Beehive, Great Head, Otter Cliffs. "Climbing can be addictive," he says. "All year long, even in the snow, you see people up there. They look like ants."

We're quiet for a moment.

"We go to bars and play Scrabble," he says abruptly. "We have sex. Get high. Go to movies, go to bars. Some people get depressed, some go to Florida."

"What about you?"

"I work on my boat," he says. "Hang out with my friends."

"Go online to meet girls."

He looks at me out of the corner of his eye, grins, shrugs. "Go online to meet girls," he says, nodding.

We are winding slowly up the mountain now. I look up at the rock face pocked with trees and the road stretching ahead. As we get higher the trees fall away, every view a postcard.

Rich pulls off the road into a scenic overlook. We sit in silence in the warm, humming truck, gazing out at the black ocean far below, the spiky coastline. Up here on Cadillac the other mountains look like hills. In the distance you can see strings of small islands, white boats like faraway seagulls, a strip of bleached sand. It's strange that I'm here, so far from what I know. I glance at Rich, as indecipherable to me as everything else. But here he is, on this journey with me, waiting for the moment to unfold.

CHAPTER 10

Any coffee shop that plays "Hey Jude" on a cold, wet Thursday morning can't be all bad. It's my third day on the island, and I have just stumbled on this place. It's called the Daily Grind, and it's in Spruce Harbor on Eider Street, between the bank and the market. I've driven through this little village several times; with its small shops, brick sidewalks, and one-room cedar-shingled library, it seems to be neither a tourist town nor an enclave of the wealthy, just a place where people live and work.

Driving down Main Street in search of coffee—I can't take Rich's watery gas-station blend any longer—I spy the placard out of the corner of my eye, down a side street. Before I park I check to make sure the place is open. I figure there is probably a fifty-fifty chance. Though it is still officially leaf season—that is, not yet November—the fair-weather stores that cater to vacationers have mostly closed up for the year. The promise implicit in its name—the Daily Grind—gives me hope. That means every day, right, not just sunny summer ones? As I get closer I am rewarded: Not only is it open, but a hand-lettered sign in the window promises "All day, every day."

Rain is coming down as if through a sieve. Water rushes to the gutters; the sidewalks are mined with puddles, awnings pregnant and sagging. Among the many things I didn't bring, an umbrella would be nice today. I dash through the front door and stand in the foyer for a moment, stamping the water from my feet. Once inside, the smell of real coffee, brewed from freshly ground beans, makes me swoon. I stagger to the counter—a drowning person toward a life raft, a thirsty person in the desert toward water . . . a New Yorker in Maine toward Colombian blend.

"Oh my God, can you really make me a latte?" I ask.

The guy behind the counter laughs. "You are officially the last tourist of the season," he says in an Australian accent.

"I'm amazed you're open!"

"This island doesn't melt into the sea when you go home, you know," he says. "Locals need caffeine as much as you people."

"'You people' are not my people," I protest.

"That's what you all say." He presses down the lever on the espresso machine and a long, slow hiss of steam escapes. After pouring hot milk into a wide white cup and spooning foam on top, he hands the mug to me.

"Thank you." I breathe, taking a sip. "Umm. Sooo good."

"Glad you approve."

"You know, you don't exactly sound like a local yourself."

"What on earth do you mean?" he says, ramping up the accent. *Whut on uth d'ye main?*

I roll my eyes and take another sip.

"Aren't we all just travelers in this journey we call life, anyway?" he says.

"That's philosophical for this hour of the morning."

He cranes around and looks at the clock over his head: 12:21. "It's afternoon. You do need that coffee."

As he talks he wipes down the counter, taps coffee filters into the sink, arranges tea packets in their slots. He's kind of short—maybe five eight—and ruddy, with reddish brown hair.

He appears to be my age or a little younger. Hard to tell with Australian men. Whatever their age, they're somehow both slightly leathery and perpetually youthful.

It is warm enough in here, but it isn't cozy. The walls are an icy yellow and the floor is checkered with black-and-white linoleum tiles. The lighting is purplish, fluorescent. The chairs are lightweight metal, with perforated seats and open wire backs; the Formica countertop is cluttered with tea dispensers and Save the Children boxes. Except for three Sprites on the bottom shelf and some grocery-store bagels puckered with slice marks, the deli case is empty. A seemingly arbitrary collection of travel-agency posters, faded by the sun, covers the walls.

The overall effect is of a waiting room in a mental hospital.

And I was wrong about the music. The Beatles were a chance selection. A radio station from Bangor is broadcasting greatest hits from the sixties, seventies, and eighties, and right now Sheena Easton is singing about how her baby takes the morning train, and takes another home again. To find her waiting for him.

I fish sections of newspaper out of a communal basket and assemble a Frankensteinian collection of parts from the *Bangor Daily News*, *Bar Harbor Times*, and the *Islander*, with classifieds from the *Ellsworth American*. Over the next half hour, I learn a lot about two sordid local crimes (unrelated but possibly part of a disturbing trend) and stumble on a recipe for pumpkin muffins involving orange rind. Pumpkin muffins—I sure could use one right about now.

A few people come in and out, announced by cold blasts of air, leaving sodden footprints in their wake. They make small talk with the Australian, whose name, I learn, is Flynn.

"Like Erroll," he tells me during a lull. "My grandma was a huge fan. He was Australian, you know."

"I didn't know that."

"Yeah. It's quite a popular name over there. Even though the dickhead told people he was Irish. And your name is—?"

"Angela."

"Nice to meet you, Angie." He disappears behind a door and comes out with a broom.

"Actually, it's—" I start to correct him, but he has disappeared behind a door.

A moment later he emerges with a broom. "What?"

"Oh, nothing." I watch him sweep the floor for a few minutes. "This is quite a popular place."

"Only place."

"Really?"

"Almost." He sweeps a pile of dirt into a dustpan with a long handle, then pours the dirt into a half-full garbage bag. "You want a refill?"

My latte is long gone. "Actually, I'm kind of hungry. Do you have anything to eat?"

"Bagels," he says, putting away the broom.

"Are they fresh?"

"Depends on what you mean by fresh. I call them Re-Fresh."

"Re-Fresh. You mean thawed?"

"That's another way to say it."

"Oh. No thanks," I say.

"I can toast one. You won't know the difference." He opens the dishwasher.

"I'm from New York. I'll know the difference."

"New York, huh," he says. "Really New York, or New York by way of somewhere else?"

"That's a funny question."

He raises his eyebrows and smiles, wiping out a glass. "I don't think you're really from New York."

"Why not?"

"You don't have the vibe." He places the glass on a shelf behind him and takes another out of the dishwasher. "Am I right?"

"No."

"You're a native New Yorker?"

"Well, I grew up just outside the city."

"Where? New Jersey?"

"Yeah."

"Aah. Thought so."

"What's that supposed to mean?"

"I just think it's funny how people from New Jersey always say they're from New York."

"That is not true," I say indignantly. "I've lived in New York for more than ten years. My entire adult life."

"Hmm," he says.

"What?"

"I'm just trying to calculate how old you are. Either twenty-eight or thirty-one, I guess, depending on how you define adulthood. Voting age or drinking age?"

"One of those," I say. "Sort of. So where do you say you're from?"

"Born and raised in Melbourne, Australia, mate, and proud of it." He shuts the dishwasher with his foot and straightens the line of spot-free glasses on the shelf above his head.

"Just not quite proud enough to stay there," I say. I don't know why I'm scrapping with him like this. Rich has been so weirdly uncommunicative that I'm starved for conversation; I'll do anything to keep it going.

"Touché. Actually, I . . . fell in love with someone, if you really want to know. He was a foreign-exchange student at university in Melbourne, and I tended bar at a place he liked to go downtown."

Ah, he. Good to know. "So how did you end up here?"

Except for us, the place is empty. Flynn throws a dish towel across his shoulder and comes over to my table with a pot of coffee. He pours coffee into my empty cup, then swoops into the chair across from me. "I used to joke that I'd follow him anywhere, and that's exactly what I did. I ended up here, on an island on the other side of the world."

"Where is he now?"

"He's here. Teaches high school over in Bar Harbor. We're just not together anymore."

"Oh, that's sad," I say. "Following someone around the world sounds like true love to me."

He shrugs. "True love is an elusive beast."

"That's poetic."

"Hard-earned wisdom often is, you know." He stretches, then pulls away from the chair back and turns around to look at it. "These chairs are rough as hell. Whose idea were they?"

"I don't know—yours?"

"I got them on the cheap from a dreary French restaurant in Ellsworth that was going out of business," he says.

"Well, maybe now we know why," I say.

The door opens with a faint tinkle, and a woman and young boy come in. The woman is small-boned and attractive; the boy looks just like her. They both have large brown eyes and dark curly hair.

"Afternoon, Flynn," the woman says.

"Hey, Rebecca. Hey, Josh. What's shakin'?"

Josh ducks behind the woman's back, and Flynn leans forward over the counter, pretending to try to get a glimpse. "Darn. Too quick for me," he says.

Josh giggles, and Rebecca pulls him out from behind her. "Be polite to Flynn," she says. "He makes Mommy's coffee."

"Ah, no, not polite!" Flynn says. "Polite is the last thing we need in this place. I think you should be really rude." He sticks out his tongue at Josh and bugs his eyes.

Josh titters again, his hand over his mouth, then sticks his tongue out at Flynn and darts behind his mother.

"Great, Flynn. Encourage him."

"Aw, he's a good kid," Flynn says. *Keed.* "So what can I get you today?"

"Um—I'll have a double tall skim cappuccino with extra foam. Oh, and a shot of vanilla. Thanks."

As Flynn fiddles with the espresso machine he says, "Rebecca, meet Angie. Angie, Rebecca."

"Angela," I say. "Nice to meet you."

"Both of you are from New York," Flynn says. "Sort of."

Rebecca smiles at me. "'Sort of'?"

"I made the mistake of growing up in New Jersey. So he thinks I'm being dishonest."

"How long have you lived in New York?"

"Ten years."

"That's a pretty long time. Only someone who's never lived there would be so literal."

"Hey," Flynn protests.

"You started it," she says.

He hands her a cup, and she gives him a twenty.

"Are you visiting people up here?" she asks me.

I nod.

"Would I know them?"

I shrug.

Flynn looks at me with sudden interest. "Yes, do tell."

"It's just a—friend. A guy named Rich Saunders."

"Holy dooley!" Flynn says, at the same time that she says, "Ahh." A look passes between them.

"Is there—something I should know?" I ask.

Flynn busies himself behind the counter.

"I don't know Richard very well," Rebecca says. "He seems like a—nice guy. He's quite good-looking."

Flynn lifts his eyebrows and pauses as if he wants to say something, but then thinks better of it. "That's true," he says.

"He gave me sailing lessons last summer," Josh announces.

All of us look at him in surprise. "That's right!" Rebecca says. "He was a good sailing teacher, wasn't he?"

"I got sick. I threw up over the side," Josh says.

"You did, didn't you?" Rebecca laughs. "I'd forgotten that."

"Next summer I'm going to science camp," says Josh.

"Good on ya," Flynn says.

Leaving the coffee shop, I walk across a small park to my car. The grass is as sodden as a sponge. Despite the rain, I wince at the glare; all the buildings in town are three stories or less, and the sky is huge and white. If I had an event tonight, I would be worrying about contingency plans: cancellations, rolls of plastic under the coat racks, rented umbrella stands. But I don't have an event tonight, or any night. I don't have any plans at all.

I think about that shared look, the questions forming in my own head. Is there something I should know?

Maybe I ought to be worrying about contingency plans.

CHAPTER 11

Rich kisses me good-bye as he leaves for work. I lie in his bed for a while longer, gazing out at the sun through the window, as distinct as a lemon in the milky sky. Ever since we went up to Cadillac a few days ago, he has been attentive and sweet. He brought home groceries last night and made dinner (well, Ragú and ziti), and later, when I slipped into bed beside him, he turned on his side toward me, ran his hand down my hip, and murmured, "I could get used to this." Afterward, when he drifted to sleep, I started to think. The charmless apartment, the seemingly deliberate cultural ignorance, the frat-boy proclivities—none of that really matters. He doesn't fit my ideal—so what? He's a nice, solid guy. Maybe my preconceptions are the real problem.

Maybe, in fact, he really is my love match after all.

I step into the shower, lather up with his manly deodorant soap, which I found repellent several days ago but now kind of like, wash my hair with his Suave shampoo that gives me static cling, and dry off.

As I'm standing there in my towel in the bathroom, the telephone rings. I run over to the phone by Rich's bed and pick it up, figuring it's probably him. "Hello?"

"Hello?" a female voice echoes.

"Hello? Who is this?" I ask.

"Who is *this*?"

"Angela. I'm—" I hesitate, wondering what I am "—a friend of Rich's."

"He never mentioned you," she says.

"And who is this?"

"Becky."

"He didn't tell me about you, either."

"Well, he wouldn't, would he?" she says.

I don't say anything, just stand there dripping, breathing into the phone.

"Fucking asshole," she says. "Just tell him Becky called. And it's the last time. I'm not calling again."

There's a click, then a dial tone, and I realize she has hung up on me.

I look at the phone as if it itself insulted me. Then I place it back in its holster. Becky. Why am I not surprised?

I finish drying off and open Rich's closet door, looking for my robe. And then it occurs to me that if there's an Angela and a Becky, there might well be an entire alphabet of women I don't know about. I glance around the closet, poking at a few empty shoe boxes and a banker's box, full of bills, on the floor. I don't feel guilty or self-righteous, just strangely calm. Pushing aside a pile of sweaters on the shelf above the hanging bar, I find a sheaf of white paper in the far back. I take it down.

As I begin leafing through the pile, I find e-mail after e-mail. Kissandtell. Women's profiles, with pictures. DogLover, Blondy, Abgirl, CutiePie. At the top of the pile is a haiku:

> *Your name is real cute*
> *I like Blondy with a Y*
> *When can I see you?*

The blood rises to my head. Riffling through the pages, I find e-mails before, during, and after our correspondence, a parallel cosmos of haikus and sweet nothings. Apparently he sent two other women the same haiku he sent to me, one that I thought perfectly captured the absurdity of our situation:

You're so far away
I'm right here, far away too
Why can't we be close?

Now that it's addressed to someone else, I see that it's as cloyingly generic as a Shoebox card.

It dawns on me that it must seem to him like random chance that I, and not another one of these women, came up to see him. I thought it was serendipity; he must have seen it as a roll of the dice. I thought I had found my soul mate; he was just playing out one of many options.

My head feels light. I have to get away from this apartment. I throw on some clothes, towel-dry my hair, and head out the door. It's still early, and the light is thin. The sun is bright, even dazzling, but the air is strangely cold. It is unsettling to see the sun and not feel it; it might as well be a picture in the sky. I pull my coat around me, frankly grateful for the brightness, the illusion of warmth.

Walking down Blueberry Cove Lane, I pass the other town houses on the left and the barren expanse of dirt on the right, in which the seeds of new condos are being planted. The few trees along the way are half plucked; leaves drift in the wind, are carried up and over, brown-yellow-gold as they twirl toward the ground. As I get farther from his house, the road slopes up and then down through fields covered with low, hardy bushes. Truth in advertising: blueberries. From the top of the rise I see a ribbon of ocean on the horizon line, dotted with little patches of land.

Gazing out at the water I take a deep breath, smell the pine and dirt. The sky is empty and pallid. In a sudden rush of feeling, like the flash onset of a fever, I am stricken with gloom—a piano scale of feeling in the key of, say, G minor, culminating in a jarring note of dread. The impulse to come here was not, as I have told myself, daring and romantic; it was foolhardy and ill-conceived. There is nothing here for me. I see that now. I am living in the town house of a guy I barely know. On a remote Maine island. With a stack of e-mails to other women, some identical to the ones he sent to me, on his kitchen table.

My thirty-three years are apportioned into boxes, a haphazard and senseless accumulation. My money won't last long; I have nowhere else to stay. All I own is an old car without a gas gauge and some books and clothes and spatulas. I keep getting it wrong, only my mistakes get bigger. Ruining my career was bad enough. Ruining my life is more than I can contemplate.

"At the same time," I say, trying to stay calm. "You were sending haikus to all these women *at the same time.*"

We are standing in Rich's kitchen. My bags are packed. He has just suggested that I may be making too big a deal about this. He shrugs, which in his body-language lexicon signifies something between annoyance at being caught and an inability to grasp why this matters so much to me. "I was keeping my options open," he says.

"I wasn't. I wasn't corresponding with anyone else."

"Look, we met online. I didn't even know for sure that you were female."

"*What?*"

"How was I supposed to know? You could've used somebody else's picture—"

"Just stop. You were still e-mailing these women after I came up to Boston to meet you."

"Look, look," he says, stepping back. "We see this whole thing differently. I was flirting. It was harmless." He turns away from me in the small kitchen, goes into the living room, picks up a ten-pound weight, and starts doing curls. "I thought you had a good time last night," he says, panting a little, "but now, I have to say, you're being a real"—*huff*— "downer." *Huff*.

The aftertaste of coffee is metal in my mouth. "By the way," I say, "Becky says to tell you it's over."

"What?" He stops doing curls.

"She called when you were out."

He just looks at me. "What were you doing picking up my phone?"

"I thought it was you."

"I don't care if you think it's Santa Claus. Don't pick up the phone in my house."

"You know what? Fuck you."

"What did you just say?" He takes a step forward, still clutching the barbell.

I wonder abstractly if he's trying to appear menacing, but it doesn't occur to me to be afraid. "I can't believe you asked me to come up here, and now you're acting like this," I say. "I—I put my whole life on hold. My stuff's in storage. My apartment is gone."

"That's not quite accurate, is it, Angela?" he shoots back. "You got fired from your job. You had nowhere to go. Saw this as a way out."

"That is not true."

"You practically begged me to let you come up here."

I am reeling. "I can't believe you're twisting it like this! You *asked* me to come."

"No, I didn't," he says. "You brought up the idea. And I said sure. I mean, yeah, why not? Take a vacation, whatever. You were a lot of fun in Boston. But then you get here and all of a sudden everything is so damn . . . serious."

I laugh—snort—in disbelief. "Well, yeah! Hello. I had all my stuff in my car."

"See, I didn't really get that part," he says.

"What do you mean? We talked about it before I came."

"I thought you were coming for a visit. I didn't know you were moving in, for Christ's sake! I mean, c'mon—we hardly know each other."

At that moment the telephone rings. I can tell we're both thinking the same thing—that it's Becky, or some other woman. He doesn't make a move to pick it up, but both of us are silent. The ringing is relentless, a shrill contrast to our own seething exchange.

"Listen, Angela," he says when the ringing finally stops. "I'm not quite sure . . ." He pauses.

"What I'm getting at?"

"No. I know what you're getting at. I'm not quite sure what you want. From me."

He says it like that, in two discrete phrases. And he has a point—they are two different, if related, subjects. But it surprises me all the same. "What do you mean?"

He shrugs. "I dunno. I just—I'm not really sure why you're here."

"I'm here because . . ." I feel a suffusing panic. Why am I here?

"Look," he says. "I don't know what you thought. I figured anyone who uses an online dating service would know what the deal is."

"What the deal is," I repeat stupidly.

He sighs, cricks his neck. Tosses the barbell onto the carpet, where it lands with a thud and rolls once. "I thought this was going to be less . . . complicated. You seemed so cool about things before."

"But we never talked about this." Then I realize what he means. "Oh—because I slept with you on the first date?"

He shrugs. Yeah, that's what he means.

I take a deep breath. Step back. All right. Well.

"So tell me, Angela," he says. "What are you going to do?"

All of a sudden the absurdity of my situation—no job, no money, no place to live—makes me smile.

"What? What's so funny?"

"I don't have any idea." Then I can't help it, I start to laugh. Being with this man was clearly an exercise in self-delusion—I conjured up the relationship out of thin air. If I had an ounce of self-respect, I'd get in my car and head back to New Jersey, move in with my father and stepmother, and start looking for a job. I'd chalk this up to an early midlife crisis during which I temporarily lost my head, and I'd very sanely move on.

"You don't need to be with me to stay here," he says, as if I've been thinking aloud.

"That's ridiculous. Why else would I stay?"

"Because it's this *place* you're really interested in. Not me."

"That's not true. I liked the—idea of Maine. I had this fantasy. But you were part of that."

"Right. Part of it. Not the first part, either."

"An important part. A crucial part."

"Nah. Just a part."

"I didn't even know you yet," I protest.

"Exactly," he says. "That's what I'm saying. You didn't come up here for me—not really. You came up here for an idea. A dream. Right?"

"But I never would have just—come here. Without a reason."

"Maybe not," he says. "But now you're here. And it doesn't really matter why you came, does it?"

In this moment I realize—as I somehow haven't until now—that he's right; I don't want to go back to New York. There's nothing there for me. I actually—how can I even separate it?—think I want to stay here for now. I'm not ready to leave. Despite Rich. And if I were honest, I would admit that I picked Rich as arbitrarily as he picked me, as much for the place as for his unique combination of attributes, many of which I blithely ignored or made excuses for from the beginning.

"Look, you can crash here with me as long as you want. But you're a smart girl. You'll figure it out. If there's one thing I'm sure of, it's that you'll find a way to do what you want to do."

"I don't know why you think you've got me pegged."

"You're not as complicated as you think," he says.

"Just tell me something. Honestly," I say. "You never had a dog, did you?"

He smiles, and we both know he's only pretending to be sheepish. "Does it matter?"

CHAPTER 12

I am sitting at a table in the coffee shop, trying to figure out what to do. When I think about what would make me happy, I am struck by how basic my desires are. I want to feel that I'm progressing through life; I want a meaningful relationship and an engaging career. I want to live in a place that feels like home. What I want is what everyone wants—so ordinary as to be clichéd. Why is that so hard to find?

"So what's going on in that pretty little head?" Flynn calls over during a lull.

I shake my head. "Ugh. Complicated."

"Try me."

"I don't want to bore you," I say, pouring milk into my coffee.

He makes a sweep of the empty shop with his hand. "I have a high tolerance for boredom, as you can see."

"All right. I'll try to make it short." I run through the highlights: Lindsay and Hot4U, the circus-themed gala, kissandtell.com, MaineCatch, haikus, Boston, the fire-eater's vendetta, a topiary in flames, the cover of the *New York Post,* Blueberry Cove Lane . . .

"You're right, that's a yawner," he says.

For the next hour we sit at the table talking. My coffee goes cold. By the end of it, he is shaking his head.

"So let me see if I've got this straight," he says. "You're staying with Rich Saunders at his town house on Blueberry Cove Lane, but he's not your 'love match.' You need to get out of there, but you don't know where to go. You should probably head back to New York, but your apartment is rented and you got fired from your job. You don't want to move in with your father and stepmother, uptight cow, in New Jersey, though you do miss your grandma. But you don't really have a reason to stay in Maine."

At this frank appraisal of my situation, I burst into tears.

He puts his hand on mine. "Honestly, I'm not surprised about Rich Saunders. Everybody knows he's a player. I'm sure that's what drove him online in the first place; the local girls are on to his game."

"Except Becky. Whoever that is," I sob.

"Oh, Becky. Well. Her." He hands me a napkin. Drums his fingers on the table.

"What?"

"I was just thinking." He pulls a cloth from his pocket and wipes a coffee stain off the little table between us. "You wouldn't be interested." *Tat-a-tat-tat.*

I wipe my eyes with the napkin. "What?"

"Ah, well—a friend of mine owns a place over in Dory Cove, a little cottage on the shore drive that he rents by the week in the summer. I don't think anybody's in there now."

A cottage? "A cottage?"

"Well, he *calls* it a cottage in the adverts; it's a shack, really," Flynn says.

"Oh."

"It's got running water and all that," he says. "The only thing is, I'm not sure there's heat. I know it has a woodstove."

"A woodstove."

"Yeah. I think it's one of those Scandinavian deals where a stick of wood heats the entire place. Gotta love those frugal Norwegians."

"I don't know anything about woodstoves," I say. "Except that burning to death is supposed to be incredibly painful."

"Well, let's not start planning your funeral just yet," he says. "Why don't I call him first and see if it's available. I mean, if you're interested."

An unheated shack with a woodstove.

In the winter.

"Let me think about it," I say.

I like Rich better now that I'm not trying so hard to like him. He seems relieved, too. He gallantly offers to sleep on the couch, but really—the bedroom floor, the couch, what's the difference? I take the couch. It's only for a few days, anyway, until I figure out what I'm doing.

Still—though we have tacitly agreed to be "friends," in the dark of night it's hard to stay downstairs on the narrow couch. When I slink upstairs he says, "I wondered when you'd come." He lifts the sheet like a bat lifting its wing, and I slide down the length of his body as he welcomes me back. I'm a little surprised, not to mention appalled, at my self-abasement, my lack of moral fiber—as well as my capacity to endure humiliation and come back for more. I didn't know how much I could take, but apparently, as it turns out, I can take plenty. His body is so warm, after all, and his hands are so welcoming.

After several days of this shameful behavior, I pull myself together.

"Okay, I'm interested." I toss my keys on a little table in the coffee shop and shrug off my coat. "Who do I need to call?"

"Excuse me?" Flynn says from behind the counter, hands on his hips. "Do I know you?"

"Hi," I say.

"Hi."

"The unheated shack," I explain. "In Dory Cove. Your friend's place."

"Aah." He nods sagely. "So Sailor Boy tossed you out."

"I beg your pardon."

"Out on your keister," he says.

"I don't think you know me well enough to be talking about my keister."

"You may be right," he concedes.

"So listen," I say. "My car is parked out front with all my stuff in it. I'm going to be sleeping there tonight unless you give me that number."

"All right, hold on. You Jersey girls are always in such a hurry." He lifts the phone receiver next to the toaster oven, punches in some numbers. "Lance? Yeah. You know I mentioned that bird for the apartment, Angie? Yeah, yeah. She is. Right here." He holds the receiver against his chest and calls over, "How long are you going to be here?"

"Is he talking minutes or days?"

"If you don't get over here soon, this chickie is going to roost on my floor," Flynn says into the phone. He hangs up. "He'll be right over." He fills a paper cup with coffee and holds it out in my direction. "Now don't get your hopes up. The place is bog standard. Four walls and a dirty floor, that's about it."

"As long as it's heated, I don't care what it looks like. Oh yeah—I forgot."

"That's the spirit," he says.

Lance is tall, rangy, and, it turns out, Flynn's former lover. "Small town." He shrugs. "What are you going to do?"

"Too right," says Flynn. "Even if Sailor Boy is a complete wanker, you'll have to get along with him 'cause you'll run into him on every bloody corner. Like I do with this mongrel."

Lance nods in agreement. "Or learn not to give a rat's ass."

"That could work," Flynn says.

"Does for me," says Lance.

"You two seem made for each other," I remark.

"Yeah, we're made for each other—like cats and dogs," Lance says.

"Original," says Flynn.

Dory Cove is a small inlet comprised of a paved loop that runs from Spruce Harbor to Mollusk Point. From this loop, tributary roads lined with houses lead to the water and into the woods. Part of the loop runs along the coastline, an eclectic mile-long sweep of shorefront dwellings, a bed and breakfast, two restaurants, and a boatbuilding company.

We pull into the driveway of Lance's house, down one of the tributaries, and any secret hope I harbored that Flynn was exaggerating is promptly crushed. Lance's house is not the cottage of my dreams. There is no trellis, no stone path, no wood-shingled roof. Instead, the squat one-story structure sports peeling hospital-smock green paint and cheap gray roof tiles. The windows are small and ill-fitting, as if stuck in place years after the house was built. Spidery cracks run through a number of panes, and several layers of paint flake off the muntins.

Is it my imagination, or does the roof sag in the middle?

"It presents better in the summer," Lance says as we park in the rutted dirt drive, stiff dead grass poking up everywhere.

"See those pots of dead flowers? They actually looked quite nice when they were alive."

We walk around to the back, an untended lot of dried weeds. Two dirty white plastic chairs are stacked on the rickety deck. I run my hand along the rail and lift it off quickly; the rough wood grain is a dozen splinters waiting to happen. Some planks on the deck still have the numbers from the woodlot stamped on them.

The creaky back door is slightly ajar. Lance pushes it open and we enter a cold, musty living area with a sagging green couch, a bargain-basement table, and a couple of wooden chairs. Broken venetian blinds splinter the meager light coming in. When I pull up the blinds, the windows are covered in grime.

"Cheery, huh?" Flynn says.

I wander through the small house, struggling to imagine its potential. The living room floor is made of wide pine planks which, though grimy, appear in pretty good shape. The dingy walls don't have any obvious problem that a little spackle and paint wouldn't solve. The only bedroom is a low-ceilinged little hole with no closet and a dank smell. A navy polyester curtain— or is that a sheet?—is pulled tight across the only window. Soiled mauve wall-to-wall carpeting covers the floor. As it turns out, there is baseboard electric heat in the little bathroom; Lance explains that he had to install it so the pipes wouldn't freeze in the winter. So that's good. And there are no leaks, from what I can see. Get rid of the venetian blinds and horrid curtain, give the place a scrubbing . . .

"I think there might be storm windows," Lance offers. "Not sure where, exactly, but I'll try to hunt them down."

In the middle of the living room sits a gleaming, red woodstove, as out of place as a spaceship in a cornfield.

"It's so—glossy," I say.

"I know. Right?" Lance says.

"It's from one of those northern countries." Lance peers at the metal manufacturer's tag. "Denmark."

"Let me explain something about Lance," Flynn says, putting his arm around me. "When he got this place, he had grand ideas about fixing it up. But the problem is, he wants top-of-the-line this and fancy that, and won't do anything halfway. So he gets overwhelmed—it's too expensive, too much bother, whatever—and ends up doing nothing."

"Hey," Lance says.

"Am I wrong?" Flynn asks.

"It's a little harsh."

"Then last summer he had renters in June," Flynn continues, "and it was cold, and they complained. So he got this stove. Which looks ridiculous here, doesn't it? But he had to get the best one on the market, even though the rest of the place looks like shit." *Sheet.*

"How do you light it?" I ask. "And where's the wood?"

"Don't ask me, I have central heating," Flynn says.

"It's pretty easy, actually," Lance says. "And a few logs will heat the whole place for hours. There are matches in the kitchen and there's some kindling and wood out back, left from last season, but you should get more. That stuff takes days to dry."

"Is there a—log store?"

Flynn sniggers.

"I don't know why you're laughing. You're as ignorant as she is," Lance says. "Yes," he says to me, "there is a 'log store.' You can order cords of wood from a place in Spruce Harbor."

I blush a bit.

"And people sell wood at the end of their driveways. Just look for the sign." Lance pushes the latch of the stove shut with his foot. "So I rent this place for eight hundred a week in the summer. I'd let you have it for a hundred a week through May, month to month. What do you think? Do you want it?"

I sit down on the sea green floral couch, sinking into its polyester depths. When I pat the armrest, a small puff of dust rises. And settles.

Virtually every aspect of this trip to Maine has turned out to be so far from what I thought I wanted that the question seems irrelevant. Do I want it? No. It is not quaint, or even cozy. It's a freezing, depressing little hovel, close enough to the ocean to vibrate with a sharp, salty crosswind but far enough away that you can't actually see water from any window. This place is to the cottage of my dreams as Rich Saunders is to my soul mate.

It is tempting to see each disappointment as part of a larger pattern, a trend. Do these momentary blows add up to a lifetime of regret? Or is weathering them part of the test one needs to pass, the successful resolution of which will make one stronger and more resilient?

To put a finer point on it: Am I moving closer to ruin, or building my character? At which point does optimism become ostrichlike foolishness?

Do I want to be alone in this Unabomber-worthy shack?

"All right. Yeah, I'll take it," I say. "But only if somebody teaches me how to start a fire. And stab an intruder to death with a knife."

"No problem," Flynn says. "Lance is skilled at both those things. Aren't you, Lance?"

"I've never actually committed murder, but I can show you how to wound someone," Lance says.

"Boy, can he ever," Flynn says.

CHAPTER 13

It takes two days to move in. Actually, it takes three hours; I spend the rest of the time shopping. At the Wal-Mart in Ellsworth I acquire a broom, a mop, a mammoth plastic jug of orange-scented all-purpose cleaning fluid, a gross of coffee filters, and a Mr. Coffee machine just like the one on Blueberry Cove Lane. Then I go down the road to the L.L. Bean outlet for two wool sweaters (sidestepping the matronly embroidered pullovers and floral dirndl skirts) and a puffy winter coat on clearance for $39.99 in a color they call "saffron," which is actually Fiskars-scissors orange.

I drive to the store in Spruce Harbor for firewood. How many cords do I need, and do I want it delivered? I say ten, which sounds like a reasonable number, though I have no idea what a cord is. The man behind the cash register, with a wispy beard that extends all the way to his sternum, peers at me over his bifocals. "Ten cords?" he booms. "How many kids you got?"

"Uh, it's just me."

"A cord is four foot wide and four foot high. Eight foot long," he says, chortling at the guy in line behind me. "Ten would fill up your whole house."

"I see." I feel my ears redden. "Well, then, let's start with one."

I wash the living room floor with a rag and the orange cleaner, scrub the crusty, charred interior of the oven with Comet. I scour the stained, dirty tub. Lance brings over some storm windows, the few he could find, and tacks them up around the house. Washing the grimy windows is a revelation: light! I find a gluey pile of feathers and bone, a dead bird, apparently, in a corner of the dark bedroom, and for a moment it gives me pause. I imagine the bird flying around like crazy, looking in vain for an exit, flying into the window and knocking itself out. Was it injured to begin with? I'm tempted to interpret this as a metaphor for my situation—confusion, loneliness, despair— but decide instead to view it as a kind of ritual sacrifice, a purification of the space.

I want to rip out the dank bedroom rug but fear that it will turn into a bigger project than I can handle, so I rent a shampoo machine from the hardware store and a lot of the stains actually disappear. I consider this a small victory.

When the house is clean—as clean as I can get it—it looks pitiful, as barren as a jail cell. I head back into Ellsworth to Marden's, a close-out store Lance told me about, and pick up some throw pillows and a floor lamp that might even pass for stylish (so hard to tell when you're standing between the overstocked Rubbermaid hampers and the fake diamonds). At the L.L. Bean outlet I find flannel sheets and an area rug, and at Wal-Mart, sheer curtains, a sofa slipcover, and a plastic shower curtain stamped with a map of the world. I am playing house.

"First you place three medium-size logs like this," Lance says. The two of us are kneeling in front of the woodstove like supplicants before a statue of the Buddha. The door in its belly is wide open; Lance places the logs inside, carefully balancing each on the other in a triangle. "Then you add these thin sticks. You can use twigs from outside, or you can buy kindling at the log store, if you want."

"They sell kindling, too?"

"Of course." He places the sticks around the logs, then tears off strips from a pile of newspapers he's brought in for the lesson. Scrunches the paper into balls, wedges the balls around and under the sticks. "That's pretty much it. You light a match to the newspaper, and in about ten minutes you should be nice and warm." He hands me the pack of matches. "Start from the back. Obviously."

"Nothing is obvious to me."

"This stove is idiotproof. You'll get the hang of it."

"You really shouldn't underestimate my level of idiocy." I strike a match and put it in the stove, and it goes out.

I try another.

Another.

"I need to get one of those ignition wands. This is tricky," Lance says kindly.

A little pile of blackened matches grows on the floor.

"I just thought of something," he says. "If you twist a sheet of newspaper into a baton, you can light that and use it to ignite the rest."

Following his instructions, I twist and light the baton, then maneuver it toward a ball of newspaper at the back of the stove. Astoundingly, the paper catches fire.

When the sticks begin to burn, he pushes the stove door until it's open only a crack. "It'll be toasty in here in a moment." We crouch in front of the stove, huddled in our coats, waiting. After a few minutes I shrug off my coat. A miracle. I feel like the Cro-Magnon whose sharp-witted cave mate first thought to rub sticks together and create a spark. Fire!

The next day, and the day after that, I wake up, in my soft flannel sheets on the double bed with the terrible mattress (add to list: new mattress) in the tiny bedroom, with a peculiar sense of peace. I hop out of bed and light a fire, hop back into bed. Skim-milky late-fall light, softened by the sheer curtain, suffuses the room. Read for a while, drift back to sleep. Take a shower in the tin stall.

Hours pass and dissipate. I have no habits in my new life; I create routines out of air. I go to the coffee shop, my one touchstone in this alien world. Get in my car and drive—along Sargent Drive, high on a ridge limning the coast, overlooking a glassy expanse of water studded with boats, into Northeast Harbor, where most of the enormous old houses I pass are boarded up. On a foggy day I make my way up Cadillac Mountain to the bleak flattop, an expanse of parking lots and deserted tourist trails, and stand in the cold mist gazing out at an Impressionist view of land and sea. In Bar Harbor, where every other shop is closed for the season, I stroll down Main Street. People on the street hustle along in their warm parkas, squinting as they come toward me—either at the dazzling midday light or the glare of my orange jacket, I'm not sure which. I meander down the aisles of the year-round grocery store, stocking up on staples. No takeout here—if I want to feed myself, I'm on my own.

The kitchen in the shack isn't much bigger than mine was in New York, but now I have time to use it. I unpack the boxes of pots and pans, knives and bowls. My old blue Le Creuset pot with a broken handle, as heavy as an infant. Three whisks, in different sizes, from the housewares section at Zabar's. An absurdly large white food processor. A bright yellow space-age silicone spatula, tinny old-fashioned metal measuring spoons. These pieces have a friendly, talismanic power, a comforting familiarity. I find my cookbooks in a box and pore over them, then gather the ingredients to make banana-nut muffins in the oversize tins I bought on Canal Street. (The oven is so small I can fit only one muffin tin on each shelf.) I cook turkey sausage in the blue Dutch oven on the electric burner with minced white onion and shreds of carrot and parsley, the juices mingling into the base of a thick soup.

I call home to let my dad know that I haven't been dragged into the woods by wild bears or, more to the point, by the sailor I met on the Internet. I'm not prepared to relate the details, so I tell him the bare minimum, keeping the conversation vague and upbeat. It didn't work out with that guy, but it's "beautiful" and "quiet" up here; the people are "really nice," I've found a place to stay for the time being, and I'm going to "see how it goes." I can tell my dad is looking for an opening, any sign of ambivalence, to push his agenda of getting me to come home, and I'm determined not to give him one.

"Sharon and I keep wondering when you're going to come to your senses, but I guess you think you know what you're doing," he says.

"Thanks, Dad," I say.

After I hang up, I call Lindsay. "I'm trying not to say I told you so. I'm biting my tongue," she says when I relate the whole wretched MaineCatch story.

"Thanks, Linz."

"Okay, so that's over. *Why* are you still there?"

I try to explain that I am taking it day by day; I want to see how things unfold; I am enjoying the solitude and the quiet, the seagulls and the evergreens.

Lindsay is unconvinced. She laughs when I tell her that the woodstove, which I have only just learned to light, is the main source of heat in my house. She tells me she's figured it out: This whole back-to-nature thing is a way for me to bond with my dead mother. I'm trying to get in touch with my inner hippie child, the way my mother did. I tell Lindsay that running off to Portland, Oregon, and living with a doctor in a cedar-shingled solar house designed by a well-known architect wasn't exactly "back to nature"—but she says I'm missing the point.

"The point is, your mother left because she said she needed to 'simplify,' right?" Lindsay says. "And that's basically what you're doing. We can never escape our mothers, Ange, even when they're dead. Maybe *especially* when they're dead."

"Where'd you get all this insight into mother-daughter relationships?"

"I'm taking a psych class at the New School," she says. "Can you tell?"

The only person I'm eager to speak with right now is Nonna, and she doesn't like to talk on the phone. I call her midmorning on a weekday, when I know my dad and Sharon are at work and Nonna is probably in the kitchen preparing dinner, cutting vegetables for *minestra* or cooking beans for pasta *fagioli,* the kitchen warming with the simmering pot.

"*Ciao?* Hello?" she says warily when she picks up the phone after many rings.

"Hi, Nonna, it's me. Angela."

"Angela! Oh!"

"Yeah, hi!" I say. "It's so nice to hear your voice."

"Oh, Angela—*mi dispiace,*" I'm sorry, she says; "your father is not here right now."

"I know, Nonna. I know. I called to speak to you."

"Me?"

"Yes. I—I miss you."

"Ach." She laughs uncomfortably. "You call me long distance?"

"Yeah, Nonna, of course."

"So expensive," she says. "You should save your money."

"No, no—it's my cell phone. It's a calling plan—with minutes—oh, whatever. It's free. I just wanted to see how you're doing."

"Free? How can it be free? Nothing is free in life."

"It's already paid for, Nonna. Like TV. You don't have to pay to watch TV every time, right? It's like that."

"Ohh," she says, as if she still doesn't quite believe me. As many times as I've tried to explain how telephone service has changed, she still thinks long distance is a luxury.

"So how are you feeling? Are you well these days?"

"*Cosi cosi,*" pretty much, she says, clearing her throat.

"Do you still have that cold?"

"No, no," she says.

"Have you been to the doctor?" I ask.

"Pah," she says with disgust. "No doctor ever told me anything I didn't know already."

Nonna's distrust of doctors, a vestige of her self-reliant peasant past, is legendary in our family. In labor with my father, she refused to go to the hospital and insisted on giving birth in her own bedroom at home, assisted by an Italian neighbor woman. The fact that my mother ran off with a doctor only confirmed and justified her worst suspicions.

"Nonna, you've been sick for a while. Promise me you'll get checked out," I say.

"Ack," she says.

"Promise."

"All right, all right," she says. "Enough. Tell me how is Maine."

"Maine is . . ." How *is* Maine? "I like it here, Nonna. It's been a challenge. But I've rented a little house, and I think I'm going to stay for a few months."

"*Buono*. And the sailor?"

"Ehh," I say.

"Not so good," she says.

"Not so good."

"Are you getting enough to eat?"

"Yes. I'm surviving."

"You have to make stone soup." She laughs, a sharp wheeze. "That will keep you warm."

"What are you making today?" I ask.

"*Non molto,*" not much, she says. "I think chicken marsala for tonight. I have lemons, so maybe a *torta al limone* for your father."

"That sounds so good. I wish I could be there."

"I do, too," she says. "But you can make it yourself, you know."

Craving the smells and warmth of Nonna's kitchen, I go back to the grocery store in Bar Harbor and roam the aisles for potatoes, ziti, plum tomatoes, carrots—cheap and hearty ingredients. Driving home I think about what I will make for dinner, anticipating the slow simmer of an evening with a good book, a nice lamp, a warm stew. Light, flaky haddock, perhaps, caught in the harbor this morning, cooked in wine with sage and shallots. Oven-roasted chicken, the cavity filled with lemons and rosemary. Or maybe just stone soup.

In my best moments, I think: This is exactly where I want to be.

In my worst moments, I think: What am I doing in this isolated place on the chilly edge of winter, with no friends and no takeout, my last hopes for romance dashed against the craggy rocks?

CHAPTER 14

Flynn is busy, busy, busy, and I am not. "You're awfully busy for a man who's not busy," I remark as he scurries around the empty shop.

"I'm good at being busy. It's what I do," he says. "Besides, part of what I'm doing is getting ready for times when I will be busy."

"You mean like next July?"

"That's funny," he says. "Actually, a bit of a lunch rush is coming up."

"You don't serve lunch."

"People come in for a caffeine jolt," he says. "Gotta get through that long afternoon."

Every morning, like a homing pigeon, I make my way to the Daily Grind. Customers holding hot cups to cold noses stand around chatting in groups of two or three. Flynn points out the different demographics as people come and go: lobstermen and boatbuilders, innkeepers and architects, wealthy people with winterized summer homes, up for a weekend; writers and painters, teachers and high school kids, retirees, the occasional stray tourist. If the flow of incoming customers has ebbed and Flynn has done enough wiping, cleaning, fussing for the moment, he pulls up a chair and plays backgammon or checkers with me.

Flynn's fingernails are bitten to the quick. Often when we're playing a board game he chews his cuticles. Between the Aussie accent and the finger wedged in his mouth, I can barely understand him.

"All artists bite their fingernails," he says when I get up the nerve to tell him to stop.

"That's baloney."

"It's well documented. Look it up."

"Anyway, you're not an artist," I say.

"I have an artist's temperament. Haven't you noticed my obsessive-compulsive behaviors—the way I wipe the counters over and over, my mercurial moods?"

"Yes, but, Flynn, you're not an artist."

"I would be if I had artistic talent," he says.

Several days later, as I'm sipping a latte and playing solitaire, he leans across the counter and says, "So, Angie, I'm guessing you're a trust-fund baby."

"What?"

"You know. Silver spoon and all that."

"That's a little rude, isn't it?" I say.

He shrugs. "Sorry."

"You're not sorry."

"Well, you'll find that people are pretty straightforward around here."

"You're not from around here," I remind him.

"I'm from around here like you're a New Yorker," he says. "So are you? A trust-fund baby, I mean."

"No. I wish." I shuffle the cards, lay them in overlapping columns on the table. "I'm living off my severance pay. Which is fast running out."

"Ah," he says. "So you'll need to get a job."

"One of these days." I've been trying not to think about it, but between the rent and the logs and the lattes, I am zipping through the two months' salary that Mary Quince charitably bestowed on me in parting.

"You know," he says, "I could actually use some help around here."

I look around at the empty shop. "Really?"

"Yeah, really. You've seen what it's like. I can't go anywhere for five minutes without closing up. Even when I'm here, it would be useful to have another pair of hands. It wouldn't be much money; I could pay you, I don't know—eight dollars an hour."

"I don't even know how to make espresso."

"You could learn. Any drongo can do it. It's not brain surgery."

"Drongo?"

"That's Aussie for 'idiot.' Not that I'm saying you're an idiot, mind you."

"Gee, thanks."

"So what do you think?"

I hesitate. "I don't know."

"Why?"

"I don't want to feel . . . tied down."

He snorts. "That's silly. You're in here all the time anyway."

"I know, but what if I want to do something else?"

"Look, it's not a prison sentence," he says. "Why don't you try it for a day or two, see what it's like? You can always quit—no hard feelings."

"Really? That's nice."

"Well, I'm a nice guy." Opening the cash register, he takes the bills out and starts counting them. "I was lying about the hard feelings, by the way." He looks up and smiles.

I smile back. "I'll think about it."

So much for thinking about it. The next morning I am behind the counter, wearing an apron, struggling to memorize the arcane lingo and processes of gourmet-coffee production. Arabica beans, *espresso breve, robusto, con panna, cremosa, chai, granito, ristretto* . . . It might not be brain surgery, but the terminology and techniques seem to me as complicated as those in a medical textbook.

Once past the blur of the morning rush, I relax and look around, inhaling the rich smell of ground beans, the tang of apricot tea. As the day progresses I am surprised to find that I like the half-brained rhythm of repetition: sweeping the floor, cleaning the condiment station (milk, cream, artificial sugar in pastel paper parcels, squeeze packets of honey), stacking paper cups, washing out the carafes, bantering with the regulars. I bring sweet lattes (caramel, mocha) to two older women, their soft bodies swathed in colorful knits, who sit at a corner table sharing a bagel. I recognize them; they come in together every day. They sit intimately, their bodies curved toward each other like schoolgirls sharing a secret. An elderly man who ordered a large coffee sits alone in the other corner, methodically reading every section of the newspaper as the hours go by. Then he folds and refolds the paper until only a rectangle of crossword is visible. Using a blue ballpoint pen, he sits until he finishes it, his cane hooked over the back of the empty chair across the table. I bring him free refills, and he beams with gratitude.

I can't remember the last time anyone ever smiled at me like that.

I like this job.

Bright and early the next morning, as I'm filling vacuum flasks with milk at the condiment station—whole, half-and-half, 2 percent, skim, soy—I feel a tug on my shirt and turn to find a diminutive masked crusader at my elbow.

"Well, hello there," I say, wondering simultaneously why this kid is dressed up as Batman and whether I just filled the soy milk container with soy milk or, god forbid, cow's milk instead. I'm holding both cartons.

"Holy smoke, Batman!" Flynn calls from across the room. "Trouble in Spruce Harbor?"

Flinging his cape over his shoulder and putting his hands on his hips, the boy says, "No worries. Everything's under control."

"No worries," Flynn says, amused. "Good on ya."

"Not so soon, Batman. Does this smell like soy milk to you?" I stick the flask under his nose.

He takes a sniff and groans. "Gross."

"Must be soy." Rebecca, the woman from New York, is standing in the doorway, and I realize that this is her son. What's his name—Ethan?

"Awesome costume, Josh," Flynn says. Oh yes, Josh. "I used to have pajamas like that."

"Might as well be pajamas," says Rebecca. "He's been wearing this costume day and night since he dragged me to Wal-Mart to get it last week."

Now it dawns on me—Halloween. I'd completely forgotten.

"Trick or treat!" Josh shouts.

"How about this?" Flynn says. "You get a trick and your mother gets a double tall skim cappuccino with extra foam."

"Marvelous idea," Rebecca says.

"No, I don't *get* a trick. I trick *you*," Josh says.

"Aah," Flynn says, working the cappuccino machine. "Well, eight in the morning is a little early for tricks *or* treats, don't you think? Come back this afternoon and we'll see what we can do."

Josh nods and Flynn raises his eyebrows at me and stage-whispers, "I'm sending you out on a mission. Find. Candy."

"Oh, you're working here!" Rebecca says with surprise. "I thought you were just a helpful customer."

"If mixing up soy and regular is 'helpful,'" Flynn says.

"Yeah, I just started," I say, ignoring him.

"And are you still seeing . . . ?"

"Touchy subject," Flynn says.

"It really isn't," I say. "But—no. I'm renting a little place in Dory Cove that Flynn hooked me up with."

"So you're sticking around."

"For now, at least."

"That's great." She smiles, taking her cappuccino from Flynn. "Maybe a real New Yorker can do something about the terrible bagels in this place."

Flynn is, naturally, a coffee snob. He orders beans from a boutique company in Vermont that roasts and sells a variety of blends. But that's all he appears to be obsessed with—that, and clean countertops. The only food in the shop, other than the cardboard bagels, is store-bought biscotti. There's a kitchen in the back, though Flynn never uses it.

"So I've been thinking," I say a few days later as I'm wiping down tables.

"Uh-oh," he says.

"Rebecca is right. The bagels are terrible."

"C'mon, they're not *terrible*."

"Flynn, they're inedible." I scrub at a spot of caramel goo. "The thing is, you've got great coffee. A good location. A nice space with a big window. But even in the off-season, people want to be able to get something to eat, don't you think?"

"Forget that!" he says, swatting the air. "I make coffee. Food is a different can of worms."

"So to speak. Well, here's the thing," I say. "I think a few breakfast items and maybe some soup for lunch would attract more customers. And I also think that with some paint and better lighting and a few other little changes, you can make this place a whole lot more inviting."

"Bloody oath," he says. "If I'd known you were such a troublemaker, I never would've hired you."

I don't know what's gotten into me. I'm not, by nature, inclined to meddle. But I have a clarity about this that has caught me by surprise. "I could help. What if we start with something easy—maybe just soup?"

He washes behind the toaster oven, taps a sludgy filter into the trash. "Look, food is not my thing," he says. "I can barely boil an egg. To be honest, I *can't* boil an egg. I've given up. They say three minutes, but do you put the egg in boiling water, or cold? And is it from the time you put it in, or when the water boils?"

I decide to bring something new into the shop for Flynn to try every day, a campaign of culinary seduction. When I get home from work that evening, I go into the kitchen and pull out the pans. I hear my grandmother's voice telling me how to caramelize garlic in a saucepan, cooking it in olive oil on low heat for forty minutes or so, until golden brown and velvet to the touch. I make chicken broth and chop canned tomatoes and soak dried cannellini beans.

"What are you having for lunch?" I ask Flynn casually the next morning.

He shrugs. "I've got some Campbell's under the counter." He glances at the clock. "I guess it's about that time, isn't it?"

"Well, actually, I made soup last night. I brought some for you, if you want."

"Really?"

"Sure."

"That's awfully nice. What kind?" He comes over to where I'm sitting and I take a plastic container out of my bag.

"It's pasta *fagioli*," I say.

"Fah-zhool?"

"Yeah, spelled f-a-g-i-o-l-i. It's Italian," I say.

"Fa-gee-oli. Fah-zhool. Weird," he says. He peers into the container. "Look at that."

"My grandmother makes this. It's pasta and white beans in a marinara chicken broth."

"Smells incredible," he says. He hops up, gets two mugs and spoons, and takes the container to the microwave to warm.

The day after that I bring apple-cinnamon muffins and barley soup with tiny turkey meatballs. The next, split pea soup and corn muffins.

By day four he is overwhelmed and bleary-eyed. But like an addict, he looks toward me eagerly. "What've you got?" he asks, and before I hand him the bag I say, "All right. Here's what I want."

"Uh-oh," he says, reaching for a cheddar and dill muffin.

"I want to make the changes we talked about."

He doesn't answer. He is busy opening the still warm container of black bean soup.

"Will you at least consider it?"

He breathes deeply, with his eyes closed. "You are a criminal mastermind."

"C'mon, Flynn—it would be fun."

"'Fun' is not what it would be," he says.

"I'll do the work. Most of the work," I say.

He sticks his pinkie in the soup and licks it.

"You'll make money."

"How do you know that?"

"Because I've been planning events for almost a decade, and I have a pretty good sense of what people want. Up here, people need a place to hang out that's comfortable, where they can have a decent breakfast or lunch without spending a fortune. You've already done most of the work; you have great coffee and a prime location. This is about adding versatility."

"That's quite a sales pitch," he says, chewing a muffin. "But the truth is, it'll be a load of work. Are you up for it? Because I'm not sure I am."

"I'm up for it," I say.

He looks at me for a long moment, and then he says, "God damn it."

"What?"

"I really don't want to do this."

I've overstepped my bounds. "Okay. I'll stop."

"Ugh." He sighs. "It's not you. I mean, it *is* you, and you should've minded your own bizzo in the first place, but now that you've brought it up . . . God damn it to hell."

"What are you saying?"

"I'm saying it makes sense. It makes fucking sense."

"So—you want to do it?"

"No, I don't want to do it. But I probably should."

"Really?"

"Yeah. We'll give it a burl."

"'A burl'?"

"A go!" he says impatiently. "We'll give it a *go*."

"Really, Flynn?"

"You are one pushy broad," he says.

I grin. "Will you help me paint?"

He nods, and then shakes his head with disgust.

"Will you reimburse me for expenses?"

He nods again.

"Are you going to nod at everything I say?"

"I'll keep nodding until you shut up," he says.

"You should never do business on an empty stomach, you know," I tell him.

"Bloody oath," he says, "I know!"

Over the next few days, I traipse back and forth to the hardware store, buying samples of colors: mellowed ivory, waterbury cream, soft pumpkin. I drive into Ellsworth to Home Depot and pick up halogen light fixtures with amber glass shades for over the counter. At Marden's I find a gigantic multicolored rag rug to cover the cold linoleum. From roadside flea markets and thrift stores, I collect upholstered chairs and round tables. I stumble on a cardboard box of old black-and-white maps of the island on sale for a dollar at the town library, and stick them in Wal-Mart frames.

The thrum of pleasure I feel these days reminds me of when I was in college, working on set design for a production of *A Doll's House.* In the final weeks I practically lived in the theater, working around the clock to finish. At one or two in the morning, I'd walk across campus to my dorm in a sleep-deprived haze. When I ran into people I knew who weren't involved in the production, I'd look at them blankly. Every waking thought was about the play: ideas for props, colors, aspects of the story I was responsible for. It was a strange ecstasy, half conscious and yet hyperaware, a sustained hallucinogenic high, the closest thing to a religious experience I have ever had.

My father thought my grades would suffer, and he was right. After the last performance he said, "Now it's over. All that hard work, and the review in the school paper wasn't even that great. I hope you've learned a lesson about what's worth spending your time on and what isn't." I crashed—stayed in my dorm room, slept until midafternoon. And my dad's words extinguished something in me. I've never had that feeling again, that sense of camaraderie and purpose.

But now, when I wake in the night with an idea, or scour recipe books, or daub paint colors on the wall, my body remembers that feverish intensity.

Flynn grumbles about the mess and chaos, but I think he's secretly pleased.

I try different soups on him: turkey and wild rice, broccoli and cheddar, vegetarian vegetable. I find a banana bread recipe on an index card, which I remember copying from my grandmother's instructions, a lemony pound cake, oatmeal chocolate-chip cookies. I begin experimenting with muffins—blueberry, pumpkin nut, cranberry orange—seeking the perfect ratio of berries to batter, spice to nuts.

A week and a half later the walls are three different shades, from cocoa to adobe; the lighting is muted and indirect; the chairs, finally, are comfortable. The counter used to run along the length of the long rectangular space, but I convinced Flynn to place it along the shorter end about two-thirds back, still accessible to the kitchen through a door to the left, so there'd be more room for tables and chairs. The deli case now holds fruit, yogurt, juices, and bottled water. Muffins are stacked in a pyramid under a glass cake cover.

"*Now* it looks like a gay man owns this place!" Lance says approvingly.

CHAPTER 15

I have been on Mount Desert Island for nearly six weeks. I have a job. I have a place to live, rented by the month. I have an ex-boyfriend, of sorts, and a new friend or two. I know where to buy groceries and lightbulbs and cold medicine. I have found a beautiful hiking trail (although sometimes, hiking alone, I have visions of falling down a ravine and not being discovered until spring, when park rangers stumble on my decomposed, half-eaten body). I have turned a hobby—cooking—into a fledgling business. In short, I am almost as settled here in this brief time as I was after years in New York.

Yet in some ways it's still hard to believe I live in this place, so different from anything I've known. I have room to think, to breathe. I also have time—maybe too much time. Days are short and nights are long. People know I'm here; it's impossible to be anonymous. I find this both comforting and unsettling.

The Spruce Harbor Library, a snug, shingled building in the middle of town, is open year-round. In midafternoon, when business is slow, I've taken to leaving the shop and strolling up Main Street to browse through the periodicals and new arrivals. The library carries the two island weeklies as well as regional newspapers and the *New York Times* and the *Wall Street Journal*. The *Times* is beginning to look distressingly dense to me, a Morse code of small black type. I read it as if I'm reading a newspaper from a foreign country—the news feels that far away.

One of the librarians, an older woman who wears her hair in a long, gray braid and appears to own a sizable collection of Fair Isle sweaters, introduces herself to me from out of the blue. "I'm Eileen Davis," she whispers loudly, leaning over my shoulder as I'm perusing the latest *Us* magazine. "You just let me know if you need anything, all right?"

"Uh—sure," I say, simultaneously swiveling around to see who it is and closing the magazine to hide my shameful scrutiny of "Stars—They're Just Like US!" "I'm—"

"Angela Russo," she says. "I already know that. I put your information into the computer when you got a library card. You live in Dory Cove."

"Wow. Yes, I do," I say, wondering what else she knows about me.

"And by the way, computer number two is free if you want to go online. That's the one you prefer, right?"

At night, after work, coming home to an empty cottage, I build a fire in the woodstove—carefully, the way Lance showed me—with a triangle of logs and crumpled newspaper. I still believe it's a miracle when the logs catch, when the fire I've made actually heats the whole place.

When the cottage is warm, I start to cook. I cut an eggplant into inch-square chunks, toss it with sea salt and a drizzle of olive oil, and slow-roast it in the oven for an hour. I make marinara, letting it simmer on the stove until the plum tomatoes fall apart.

One afternoon someone from the local animal shelter posts a sign on the coffee shop bulletin board that tugs at my heartstrings: "Docile Lab mix needs a home. Five years old. Loving and lonely. Answers to Sam." Sam! When I call the number I ask, "Is that Sam-short-for-Samantha?" Apparently not; this Sam is a he. I drag Flynn to the shelter with me, and the dog looks up at us through the wire fence with its glistening (rheumy?) eyes. Sam has a dull chocolate coat with tufts of hair missing. He appears to be starving; every rib is visible. I fall in love with him at first sight.

Not that I believe in falling in love at first sight.

Flynn teases me that this is only the beginning. I will start to collect animals; I will be branded the Woman Who Takes in Strays. But when I ask, Flynn agrees (hesitantly, conditionally) that I can bring Sam to work with me. Then he accuses me of manipulating him by bringing him to the shelter, a place where anyone with half a corroded heart is going to give in.

So here I am with a shy, malnourished dog and a house and a job, more settled than I have ever been, and yet not settled at all. The Big Questions hover in my head. But with butternut squash soup simmering on the stove and Sam lying like a sack of flour on the rug, those questions have lost some of their immediacy. Here I am, building a life—not just waiting for my life to happen. I am breathing in and out, living day to day. It requires so little effort I barely have to think about it.

All of a sudden it is freezing cold. Lying in my bed, early in the morning, I can see my breath. I sit up, exhaling like a smoker. Wind seeps through the cracks between windows and window frames, rattling the panes. I don't make a fire or take a shower; I throw a sweater on top of a sweater, coax the dog into the car, and head straight for work. "This is insane! It's only November!" I wail to Flynn when I arrive.

"It's November. There's no 'only' about it."

"Is this the way it will be? From now on, until spring?"

"Oh no," he says. "It gets a lot colder than this, believe me. What'd you expect? You're on an island in Maine. In the winter."

"I don't think I'm up for this."

"C'mon, it's not that bad."

"That's easy for you to say. You have central heating."

"Buy yourself some good thermal socks." He looks over at Sam. "And feed your dog, will ya? He's going to need some body fat to get through this winter. Here, give him a biscotti. It's stale anyway."

"I have this image in my mind of you at the end of a long pier, yearning for your sailor, like in *The French Lieutenant's Woman*," Lindsay says. We've started talking on the phone again every few days, having negotiated an unspoken truce: She is fascinated and appalled by the details of my quiet life, and I am likewise fascinated and appalled by her blossoming relationship with Hot4U.

"As far as I'm concerned, my sailor is lost at sea," I say. "Good riddance."

"Well, I can't say I'm surprised. Do you ever see him around?"

"Never," I say, but as it happens, when I report for duty at the Daily Grind the next morning, there he is.

"Oh—hi," Rich says. He's standing at the counter, looking up at the menu on the wall. It's not even seven o'clock; he's the only customer. "I just came in to grab a coffee."

"As good a reason as any to go to a coffee shop," Flynn remarks.

"Hi," I say. I know that Flynn is mocking Rich for my benefit, and I'm secretly pleased. I hang my orange parka on a peg and go into the back room to get an apron.

Uncomfortable pause. "Sooo—you two know each other?" Flynn asks innocently.

"Yeah, we do," Rich says. "Pretty well, in fact."

I come back out to the front, swatting Flynn as he passes me on his way to the supply closet. It's funny seeing Rich—funny strange—outside the Petri dish of his apartment, separate from me. On the other side of the counter.

"What can I get you?" I ask, tying my apron in the back.

I'm a little startled by how good looking he is, having chosen to remember him at his worst. He's wearing a blue-specked fisherman's sweater that makes his eyes look even bluer, and a red parka that accentuates his broad shoulders. All those things that attracted me in the first place—the sly smile, strong forearms, slightly crooked nose—are fully in evidence.

Despite myself, I feel insidious stirrings.

"Uh, I don't know. Just a coffee, I guess. I don't even know what all those things are," he says, motioning toward the coffee board above my head. "Double chai soy latte? What language is that?"

"It's pidgin yuppie," I say. "Why don't you try a latte—espresso with steamed milk?"

"I've had that before," he says. "Okay, thanks."

While I'm busy at the espresso machine, Rich looks around and says, "There's something different about this place. You—painted?"

Flynn pokes his head out of the closet. "Your ex-girlfriend has been fixing up the joint. Good thing you ditched her when you did, or she'd be doing this to your house."

I cringe at his breezy betrayal of my confidence. "He didn't ditch me," I protest, shooting him an evil look.

"I didn't," Rich says. "She walked out on me."

"Yeah, but only because—oh, forget it. Let's not go there," I say.

"Yeah, let's not," Rich says. He peers through the glass bell over the muffin display. "So what kind of muffins do you have?"

"Blueberry. Maple walnut. And these are cinnamon scones," I say, pointing at another glass pedestal.

"I'll take that."

I wrap a scone in waxy paper and he takes a bite. "Iss guud," he grunts with his mouth full.

"She would've been making these for you, if you'd played your cards right," Flynn says.

I glower at him again, and he pantomimes surprise: What'd I do?

Rich, watching us, wipes his mouth with the dissolving paper, then wads it up and stuffs it in his pocket. "That's okay. I guess I deserve it."

"Well—whatever, Rich," I say. I hand him the latte.

He takes a sip, and all at once I'm aware that he seems a little nervous. "I guess you're wondering why I'm here," he says, putting the latte down.

"Not really. Everybody needs coffee, don't they?"

"Yeah." He laughs a little. "But you know I drink—what'd you call it?—swill."

"Never too late to develop a palate," Flynn says.

Rich gives me a look, like Flynn is driving him crazy. "Could we—could we go somewhere? Somewhere private, to talk?"

I shrug. "I'm working."

"After work?"

"I don't know," I say. "I don't know what we have to talk about."

Flynn crouches down on the floor behind me, opens a cabinet door, and pulls out all the coffee filters in an ostentatious display of busyness.

"So I guess you're staying on the island," Rich says, reverting to small talk.

"Yep. For now, at least."

"That's great," he says. "So you—you have a place?"

"Uh-huh."

He pauses, waiting to see if I'll continue. When I don't, he asks, "Where is it?"

"Dory Cove."

"Oh. Good."

"Yep," I say.

"So . . ." He laughs a little. "Can I ever see it?"

"What do you mean?"

"You know. Stop by. Say hello."

"You're saying hello now."

"I know, but . . . I thought maybe we could have dinner together. I could make you dinner."

"Rich—," I start.

"Look, I came in because I heard you were working here," he blurts out. "I wanted to see you."

Flynn, crouching under the counter, pokes my leg, and I kick my foot in his general direction.

"So how is 'Blondy with a Y'?" I ask Rich. "Or—who's the one who called? Suzy?"

"Becky, I believe it was," Flynn says.

Rich shakes his head. "That's in the past."

"Oh, really."

"Yes, really," he says. "I'm a single guy these days."

"Aww," Flynn stage-whispers, and I kick him again.

"This is awkward," Rich says. "But I guess I'll just say it. I was hoping maybe we could just—well, try again."

"What? Are you serious?" I say.

Flynn pokes his head above the counter. "Very bold, mate. I like it. But I don't really see how she can go out with you again after you treated her like you did."

"Flynn, I can handle this," I tell him.

"Are you ruining my good name?" Rich asks me.

"Did you have a good name?" I ask.

"A fair to middling name, I'd say, at least," Flynn says.

"Thanks, Flynn," Rich says.

"No problem, Rich," Flynn says with a smile.

"Okay then," Rich says to me. "I guess I've made a total ass of myself. But I wanted you to know I've been thinking about you."

"You mean, you wanted her to know you're between girl-friends," Flynn says.

Rich looks wounded and irritated at the same time, and I almost jump to defend him. But I don't. I came to this place wanting to believe that I was the heroine in my own personal fairy tale, and that this man with the sun-kissed face and ice-chip eyes was my prince. I thought I was stepping into the picture tacked to my office wall. Part of me still yearns to believe that this particular story can end happily ever after, and for that reason it's safer for me to keep my distance, on this side of the counter.

On a typical day I wake up at five forty-five to get to the shop by six thirty. I mix the dry ingredients into the wet for muffins and scones, all apportioned and sifted during slow moments the day before. Flynn bustles around, getting the coffee going. Sam sleeps on a piece of carpet in the back room near the furnace, and then, as customers begin to arrive around seven, comes out to loll by the front door, greeting people with a tentative wag of his tail. As soon as the last batch of muffins is in the oven (and it's taking longer now, since the baked goods started selling out by nine and I had to double the recipe), I begin working on the soup, using stock I made at home on Sunday for the base.

Then it's midmorning, and I'm checking the soup and tend-ing the counter for the occasional customer. Like a man whose wife insists on having a child he says he doesn't want, Flynn has progressed from exasperation with the whole idea to grudging acceptance to something like pride. Sometime in the third week, he announces that after deducting expenses—the paint and lighting and other improvements, the pots and pans and grocery supplies—he's about to break even.

By twelve fifteen the line is almost out the door. Customers order soup and linger at the tables, paying bills and filling out college applications, having political arguments and meeting their kids after school. And like characters in a recurring dream, both Rich and Lance start coming in regularly. "You know, when you break up with somebody in New York, at least you'll probably never see them again," I complain to Flynn after Rich leaves with his scone one morning.

"Yeah, it's the opposite here," he says. "You're tormented by them for the rest of your life, until one of you dies."

In the afternoon I go outside to clear my head. I put Sam on a leash and walk up Main Street to the small park with the fountain turned off for winter, the flagless flagpole. After tying Sam to the bench out front for a few minutes, I step into the library.

"Hello, Angela!" Eileen Davis trills when she sees me. "I notice you took the new David Sedaris out a few days ago," she says. "What do you think of it?"

"I like it," I say. "He's so dry."

"Isn't he?" she says. "You know, I was thinking—if you like him, you might want to try P. G. Wodehouse. Very different writing style, but similarly outrageous. I found myself laughing out loud."

"Thanks. I'll give him a try."

"If you've never read Wodehouse, I'd say start with *The Inimitable Jeeves*. Here—I saved it for you." She hands me the volume from the shelf of reserved books behind her head. The book is wrapped in white paper with my name on it, secured with a rubber band.

In New York I might have contemplated taking out a restraining order at this point, but here I just take the book and sign it out. This small-town friendliness is hard to get used to, but I'm learning to adapt. Years ago I started a Wodehouse book, perhaps this very one, and couldn't get into it. But who knows? Maybe this improbably friendly woman has a better sense of what I might like than I do.

At home after work, I read in bed until I fall asleep. I wake to a loud rattling noise and sit upright. It's dead dark. I've never seen this kind of darkness—a darkness of shapes and shadows, with depth, a lake of darkness. The wind whines under my window, a low complaint; I hear the compliant rustle of the curtain, the thud-thud of my heart. At the foot of the bed, Sam whines in his sleep, then raises his head, his ears instantly up and alert. I am afraid. I tell myself I'm being ridiculous—what could happen? But things happen.

I shiver, trying not to look out the window. What am I proving, so far from home, vulnerable to unknown, unseen intruders? There's a reason people used to live in villages all their lives, surrounded by family and extended family, marrying at twenty a boy they'd known since childhood. They might have felt stifled, but at least they didn't have to face this silence filled with noises, this stark terror of being alone. Even in New York, behind my metal front door with multiple locks, I felt safer than I do here, where my flimsy glass-paned door opens onto a dark road and my guard dog is more nervous than I am.

CHAPTER 16

I miss my television. I can visualize it, on the floor of my dad's garage in a cardboard box. I miss talk shows and hour-long dramas with wisecracking banter. I need a break from all of this reality.

"I am craving TV," I confess to Flynn.

"TV is evil," he says.

"Yes, and I need to watch it."

"So come over," he says. "But you have to watch what I want. Tonight is *Lost.*"

Sitting on the couch in Flynn's cozy heated apartment above the ice-cream store on Main Street, flipping channels, is glorious, even if Flynn's the one controlling the remote. "Stick those idiots on *this* island and let's see how they do!" he heckles the TV.

After *Lost* we watch *Sex and the City* reruns. "So which one were you?" Flynn asks, twisting the top off a Bar Harbor ale and handing it to me.

"This is the same beer Rich drinks."

"It's the same beer everybody drinks," Flynn says. "Don't say Carrie. Everyone says Carrie."

I take a sip. "But I was Carrie. Well, without the designer wardrobe. Or the five-hundred-dollar shoes or the great apartment. Or, for that matter, the sex."

"Yeah, you were *just* like her," Flynn says, opening a beer for himself. "Here's a better question. Who did you want to be on *Beverly Hills 90210*? I wished I was Luke Perry, but I was probably more Brian Austin Green. You know, if they'd had any courage they would've made that character gay."

"He was so gay," I agree. "You got that show in Australia?"

"Oh yeah, baby. All your American trash washes up on our shore. So who did you want to be? And don't say that Goody Two-shoes Andrea."

"You have a lot of rules."

"Andrea bugged the shit out of me."

"Why, because she wasn't a Barbie like the others?"

"Nah. Her personality was *actually more annoying*. By the way, that's an important thing I've learned from TV," Flynn says. "Plain-looking people are less tolerable than good-looking people."

"Well, that's true," I say. "And brains require glasses."

"And brunettes are smarter than blondes."

"Obviously. And people with curly hair are quirky."

"Andrea had it all," he muses. "The plainness, the glasses, the curly brown hair. A triple whammy. Poor kid—the deck was stacked." He's quiet for a moment. "Maybe that's what I hated about her. She was so vulnerable. Kind of the way I felt as a kid."

This confessional nugget startles me out of my TV haze. I put down my beer and pull myself into a sitting position. "Really?"

"Or maybe I hated her because she was so frigging annoying."

"You're not getting off the hook that easily. You were about to say something real."

He takes a long swallow and holds the bottle up to the light. It's empty. "I was joking," he says. "Time for more amber fluid."

A few days later, during a slow afternoon at the shop, I ask, "So what happened with you and Lance?"

"You're just bored," he says. "You don't really want to know."

"Yes, I do."

"No, you don't."

"Can't I be bored *and* really want to know?"

"But you don't really care."

"Stop," I say. "You're picking a fight to avoid the question."

The next day, after the lunch rush and before the late-afternoon pick-me-up rush, Flynn says, apropos of nothing, "It's that old cliché. We had different goals."

I'm chopping green pepper. "What?"

"He was into the whole gay-marriage thing. I just wanted to shack up."

"Why didn't you want to get married?"

He takes the knife from me and starts mincing the pepper strips into little squares. "My family had a hard enough time with my being gay. That's ultimately why I left Oz. But marriage—that seems like a statement for the sake of making a statement. It seems—contrived."

"Maybe you were afraid of making that kind of commitment."

"Yeah, maybe. It's hard to commit to someone—anyone—forever. And there are some things about Lance that I wasn't sure I wanted to live with for the rest of my life."

"Like—?"

"Well, for one thing, he's a recovering alcoholic. I always felt guilty having a beer around him."

"That doesn't seem like such a big deal."

"And he snores."

"Oh, come on. Everyone snores."

"They do not."

"Sure they do. I mean, even *I* snore."

"Why does that not surprise me?" he says.

"Flynn this, Flynn that," my friend Lindsay says. "So he's your new best friend now?"

"Of course not. Speaking of which, when are you coming to visit?"

"Is it still winter up there?"

"Oh, come on. It's not even December yet. Besides, the Gulf Stream—"

"Yeah, yeah, the Gulf Stream, blah blah blah. You can lie about how warm it is up there all you want. There's a reason people call that place *Vacationland*. You aren't supposed to actually *live* there. Just visit. In August."

"That doesn't sound like something a true friend would say."

She laughs dryly. "It's something only a true friend would say. So tell me," she says. "Is your quality of life better? Are you happier?"

Am I happier? What a question. My shack is cold, I'm working at a coffee shop for just above minimum wage with a small, caustic gay man as my only companion, I've adopted a sad, starving dog, the sky has been relentlessly gray for the past five days. "Happiness is overrated," I say. "I'm having an adventure."

"You're clinging to that little island for dear life. That's not adventure. It's hibernation."

"Make fun all you want," I say. "I'm glad I'm here."

"That's your story, and you're sticking to it," she says.

"So," I say in an attempt to change the subject, "how's Hot4U treating you?"

"Peter is *great* in every way," she says, enunciating emphatically. She has warned me that I'm not allowed to call him Hot4U anymore, but sometimes I can't resist.

"Well, that's *great*," I say.

"Go ahead, tell me more stories about Flynn," she says. "I know you want to."

Every few days a tall, diffident man in paint-splattered jeans and a white button-down shirt comes in and orders a small black coffee to go. He has fine lines around his eyes and an intense gaze, and appears to be in his late thirties.

After several weeks, he says, "You're new here, aren't you?" as I hand him his change.

I look into his eyes and stammer, "Uh—yeah."

When he leaves, Flynn says, "Smooth."

"Shut up." I neaten the rows of muffins in the case, sweep away the crumbs. Then I say, as casually as I can manage, "So who was that?"

Flynn claps his hands. Smugly. "I made a bet with myself that you'd start sniffing around that guy by the end of this week."

"You're a strange little man," I tell him.

"Flattery will get you nowhere," he says. After holding out for a few moments, Flynn says, "His name is Tom Martinelli. He's a woodworker. Been here a few years. Came from California, I think."

"So is he married?"

"Is he gay, more important," Flynn says.

"Gay?"

Flynn shrugs. "I'm not getting the usual signals, but then again I'm not so familiar with West Coast karma."

"What kind of gay man are you?" I say. "Can't you identify your own people?"

"You're one to talk," he says. "You thought Rich Saunders was your soul mate."

The next morning I am lifting cooled chocolate-chip muffins from the baking tin to the display tray when Tom comes in. He's wearing oilcloth overalls and a down-filled green jacket, a black knit cap pulled low over his ears.

"Ahoy, matey," says Flynn. "You look like a longshoreman."

Tom glances down at himself. "I feel like one," he says. "I have to get over to Little Cranberry Island today, and it's going to be damn cold." I read about Little Cranberry Island in the free tourist guide; it's a mile-wide landmass about three miles from Mount Desert, accessible only by boat. Thirteen kids attend its one-room schoolhouse.

Out of the corner of my eye, I covertly inspect him. Tom is sinewy, like a long-distance runner, with thinning hair cropped close. His mouth looks several times too big for his head, and his teeth are California white. His skin is rough and his nose beaky. He's tall, and looms a little. You wouldn't call him handsome, though something about him is compelling—his intensity, his inquisitive gaze. If he were a bird, he'd be a bald eagle.

"Business or pleasure?" I ask.

"I'm doing a project out there in the spring for a new client, and I need to scope out the property. So it's business." He shrugs. "But—you know. Business is pleasure."

"Is it?" I can't tell if he's serious. After all, it's frigid out there on the open water. "Black coffee?"

"Yeah, thanks," he says. I hand him the coffee, and he puts a handful of change on the counter. "Sure; you have to like what you do. Otherwise, what's the point?"

"Some people might say the point is—oh, heck, I don't know—buying groceries? Paying the rent?" Flynn says.

"Yeah, of course." Tom nods. "You gotta take care of Maslow first."

"Huh?" Flynn says.

"You know—Abraham Maslow's hierarchy of needs."

Flynn and I look at him blankly.

Tom takes a sip of coffee. "Maslow was this humanist psychologist who said that you can't expect to have a civilized society until humans' basic needs are met—water, food, safety. If you don't have a roof over your head or food in your stomach, you're not going to be asking existential questions about autonomy and personal happiness, right? So of course I'm talking about a situation where my needs are met, more or less, and I have choices about what kind of life I want to lead. Within that context, yeah, I wouldn't do the work I do unless I found it exciting and intellectually fulfilling."

"Well," Flynn says. "Good on ya."

"Was I just a total blowhard?" Tom asks.

"Kind of. But I get your vibe, man—your groovy West Coast vibe. I dig it."

Tom laughs and rolls his eyes.

As I slide the muffin tray back into the display case, I wonder, Am I doing enough existential thinking about my own autonomy and personal happiness?

"Are those raisin?" he asks.

"Chocolate chip."

"I'll take one. Thanks."

I hand him a muffin and a napkin and he digs around in his pocket for change.

"Don't worry about it," I say. "That muffin was squished. But it should meet your basic needs just fine."

"I'm sure it will. Some of them, anyway," he says, grinning.

There are few options for eating out, even in Bar Harbor, so despite the fact that Flynn and I spend most of our waking hours together, I have begun inviting him over for dinner after work. He's in charge of fire and I'm in charge of food. Flynn doesn't know how to cook, but has impulsively decided that he wants to learn. At least a few things, he says, to impress prospective paramours.

"Teach me how to make risoda," he says one evening, sprawled on my couch sipping fumé blanc.

"Risoda? You mean risot-to?"

"Yeah, whatever. That's an impressive one, isn't it?"

"Maybe, but it can go horribly wrong. If you stop stirring—and you have to stir it constantly—you'll end up with a sticky mess. Also, if you're trying to impress a hipster, you should know that risotto was trendy in the nineties but is now considered a little passé. It's been around for centuries, of course, but like quiche and pesto, it got caught in an unfortunate trend warp."

"That's sad," he says. "Why can't a risotto just be a risotto?"

"You wouldn't want someone who's that superficial anyway."

"Uh—I might," he says. "My options are limited enough as it is. Beggars can't be picky."

"Choosers," I say.

"What?"

"Choosers. Beggars can't be choosers."

"God, you're annoying," he says. "It makes it really hard to like you."

"Only two shopping days till Thanksgiving," Lindsay announces the next day when we're on the phone. "Who are you spending it with?"

I've been doing my best to ignore this holiday-of-all-family-holidays, a task made infinitely easier by the fact that my only real friend on the island is Australian. I'm feeling surprisingly unsentimental: I don't want a turkey, stuffing, or any of the trimmings. But I decide to celebrate my own way—by teaching Flynn how to make risotto.

Which is how, at five o'clock on Thanksgiving Day, Flynn

comes to be in my kitchen, stirring minced garlic and onion in olive oil with a wooden spoon. I pour sauvignon blanc in two glasses, hand him one, and clink mine against his. "To family. Wherever they may be."

"Far from here," he adds.

"Don't let the garlic burn," I warn him.

Keith Urban is crooning some sexy country song on my CD player—I've never heard him before, but Flynn is an avid fan—and the Danish stove is doing its efficient thing, warming the whole place. Despite the fact that it's just the two of us, and we're cooking risotto, it feels somehow festive, like a real celebration.

So festive, in fact, that after one glass of wine I am moved to say, quite suddenly and without provocation, "You know what, Flynn? I am really happy."

Flynn looks at me sideways. "Oh dear. Is this like training with a drunk flight instructor? Am I going to have to do this rice thing by myself?"

"Don't be silly," I say, slapping his arm, "I'm not drunk." Eyeing my empty glass, I pour both of us a little more. "So I have a question for you. Are you living the life you always wanted to lead?"

"Oh, here we go," he says.

"Is that a bad question?"

"I thought we were just making risotto."

"We are," I say, taking a sip. "I just wondered."

"Two cups?" he asks, holding up the bag of Arborio rice.

I nod.

Flynn measures the rice into a bowl. "Well, I'll tell ya. My only aspiration was to get out of Dodge—I mean Australia—and open a coffee shop. And find the love of my life. Not very ambitious, really."

"But you've done it," I say. "Most of it."

"Not the most important part."

"Who needs love when you've got great coffee?" I say.

"I do," he says. "All right. Your turn."

"Well," I say. "I wanted to be a chef."

"Really?"

"Yeah."

"Why didn't you ever do it? I mean, you obviously like to cook. And you're not bad at it."

"My dad didn't think it was practical to cook for a living."

"And he thinks it's practical to move to Maine for a guy you met on the Internet?"

"Hardly." When I pour the rice into the hot pan with the garlic and onions, plump stray grains hop and jump. "Stir that to coat the rice in olive oil," I tell him. "Then start adding chicken broth." Flynn stirs dutifully. "It was a long time ago," I say. "I was in my early twenties. My dad's opinion carried a lot more weight back then."

"Well, it's too bad you listened," he says. "Though maybe things happen for a reason. You'd never have come here if you'd followed your dream back when you wanted to."

"Keep stirring," I say.

"I think that if you really want to do something, sooner or later you'll find a way to do it."

"Or not. Stir," I say.

He stirs, and I begin adding chicken broth in a slow stream. "You should open your own restaurant," he says.

"Flynn, I make muffins. I don't know the first thing about running a restaurant."

"Not yet. But you can learn. God, you weren't kidding about all the stirring. My arm is getting sore."

"Okay, turn it down to a simmer," I say. "And can you see why this might not be the perfect date-night dinner?"

"Abso-bloody-lutely," he says.

When we're finally at the table, eating the risotto and sharing a bottle of pinot grigio, he says, "You know what? I think we should put up a sign."

"What do you mean?"

"You should offer a cooking class. We'll put a flyer in the shop. And the library. It'd be something to do, huh?"

"A cooking class? For who? There's nobody around."

"Isn't it 'for *whom*,' grammar queen?" he says, pouring more wine in our glasses. "There are plenty of restless natives."

I think for a moment. "But where would I do it?"

He sweeps his hand around with a flourish. "Here, of course."

"Here? But I have only two burners. And a tiny oven. And no serving utensils. Or heat."

"So what? Nobody's going to care. Body heat, baby. You'll get four or five people who are desperate to get out of their own houses on a cold winter night. They're not going to care how many burners you have. You'll make a little money. Hopefully a friend or two. Maybe even find me a boyfriend."

"I don't know," I say doubtfully.

"About the idea, or about finding me a boyfriend?"

The next day Flynn tacks up a notice:

Cooking class in Dory Cove—a dinner party a week!
(Southern Italian with an American accent)
4 Wednesdays starting November 29
6-9:30 pm
$15 each class
Bring a bottle of any kind.
Sign up below, or see Angela at the Daily Grind.
(Ask for directions)

CHAPTER 17

The day of the first class I wake with my stomach in a knot. Five people, including Flynn, have signed up, and I own three chairs and four mismatched forks. The kitchen in my shack is barely functional, the stove a glorified hot plate. I've never taught anybody anything in my life.

What am I thinking?

"You have nothing to worry about," Flynn says. It's nine fifteen, just after the morning rush. He screws the top off a glass salt shaker and dumps the contents onto a growing mound on a paper towel, then tosses the empty shaker in soapy water in the sink. I watch it plummet to the bottom with the others, a shipwreck of shakers.

"I don't know how to teach anybody to cook," I fret.

"Sure you do. You taught me how to make risot-*toe*," he says.

"But the only thing you learned is that you never want to make it again." I rinse out the shakers one by one and set them on a towel to dry.

"It had nothing to do with your skill. It was about the logistics of trying to bag a hottie and stir rice at the same time."

"My kitchen is the size of a hamster cage," I say. "There's nowhere to sit and nothing to sit on. Why did I leave all my stuff in my dad's garage? I could've at least brought *forks*."

"Yeah, why didn't you?"

"I was trying to carpe diem."

"And you couldn't carpe some forks on your way out?" Flynn holds his arm out straight and waggles his fingers at the window. "Look."

I look. A thick fog hangs over the street, windswept and deserted, like a Main Street out of a black-and-white Western. An old man hurries by, half obscured by the mist, huddled in a coat with his woolen hat pulled down low.

"It's miserable weather. Nobody wants to be outside. You don't have to do much of anything but open the door of your humble abode and invite folks in."

"Humble is right."

Flynn strolls over to the sign-up sheet. "Let's see who's on the list." He scans it for a moment, then says, "Why, it's the Land of Misfit Toys! Okay, Rebecca Zinsser. You know her—mother of Josh, single mom, moved here from New York. Double tall skim cappuccino. I'm guessing she lived on sushi in the big city and now defrosts Lean Cuisine for herself and tater tots for the ankle biter. Aah—our good friend Tom Martinelli. Small coffee, black. We can fight over him. Eileen Davis. Herbal tea with a mound of sugar packets. There's an odd gal. She showed up last summer from out of nowhere. What's with the gray braid?"

"I like the braid," I say. "Besides, she's really nice to me."

"So maybe we *won't* be fighting over Tom," he says. "Lance. Vanilla latte. Hmm. Is this going to put a cramp in my style?"

"Crimp," I say. "*Crimp* in your style."

"Mother of God, give me strength," he says.

"Promise me you'll come early," I plead.

"What did I do to deserve this woman?" he says, shaking his fist at the pocked ceiling tiles.

A simple dinner, I'm thinking, something that won't be too stressful. Something familiar. I came up with a menu last night: chicken marsala; a salad of field greens, sun-dried tomatoes, pine nuts, and goat cheese, with herb vinaigrette; roasted peppers; and a *torta al limone*. As a teenager I often helped Nonna make chicken marsala—one of my father's favorites—so I have a fairly good idea of what I'm doing, but I called her to make sure. "I'm teaching a cooking class tomorrow," I told her.

"A class!" she said with surprise.

"Yeah, I'm kind of nervous. I posted a notice for it in the coffee shop where I work."

"How many people?"

"Five. Six, including me."

"What will you make?"

"Well, that's why I'm calling. I'm thinking chicken marsala. I want to go over your recipe to make sure I've got it, if you have a moment."

"I think I have a moment," she said with a dry laugh. "But I don't have a recipe. You know I never wrote anything down."

"I know. But I'm not as clever as you are, Nonna. If you talk about how you make it, I can take notes."

"Well," she said. "Do you have a meat pounder?"

"No. I do have a Progresso soup can."

"That will do, I suppose."

"This is kind of improvised, Nonna," I apologized.

"That's all right. You know what you're doing."

Just hearing her say this made me feel better. "So you start with chicken breasts," I prompted.

"Good-quality chicken breasts," she said. "Boneless. Or you debone them."

"Okay."

"Slice the breasts in half through the middle, then pound the chicken pieces with a mallet—*scusilo*, can of soup—between two sheets of plastic wrap. Do you have Wondra flour?"

"I can probably get it."

"Wondra, or regular if they don't have it. Sifted. Dip the chicken pieces in flour and cook them in butter. Hot butter. Sizzling. Real butter, not that *roba fasulla* your stepmother uses."

"Uh-huh, uh-huh." I scribbled notes on the back of an envelope.

"Okay, now you boil button mushrooms with a dash of lemon—just quickly—and then drain. When the chicken is no longer pink you remove it. Add the mushrooms, garlic, a few slivers of prosciutto, and the juice from the chicken to the pan, for taste. Then stir up the pieces with your spatula—you know how to do that—"

"Yes, I know."

She told me anyway: "—you scrape the pieces up and add *liquido*, a little chicken stock and marsala wine. Add pepper and salt. When the liquid is gone, add more chicken stock and reduce some more. Add the chicken pieces and heat. *Ciò è tutto.* That's all."

"Then I just plate it and sprinkle parsley over it, right?"

"I serve with potatoes."

"I know. But I'm thinking linguine for this crowd."

"Not authentic, you know. But linguine will do," she said. "What else are you making?"

I recited the rest of the menu, and she said, "Just remember. Only a few rules. The rest is—how do you say?—*improvvisazione.*"

"Improvisation."

"Yes, improvisation."

At the end of our conversation, Nonna gave me a little lecture. Cooking skill, she said, is as much about preparation as it is about talent. It's about buying the right ingredients and taking time to mince the garlic fine, cut the potato into thin slivers. You must have a quality of watchfulness; you must be vigilant that the butter doesn't burn or the garlic turn bitter. As she talked I remembered school-day afternoons sitting at the Formica table in her kitchen, cutting carrots and celery, weeping over the onions while she scolded, "I told you to peel them under running water, *la ragazza sciocca*," silly girl. I was a clumsy, absentminded child, always spilling milk or sneezing into the sifter, trying her patience. She'd set a simple task and I'd half-finish it, trailing dirty dishes and garlic husks behind me.

When she finally decided I was ready, Nonna gave me a lump of my own bread dough to knead. For a long time I couldn't get it right; my lump was grubby and dense. But when Nonna saw that my dough was beginning to rival hers, that I had learned the trick of patience and the rhythm of timing, she surrendered more control. She taught me to braid loaves the way she braided my hair on Sunday nights in front of *60 Minutes*.

"You will be fine, Angela," she said last night before we hung up. "*Il regalo*. The gift. You have it, remember?"

At twelve thirty, when I leave the shop, I drive off the island to the Super Shaw's in Ellsworth to rustle up ingredients. I can't find marsala wine. The store clerk suggests I try the boutique wine shop in the old downtown, which is, capriciously, closed for inventory. Pine nuts are nowhere to be found, and the fresh herbs are wilted, the leaves curled and charred. Red peppers are out of season and unavailable, and inexplicably there are no fresh lemons. The only sun-dried tomatoes I can find come in a tiny jar for six dollars. I need to rethink the whole menu.

Wandering through the produce department, I stumble on

unexpected treasures: root vegetables, parsnips and turnips and organic carrots; a shipment of oyster mushrooms. I find almond paste in the international foods section. My panic subsides and I begin to enjoy myself. This reminds me of how Nonna shops, figuring it out as she goes. "Pah. Who needs a list?" she says. "You find fresh, you have your dinner."

I hear Nonna's voice in my head as I drift down the aisle: *It's all by feel,* she says. *If a cantaloupe is too soft, it may have been frozen. Check asparagus to be sure that the cut ends of the stalk are damp, like a dog's nose. Press a plum tomato; if it isn't firm to the touch it will taste mealy. Buy only top-quality chicken; you will waste less and the flavor will be better.*

On any given day, Nonna has these ingredients in her larder: fresh and smoked mozzarella, provolone and Pecorino Romano. Occasionally *impestata,* a dry ricotta, from the local Italian market. Soppressata, hot and sweet, and pepperoni. Thin-sliced prosciutto. Cherry peppers, *peperoncino,* roasted red peppers in oil. Sicilian and Greek olives. Tomatoes, in season. Extra-virgin olive oil and virgin olio, a mild olive-oil blend she makes herself by combining extra-virgin olive oil and canola oil. Canned cannellini and garbanzo beans. Dried pasta of all kinds—ziti, penne, orecchiette, linguine, fettucine. Sea salt and peppercorns.

A surprising number of these things are available at Shaw's. I gather a mound of fresh mozzarella, plump as a water balloon, a knotty salami, Sicilian olives, and a jar of fire-roasted red peppers—not as nice as fresh, but they'll do—for an antipasto platter. For the chicken I find button mushrooms and prepackaged prosciutto; at the in-store bakery, two baguettes. Tonight I won't make pasta from scratch, so I buy two boxes of dried linguine. For the marsala I substitute merlot. My total at checkout is $104; I'm already operating at a deficit. I leave the store at four-thirty, and the drive to Dory Cove takes forty minutes. People are due at six. I run through a quick checklist in my head; the shack is clean enough. All that remains is the prep work.

Driving across the scant stretch of road that grafts the mainland to the island, I exchange one civilization for another, like stepping through the wardrobe into Narnia. Though only a breath away, the island's weather and terrain are different. The landscape is exposed and bleak; snow doesn't linger. Glowing lights in the windows of the houses I pass remind me of long-ago settlers, homesteading craggy patches of inhospitable earth.

Pink granite, slate gray, patches of ice: the island mimics the colors of sea and sky. Driving into its depths is like diving into a shipwreck; it is quiet and eerie and feels haunted by ghosts. It feels timeless. Rocks shift, trees fall, people come and go; the island remains.

CHAPTER 18

It's 5:39, there's a knock at the door, and my hands are covered with raw chicken goo. Oh, *shit*. I rub my hands together under the running water in the sink, and dry them on a bath towel. Before I can get to the door, Flynn opens it. "Thank God it's you," I say.

"Are we having fun yet?" he asks. He deposits a bottle of wine on the counter with a clunk. "White burgundy. Chardonnay is *so* last year. And I brought forks," he says, pulling a bouquet of white plastic utensils out of his jacket.

"Flynn. These are sporks."

"I know, I took them from the shop. Handy, huh?" he says.

I'm too frantic to be hospitable. Grocery bags litter the floor, boneless chicken breasts flop over the edge of the cutting board like mutant slugs. Water runs in the sink, splashing over vegetables onto the floor. "Can you—?" I motion spastically toward, well, all of it.

Flynn gives me a look of mock exasperation and starts swiping plastic bags off the floor.

"I didn't plan my time right," I mutter, slicing a breast in half lengthwise. "I forgot how long all this takes."

"Didn't you do this kind of thing for a living?"

"That was different!" I say, getting down on hands and knees to mop water off the floor. "I just devised the game plan. Other people did the actual *work*."

"That sounds nice. And you left why?" Flynn says.

"Because I got fired. Thanks for bringing it up."

"Whoops. Forgot that little detail. Well, tonight's going to be just fine. No worries."

Despite myself, I look up at him and smile. "I've been waiting to hear you say that since I met you."

"Saving it for a special occasion. *Hakuna matata*, baby," he says. He wads the plastic bags together in a ball and steps around me to stuff them under the sink.

I'm lighting votive candles, the better to disguise the shabbiness of—well, everything—when the first real guest knocks on the door: 5:58. I take a deep breath. Okay, I can handle this. "I'll butler," Flynn says, and springs to the door like a kangaroo. "Rebecca! Welcome to Casa di Angela," he booms.

"Hi, Flynn," she says. She squints into the semidarkness of the living room, and I see the space as it must appear to her: rustic, cramped, haphazardly decorated, way too many cheap candles. "What a cozy space," she exclaims.

"What a forgiving adjective," Flynn says.

Rebecca has a cat's quiet watchfulness. Her clothes are tastefully conservative: a pink Talbot-y sweater set and black jeans and black suede boots, a string of pearls.

Upper East Side, I think. After chatting for a few minutes, I ask where in New York she lived.

"Gramercy Park," she says, and I know what that probably means: young old money, key to the park, Town Car and driver, live-in nanny.

"And you're here year-round now?"

"Yes." Long silence. "What about you? Will you be staying year-round?"

Now I'm the reticent one. "Umm, well, I don't know. Basically my life fell apart, and here I am."

"Yeah, that's my story, too," she says, smiling. She seems relieved by my frankness.

Another knock on the door, and soon the little house is full of people: Tom-the-woodworker and Lance-the-ex and Eileen-the-gray-braided-librarian. Tom and Eileen clutch bottles of wine, and Lance holds a six-pack of Mug root beer.

"Nice place," Tom says, eyeing the room.

"Why, thank you," says Lance.

"Are you being sarcastic?" I ask. "It's a wreck."

Tom grins. "I like wrecks. I like—potential."

Once everyone has settled in, I usher them to my rickety table. Earlier in the day, Flynn brought over three discarded metal chairs to add to my three flea-market finds, and we crowd around the table as Flynn opens Eileen's red zinfandel and doles it out in wineglasses I bought at Marden's. "I can't pretend to be a real chef," I say by way of welcome. Flynn gives me a *what the fuck?!* look, and I amend my approach. "But I think I might be able to show you a few things."

I talk about how I grew up peeling potatoes and kneading dough in my grandmother's kitchen while she told stories from her past, from Italy. My grandparents' village of Matera, in a region now known as Basilicata, was a place of *cucina povera,* the cuisine of poverty. They lived in houses with wood-burning hearths where the women baked their own bread, grew tomatoes in the backyard, made mozzarella from goat's milk, picked olives off the trees to marinate in oils and spices. But the land was parched and rocky. Wine was cheaper than water. Flour was so scarce that even the bread was poor. My grandparents were called *terrone*—of the land, a term Italians from the north used to describe the other Italy, southern Italians, whom they considered crude, uncultured, ignorant.

In hard times my grandparents learned to live with hunger; they made soup from root vegetables, salads from bitter herbs. They ate stale bread soaked in water and olive oil. Each family had one pig a year, which they rationed carefully, using every scrap to make the spicy sausage of the region called *lucania,* the garlicky pressed salami called soppressata, the *pezzente,* or beggars' salami made of the least desirable parts. They made lard from the pig and flavored it with *peperoncino*, small pickled peppers, then stored it in jars to use for cooking or to spread on bread.

As I talk, I rub garlic between my palms to remove the stubborn papery husk. I pass around an ordinary plum tomato, explaining, as my grandmother explained to me, that while it might be as waxy and tasteless as a raw potato, its dense heft makes it the best kind for sauce. Though the tomato is familiar to everyone, my guests handle it as if they've never seen one before, examining its eggy shape and weight, nestling it in their hands. With surprise, I note genuine curiosity on their faces, and it dawns on me that these things that have come to seem intuitive to me aren't necessarily obvious to everyone.

The small space is filled with bodies, and for a few minutes we bump clumsily around each other as I devise tasks for people to do. Lance opens the olives and roasted peppers and removes the mozzarella from its filmy sac; Tom slices the salami and cheese and cuts a baguette into chunks, which he tosses in a basket. Rebecca cuts the boneless chicken breasts lengthwise, into medallions. I help Eileen arrange a classic antipasto platter, layering the cheese and meat and vegetables and olives so they appear unstudied and yet pleasing to the eye: fresh mozzarella, sliced a quarter-inch thick, rolled into a cylindrical shape. Plain and spicy soppressata next to it, then cubes of provolone, cherry peppers, *peperoncino,* wedges of roasted peppers, and sliced pepperoni, with oil-cured olives heaped in the middle. I drizzle the olive oil that I brought from the Italian market near my dad's house in Nutley and place the platter on the table with the basket of bread.

As we discuss the menu, I nibble a piece of soft mozzarella. It is tangy, tougher than the barrel-fresh cheese I'm used to. The rest of the antipasto platter isn't much better, the peppers limp and the olives bland. But there's nothing I can do about it; I just have to let it go. The shack is warm, everyone got here, and, miraculously, they seem to be enjoying themselves.

"What should I do with this lemon zest?" Before tonight, Eileen thought lemon zest was a soft drink. Now she lifts the snow-drift of grated rind on a paper towel as I direct her to the whole milk simmering on the stove. "You said your grandma doesn't use recipes, but I wish you would," Eileen tells me. "I'm a methodical person. I like to know what I'm doing every step of the way."

"I understand. I'll write out some recipes next time. Stir the custard so it doesn't stick," I say, watching Lance as he rolls out a marzipan pie crust, leaning into the rolling pin like an expert. Tom flattens chicken breasts with a Progresso soup can, and Rebecca combines flour, salt, pepper, and crushed oregano in a bowl. She dredges the chicken pieces in the flour mixture before placing them in sizzling butter. Tom nudges her aside to check the root vegetables roasting in the oven. When the chicken is cooked on both sides, Rebecca removes it to a plate under a wide lid to keep it warm.

I demonstrate how to parboil the button mushrooms with lemon, and slice garlic the way Nonna taught me, *taglilo sot-*

tile. Lance combines the mushrooms and garlic with slivers of prosciutto in the pan and the juice from the chicken, cooking it all quickly. I deglaze the pan, adding seasoning and then wine. When the sauce is reduced, Lance adds a long, slow stream of chicken broth, whisking until it thickens.

Meanwhile, Flynn sits at the table helping himself to wine. "We're cooking with gas!" he remarks. "No need for me to get in the way. I'd be as useful as tits on a bull."

"Just sit there and entertain us with charming Australian colloquialisms," Lance says.

"I'm a fabulous taster, if anyone needs an opinion," Flynn says. Eileen offers him a spoonful of lemon custard, which he accepts, looking serious as he considers the balance of flavors. "Needs Tabasco," he pronounces. Eileen clucks and turns away, putting a quick end to Flynn's tasting career.

When the chicken is back in the pan and the pasta water is simmering, we sit down for a salad of field greens with roasted peppers, walnuts, and goat cheese. The antipasto platter and two bottles of wine are empty. For the first time all evening, I begin to relax. By the time we get to the chicken marsala, I'm on my second glass of wine, and I'm not the only one; candlelight glows on flushed, animated faces. It feels like a major accomplishment to have assembled a collection of virtual strangers on this frigid night.

Rebecca is tapping her wineglass with a spoon. "I didn't know what to anticipate," she says, looking around. "I have to admit, my expectations weren't very high—I just thought it would be something different, and that's always welcome at this time of year, isn't it? But I actually learned something. And the food was delicious. So thank you, Angela. I'm looking forward to the next time." She raises her wineglass in my direction.

Flynn stands up and leads a little round of applause. "And a standing O," he says, circling his arms over his head like a pre-school ballerina.

It's been so long since I've been thanked for anything—since I've done anything worthy of thanks—that I don't know how to respond. I stammer, "The truth is, I only did it to make friends."

Flynn rolls his eyes.

"There's one more thing," Rebecca says. "I'd like to offer my kitchen for the rest of the classes. If you'd consider it, Angela. This little house is charming, but I have a big empty place in Egret Bay with a kitchen I barely use and a huge range my husband insisted on. And a dishwasher. And a seven-year-old son who won't need a babysitter if we relocate."

"Are you sure?" I ask. "It's a lot of mess."

"Don't worry, we'll all clean up," Flynn says quickly.

"I'm not worried about that. It'd be fun. If everybody likes the idea."

People nod and shrug with controlled enthusiasm. Afraid of hurting my feelings, or possibly Lance's, I suspect they don't want to appear too elated at the prospect.

"What's not to like?" Flynn cajoles. "C'mon, people!"

"I say yes," I tell Rebecca.

"Settled," she says.

At the end of the evening, after the *torta al limone* and the good-byes, Flynn and I collapse on the lumpy couch and survey the damage. "You were right. What a mess," he says. Flour dusts the floor, oil spatters the wall, dirty dishes and silt-glazed wineglasses are everywhere. Flynn wants to gossip, but the evening is such a blur that I have little to say. I'm relieved to have made it through without a disaster—an oil fire or salmonella poisoning, or, worse, being exposed as a fraud.

"There's something mysterious about Rebecca," he muses. "What happened to the husband?"

"Sure was nice of her to offer her kitchen. Lance is sweet."

"Lance is sweet," he agrees.

"You belong together."

"I'm more into the bad-boy type, you know."

"Take it from me," I say. "You're making a mistake." With effort, I hoist myself off the couch and start collecting glasses.

"Whoa, Nelly," he says. "Do we have to do that yet?"

I sink back onto the couch.

"So was anybody here tonight who didn't come from somewhere else?" Flynn muses. "Rebecca's from New York, Lance from Virginia. Tom's from the West Coast somewhere. You're from Jersey."

"Flynn—"

"You know what? This whole night was about your being an Italian girl from Nutley. Claim it." He takes a swig of wine. "So what do we think about Tom? Gay? Not gay?"

"Don't ask me," I say. "As you well know, I'm no judge of character."

"Aw, don't be so hard on yourself," Flynn says. "That Saunders guy is a professional manipulator. It's to your credit that you weren't hard-boiled enough to see it."

I glance at Flynn, with his freckled nose, teasing eyes, and two-day orange stubble. "Excuse me, perhaps I'm mistaken—was that empathy?"

"Nah, couldn't be," he says.

"Well, anyway," I say, "I've sworn off men for the time being. I need to, as they say, 'find myself' before I start looking for someone else."

"Find yourself?" He gives me a skeptical look, then nudges me with his shoulder. "Perhaps *I'm* mistaken—but it seems to me that you're right here."

CHAPTER 19

"There's something I can't figure out," Tom says, craning his neck over the coffee shop counter early on the morning after the cooking class. "What are you doing here?"

I peer up at his smiling face. "Hi, Tom. I'm restocking the deli case."

"I see that," he says. "Italy to New Jersey, I understand. New Jersey to Mount Desert Island? Can't make sense of it."

"I know," I say, straightening a row of fruit cups. "I'm not so sure myself."

"Don't lie," says Flynn, pouring Tom a small coffee.

"I'm not lying," I snap, irritated by his intrusion.

"Love pays geography no heed," Flynn stage-whispers to Tom.

"It was love?" Tom asks.

I pinch Flynn's calf. "Well, in her case, lust," he replies blithely, shaking his leg and handing Tom the coffee.

"Don't you have anything better to do?" I ask.

"Excuse me." Flynn motions toward Tom with a flourish. "I'm serving a customer."

"Lust, huh?" Tom says.

"No." I slam the door to the deli case shut and haul myself up off the floor. "I mean, yes, I was briefly involved with someone. But that's not the reason I came. Not the *only* reason."

"She just lo-o-oves the bracing winter air," Flynn says.

Ignoring him, I turn to Tom. "What about you? How did you end up here?"

He takes a sip of coffee. "I came here one summer to visit a college friend whose family owns a house in Seal Harbor. Then I moved to California, and when—well, it's a long story. But after a while I didn't need to be there anymore. I didn't need to be anywhere in particular. And I remembered this place."

"So you came here randomly?"

"Sort of. I like working with my hands, and I thought I could do that here."

"You're a woodworker."

He nods. "Yeah. Furniture maker."

"He makes these exquisite chairs and tables out of cherry and maple," Flynn says. "They're like—art."

"Can I see your work? I—I used to work in a museum." As soon as I say this, I cringe. First of all, working in a museum has nothing to do with Tom's furniture, and second, it has nothing to do with what I actually did. I might as well have been plan-ning events for a pharmaceutical company. I expect Flynn to ex-pose me—he's usually quick to root out phony posturing—but he's uncharacteristically quiet.

"A museum? That's interesting." Still, Flynn says nothing. "Drop by my studio in Deep Spring Harbor anytime. It's open most days."

"I will."

"By the way, last night was fun. I learned a lot." He laughs. "I have a lot to learn."

"Good," I say awkwardly.

"I didn't mention this, but I'm half Italian, too," Tom says.

"Martinelli. Of course," I say. "What's the other half?"

"Jewish. My mom's Jewish, so I'm Jewish. But you can't beat Italian food. Speaking of which, I'm going to get the ingredients for last night's menu and surprise my girlfriend this weekend. She's going to be impressed."

I nod and smile, hiding a prickle of disappointment.

When he leaves, the little bell in the door tinkling behind him, Flynn turns to me and says, "Girlfriend? What the *fuck*?"

I sigh. "Whatever."

"Not whatever," he says. "He was definitely flirting with you."

"You know what? It doesn't matter. I've sworn off men, re-member?"

"Uh-huh," Flynn says, nodding, "right."

I am lying under a blanket on the sofa with Sam, reading Wode-house, a cozy fire in the stove and a cup of tea in my hand, when Rich appears at the front door of my shack with a six-pack and a pizza.

"I was in the neighborhood," he says.

"With a pizza?"

"I remembered you like mushroom and sausage." He holds it aloft. "Hungry?"

If the book were more my style (I'm still not loving Wode-house), or the pizza didn't smell so tempting, or Rich weren't wearing those old, faded jeans with the hole in the knee that hang on his hips like boxers, I would never have let him in.

"So you got a dog," he says, putting the pizza on the coun-ter and the beer in the fridge. "Cute little fella. Kinda skinny though, huh? What's his name?"

"Sam," I say, a little smugly.

He grins, unfazed. "You found my dog."

Here's the thing: Sex with someone you don't know very well is usually a brief flash of pleasure cloaked in a before-and-after of awkwardness. How do I look? What is he doing? Why is he doing that? It can be all elbows and knees, poking and prodding, rough hands, clammy skin, coffee or cigarette breath, or worse. With Rich, there's none of that. His hands are a revelation—sensitive to nuance, attuned to ambiguity. Our bodies' perfect fit makes me want to spend all my time with him entwined and naked.

The fact that I've already had sex with him means, in my own relativistic ethical scheme, that I'm no more morally compromised by sleeping with him again than I have been already.

"Despite yourself, you still like me," Rich whispers, nibbling my ear.

I shift away, putting a pillow between us. "I'm not sure about that."

"You can't resist me."

Sadly, this appears to be true. Something base in me is drawn to something base in him. Never have I experienced such disconnect between mind and body, which both craves and yields to him without consulting its better, higher half. Rich is shallow, self-involved, unscrupulous, and remarkably ignorant of the references that populate the brains of most intelligent people. Yet he can be witty. He knows the meter of a haiku. He sails complicated boats and reads the weather and sea with precision. He is all casual physical charm; sex is no big deal, yet it is everything.

But this can never work. I sit up and throw back the covers.

"I can't believe I'm sleeping with you again," I mutter, as much to myself as to him. "This is crazy. You have to leave."

He pulls the covers up and pulls me closer. "I like you, Angela. There's something about us that feels right. I know you feel it, too. Why can't you admit it?"

Why, indeed . . .

A few days later, after another such encounter, we are sitting at a bar in Bar Harbor, eating hamburgers and drinking beer. "So what are we doing, Angela?" Rich says.

"Uh . . . Eating hamburgers and drinking beer?" I say with my mouth full.

"You know what I mean."

"Not sure I do."

He shifts on his stool. "Maybe it's time to talk about where this is headed."

"Where this is headed?"

"Where we're headed."

"We're headed somewhere?"

"You're not taking me seriously," he says.

It's true, I'm not. I take a sip of beer. "Last I knew, you wanted to keep your options open," I say.

"So maybe I changed my mind."

Nibbling a french fry, I ponder this revelation. Ideally, he would have liked to keep his options open, but it's winter, and frankly, there are few options loitering around. Having my own place and interests takes off the pressure. As for me, I'm playing this game with his rules, and feeling just fine about it.

"Don't you think it's a little soon to be having this conversation?" I say.

"What do you mean?"

"Shouldn't we take it slow?"

"You call sex in three different positions in one night 'taking it slow'?" he says, his voice rising.

"Jesus, Rich," I yelp, looking around. "Keep it down."

"I'm just saying. It seems to me we're pretty involved already."

"Well, maybe. But last time we were 'involved' like this, you were still e-mailing five other women."

"Not that many," he objects.

"I should think that you, of all people, would be able to differentiate between sex and a relationship."

He looks wounded. "That's a low blow."

"Why?"

"Look, Angela, I'm trying to turn over a new leaf here." Reaching across the bloody remains of my burger, he grabs my hand. "I think we should give it a try."

"But you—you're the one who couldn't commit," I sputter.

"Everything was happening too fast," he says. "I needed to think. So—I thought. And what I thought was, What the hell? We should try to make a go of it."

"C'mon, Rich. Let's admit that this is a nice little diversion, and leave it at that."

"Wow." He sits back on his stool. "You really are cynical, Angela."

"*You* told *me* to take a hike. For you to say, 'What the hell, we should try to make a go of it' a month and a half later seems, well, thoughtless."

"Maybe it should be. Maybe you think too much," he says.

His dimness irritates me. "'Thoughtless' is the opposite of 'thoughtful.' It is not the same as 'thinking less.'"

"Whatever," he says. "Sorry I'm not an English major."

Leaving the bar, we bump into Tom and his girlfriend. Literally—trapped awkwardly in the doorway as they're coming in and we're going out.

"Oh, hello!" Tom says with evident surprise. Despite the few people around, the island is so spread out geographically that it can be startling to run into someone from the other side.

"Hi!" I say. Tom is wearing a green-and-black-striped knit hat pulled low and an orange sweater, and looks pretty goofy. Actually, it occurs to me that he resembles Goofy, the Disney dog. "You look—" I start, and think better of it. "Never mind."

"What?"

"Nothing."

"No, what?" Tom says.

"Augh," I say in exasperation. I don't really want to admit to this silly observation, but I can't think of anything else to say. Standing there in the unheated vestibule in our coats, we're stamping our feet like ponies. His girlfriend is talking on a cell phone, and Rich's attention has wandered to the football game on the TV above the bar. "I was just going to say that you—you look a little like Goofy. Your . . . sweater and hat. Sorry. It's dumb."

He looks down at himself. "You're right. That's pretty funny," he says. "I wonder if it was subconscious. I always identified with Goofy as a kid. He was so—goofy. And so was I."

We both laugh.

Girlfriend snaps her phone shut. She sports straight, blunt-cut blond hair and angular black-rimmed glasses designed for maximum hipness. "What?" she says.

"Ah, nothing," Tom says. "Angela, this is Katrin. Katrin, Angela is—"

"The Italian chef," she says in a throaty voice.

"*Muy bueno,*" he says with a big smile. She's a good girlfriend, this Katrin, to keep track of people he's mentioned.

"Nice to meet you," she says. We've migrated to the foyer, where we huddle in our coats, moving like bumper cars as people come and go around us.

"I'm not really a chef," I tell her.

"She only plays one on Wednesdays," Tom says.

"Uh, hey." Rich breaks in belatedly, having followed an exciting long drive that ended in a fumble. He reaches out his hand to Tom. "Rich Saunders."

"I'm Tom Martinelli. And this is Katrin Winters." Tom raises his eyebrows at me: *Is this the guy?*

I feign incomprehension. Beside me, Rich holds Katrin's hand a second longer than necessary. She yanks it away. "Don't think I've seen you around here," he tells her. "I'm sure I'd have noticed."

"I think I've seen you," she says. "Do you hang out at the Thirsty Whale?"

"Ah, sometimes," he says, clearly uncomfortable about where this is going.

She squints, steely-eyed. "Yeah, that's it. Didn't you go out with a friend of mine, Melanie?"

He has to think. "Melanie. You mean Melody?"

"No. *Melanie*. Melanie Guest."

"Ohhh, yeah. Melanie. That was a while ago."

She barks a laugh. "If you call two weeks 'a while ago.' I guess now we know why you haven't called."

Rich looks like he's been caught with his hand in another kid's piggy bank.

"Oh, no, no," I say, laughing and shaking my head. "This isn't a *date*. We're just friends. It's probably not my place to say this, and Rich never would, but he hasn't felt well for the past few weeks." I put my hand on Rich's arm. "He even went to the emergency room. A weird virus, right, Rich? He's just starting to feel better, aren't you?"

I see the gears shifting as Rich catches on. "Ohhh, yeah. It really sucked. Tell Melanie I'll give her a call in the next day or two."

Tom turns to me. "Well, I'll see you on Wednesday. What kind of wine should I bring, red or white? Italian, don't you think?"

"Sure. Either. I haven't decided on the menu yet. It all depends on Super Shaw's. The pickings are slim these days."

"Hmm," he says.

"What?"

"I'm just thinking. Did you know there's an indoor farmers' market in Blue Hill? Tuesdays and Fridays."

"No, I had no idea."

"Yeah, it's pretty cool. I'm actually going there Tuesday. I have to drop a table off in East Blue Hill. If you want, I could stop by and see what they've got."

"Or maybe I should just go there myself, if you tell me where it is."

"Or . . . hmm," he says.

"What?"

"Well, if you want, we could go together. The delivery will only take a few minutes. I could drop you at the market and pick you up."

"Really?"

"Why not? I have to go anyway. I'd like the company."

I glance at Katrin, who is checking out of the conversation, and Rich, who is checking out the female bartender. "Okay. That'd be great. I'll be at the coffee shop all day, if you want to stop by."

"I'm thinking early afternoon."

"Could we make it after the lunch rush? Say, one thirty?"

"Good."

"See you then. Nice to meet you," I say to Katrin, who gives me a tight smile and pulls Tom toward the bar.

In the car, Rich says, "So why didn't you invite me to your cooking class?"

"You knew about it," I say. "You saw the sign-up sheet."

"Well, I didn't know it would be *fun*," he says.

"Katrin is not in the class," I say pointedly.

"She isn't? I thought—"

"No."

"Oh," he says.

A wave of indignation washes over me. "This is a girl who's clearly angry with you for dissing her friend—and she's with another guy—and you're with *me,* who just saved your ass, and *you're scamming her*?"

"Of course not," he says defensively. "But you're the one who said we should keep our options open."

I'm not—but it's hardly worth fighting about.

At home, I stoke the woodstove, and in a few minutes the living room is warm. Sam jumps up on the couch expectantly. When I sit down beside him, he shoves his wet nose under my hand, demanding to be petted. I stroke his head and think about the evening—Rich's quasi invitation to move back in, the encounter with Tom and our plans to go to Blue Hill, Katrin's disgust with Rich and, by association, with me.

Though we didn't actually say the words, Rich and I both know we're through. I feel unexpectedly melancholy. My bond with him was the only connection—however tenuous—to my original impulse to come to this island. The path I followed to get here has been swept away by the tide.

Perhaps it's time to let go of the fantasies that brought me here. Perhaps I can learn to glide contentedly, alone, from one momentary pleasure to the next—the softness of a down pillow against my cheek at night, the beanbag weight of my dog curled against me on the couch, the warmth of a fire I made myself. The rich smell of just-ground coffee. Blueberry muffins fresh from the oven. Life's small details are the ones that interest me, anyway. The big questions are too hard to parse.

CHAPTER 20

"So what kind of stuff does he do?" I ask Flynn at the shop on Monday.

"What kind of stuff does who do?"

"Tom. What kind of furniture?"

Flynn raises an eyebrow. "Thinking about him, huh?"

"I'm just curious," I say nonchalantly, wiping the counter. "I'm tagging along to Blue Hill with him later this week. Apparently there's a farmers' market on Tuesdays."

"Uh-huh," Flynn says. "And what about the girlfriend?"

"It isn't like that."

"Uh-*huh*." He wipes down the espresso machine, taps the filter into the sink, puts the milk away in the minifridge, generally takes his time.

"So."

"So?"

"The furniture."

"Oh, yeah, the furniture," he says. "Well, it's pretty high-end stuff—tongue and groove, inlaid wood, dovetail joinery, all that. I went to Tom's workshop once—it's basically a converted barn. He has this revolving group of acolytes, mostly from art schools, who sand and treat the wood and help put the pieces together. They're a funny bunch. A little woo-woo. When they're not working, they sit around and practice Zen meditation, listen to harmonious music on the high-tech sound system. One teaches a yoga class. In the summer somebody—maybe Tom—plants a garden out back. And they open the doors to the neighborhood kids, give them blocks of wood to paint on, teach them how to make macramé bracelets."

"Oh," I say. Groovy workshop, Zen meditation, edgy girl-friend with black glasses. It's all so much cooler than I am that I promptly lose interest, which is, I've found, a useful coping mechanism. One that has served me quite nicely over the years.

"Ready to go?" Tom asks. It's early Tuesday afternoon, and he's hovering in the doorway of the coffee shop. He looks dorkier than necessary, with his trucker cap on backward. The char-treuse sweater he's wearing is not the best color on him. I am instantly at ease.

"Give me a sec," I say, untying my apron. Crouching on the floor, I riffle through my bag to make sure I've got the essentials: wallet, cell phone, sunglasses. Breath mints. Hmm, as long as I'm here . . .

"What's that rustling?" Flynn says, standing at the counter beside me.

"Nothing," I hiss. Why do so many of our exchanges take place like this, under the counter?

"Could that be—Altoids?" He reaches for one, and I slap his hand. He motions toward Tom, standing near the door read-ing the notice board, threatening to expose me as a breath-mint popper right before an alleged nondate. I hand over the minty bribe, and put the Altoids in my bag.

"Be sure to get her back before she turns into a pumpkin," Flynn calls over to Tom. "She's not much good in that condition."

"Useful for muffins and soups, perhaps, though?" Tom says.

"Nicely played," Flynn remarks approvingly.

Tom opens the passenger door of his Jeep. I think his gesture is quaintly gallant until he bends down and begins tossing items in the backseat: carving knives, a can of putty, two jackets, *New Yorker* and *Wired* magazines, old paper coffee cups, a mitten. "I should've done this earlier," he apologizes.

"No problem." The day is mild and clear, the winter sun low. The yellow-and-blue-toned sky is as vibrant as an illustration in a children's book, and I'm in an unusually good mood. Feeling the transformative glow of the sun, I tilt my face upward and close my eyes. The world is orange, the sun warm on my lids. For the first time in weeks I remember—my whole body remembers—what summer is like. I think of lazy beach days, picnic baskets with canteens of fresh-squeezed lemonade, sand as thick and crumbly as brown sugar, and I sigh.

"I know. I'm such a slob. Sorry," he says, half turning around.

I laugh. "I'm not sighing at you, I'm just enjoying this beautiful day."

Tom ushers me into the Jeep with a sweep of his hand. Ensconced in the heated leather passenger seat, I glance around. The interior is cluttered, but also clearly new and expensive. Fancy sound system, airplane-style control panel, tinted skylight. "Nice car."

"Thanks," he says, shutting his door and turning the key. The car hums to life. "I got tired of driving a beater. Didn't think I could face another winter without four-wheel drive."

"The furniture business must be good."

He shrugs noncommittally. "Can't complain."

As we drive off the island, sun glitters on the snow. We drive past the now familiar tourist shops, cheap motels, hardware stores. Tom puts in a CD, and I recognize the smoky voice and jazzy refrain.

"Oh, Nina Simone," I say. "I saw her in concert at the Beacon in New York."

I glance over, wondering how old Tom is. Nina Simone is something of an acquired taste, usually appealing to an older crowd. At the concert I attended, most of the audience were in their forties and fifties. Looking closely, I see crow's-feet, thinning hair, a few laugh lines. In some ways Tom seems surprisingly youthful: He has the frankness and curiosity of a twenty-year-old. But he also possesses a world-weary air.

"Trying to guess how old I am?" he says.

"No, of course not!"

"You were."

"Well, now that you've brought it up—"

"Guess."

"Not so old."

"Let's just say I'm old enough, theoretically, to have figured out some of life's big questions."

"Such as?"

"Such as, you know. Marriage. Family. Career."

"Oh, *those* big questions."

"Yeah, those big questions."

"And have you?"

He drums his hand on the steering wheel. *Bah dump dum.* "Not even close."

"Ever been married?"

"Yep," he says.

This surprises me. "Really? When?"

"In my late twenties. For quite a while, actually—I was twenty-eight and Beth was thirty. An older woman," he says with a rueful smile. "We divorced right before I came here."

"You met in San Francisco?"

He nods. "I have to say, she was—is—a wonderful person. I was—am—the jerk."

"It's rarely one person's fault, though, right?"

He shrugs, shakes his head. "I take full credit for this one."

Passing through Ellsworth, we stop at one red light after another. Usually I'm impatient on this stop-and-go stretch, but today I'm content to take it slow. "So what happened?" I venture.

He looks over at me and raises an eyebrow. "Do you really want to know?"

"I don't mean to pry."

"I don't think you're prying," he says. "Or maybe I do. But I don't mind." He stops at yet another light. "I didn't really know how to have a relationship. For one thing, I was working way too hard. I practically lived at work during that whole mid-to-late nineties period. A friend and I started a software company on the waterfront—one of those Internet companies that boomed and eventually went bust. I worked ninety hours a week when we were doing well, and a hundred hours a week when we started to crash. It was brutal, and our marriage didn't survive it."

Tom turns left down Main Street, crosses the stream at the bottom of the hill, and forks another left at the sign for Blue Hill. "I can be a single-minded bastard," he continues. "I've been that way since I was a kid. First I was obsessed with dinosaurs, then baseball cards, then music. With the whole dot-com thing, I felt like a pioneer, setting off into uncharted territory. I mean, we all did. Every day was brand new. You know?"

I nod. A part of me can relate to this kind of obsessiveness. Or maybe a part of me can relate to him.

"Beth was—is—a midwife. A very different profession from mine. I think after a while it wasn't just my hours that she'd had enough of; she also thought my work was morally and spiritually bereft."

"Did you agree?"

"Not at first," he says. "I was furious with her holier-than-thou attitude. Above the fray. Of course, what I was really angry about was that somewhere along the way, she'd fallen out of love with me." He looks over and gives me a wry smile. "My business partner and I got out at the right time, managed to sell the company before everything fell apart. But I couldn't let go—didn't want to give up the adrenaline rush. After Beth left and there was nothing else to distract me, I took a good look at myself and realized she was right. I *had* changed—I'd become someone I didn't like that much. So I decided to make a clean break. My grandfather's hobby was woodworking, and I'd grown up spending summers in Washington state with him in his workshop. I cashed in my chips and moved to Bellingham, the town where my grandparents live, and persuaded him to let me apprentice with him. I stayed for a year and took classes at the local college in furniture design and craftsmanship. Afterward, I wanted to go somewhere on my own. That's when I remembered this island. And I just did it—I came here, two and a half years ago."

I listen, struck by the similarities between our stories—big city, desire to simplify, craft learned at an Italian grandparent's side, impulsive move to Maine. In the same instant, though, I remember my tendency—as with Rich Saunders—to invent connections that don't exist, just as one invents recognizable shapes in the clouds.

"So I got some of your story the other night," he says. "But tell me more. Who are you, Angela Russo?"

"That's an awfully big question." I look out the window, wondering how to answer. I don't think I *can* answer. Inevitably, the stories we tell about ourselves are filled with half-truths, distorted recollections, and blind spots as well as occasional moments of insight, I think. It's all in the spin, isn't it? The emphasis on this particular event, that milestone, revealing more about how we want to see ourselves than who we really are. Not just in the stories we spin to other people, but in the stories we tell ourselves—the narratives we craft from memories to convince ourselves that our lives have order and meaning.

We pull into the parking lot of the Blue Hill Armory.

"You're off the hook," Tom says. "For now. But don't think I'm not going to make you tell me, after I've spilled my guts to you." He looks at his watch. "I'll be back in about half an hour. You have my cell phone number, I have yours. All set?"

"Don't forget me," I say, hopping down from the Jeep.

"Of course not," he says. "I'd have to answer to Flynn."

Squinting, I enter the dim, cavernous barn that houses the farmers' market. Expecting little on a December Tuesday—perhaps some dry tubers and greenhouse tomatoes, a few jars of blueberry jam—I find instead a vibrant emporium with twenty-odd vendors selling everything from organic spinach and baby lettuce to free-range eggs and chickens, honey and maple syrup, dried blueberries and cranberries. As I wander up and down the aisles, passing stalls with low-fat granola and whole-milk yogurt, goat's milk cheeses and roasted soybeans, I chat with farmers and examine the produce.

Before I know it, Tom is at my elbow. "Look at this beautiful eggplant." He holds it aloft. "I can see my reflection."

"Back already?" I say with surprise.

"It's been half an hour," he says. "I'm a man of my word. Today, at least." After strolling around for a while longer, he helps me carry bags to the car: asparagus, Parma ham, eggplant, eggs, parsley, ricotta and Parmigiana, hearty tomatoes. I'm envisioning a menu of small courses for tomorrow night, each a different taste of Basilicata. All that's left is to pick up clams and mussels, ocean fresh, at the harbor in the morning.

On the way home, we stop at the Riverside Diner and Tom orders a roast beef sandwich—"Don't rat on me to the vegans," he says—and I ask for a BLT. We settle into a booth by the window, and the waitress brings over a pot of hot water and two green-tea tea bags (Tom says to counteract the oxidants in the bacon; I suspect to alleviate his guilt). I tell him more than I intend to about New Jersey, my parents' divorce and mother's death, the debacle at the museum that propelled me out of the city. We linger as the waitress clears our plates. I order a coffee and we share a giant oatmeal-raisin cookie as I describe the picture of the cottage on my bulletin board and the assorted sordid details of my recent adventure.

I stop short of Blondy with a Y and the generic haikus. I have my pride.

"So you did it," he says. "You came and found your dream cottage."

"Yeah, right."

"You scoff, but that place has potential."

"I really don't think so."

"Sure. Knock off the back deck and build a new one, redo the kitchen, patch and refinish and paint. It just needs a little TLC."

"That shack is a metaphor for my life," I tell him. "I have an ideal image in my head, and the reality turns out to be completely different."

He tears off a piece of cookie and pops it in his mouth. "Well, you can't expect your dreams to materialize fully formed. Maybe you just need to move the two extremes closer together. Adjust the way you think. Let me ask you something," he says. "What do you really want to do with your life?"

"Oh, God." I think for a moment. "I like to cook, but cooking has always been a hobby, at most. Then I moved here, and all of a sudden I have the time and—I don't know. I've become possessed. When you talked about your job in California, I recognized that passion—a glimmer of it. Even though I've never felt anything like it before."

He nods, tearing off another piece of cookie.

"I guess my dream is someday to open a restaurant. That sounds crazy, doesn't it?"

"What's crazy about it? It seems like a logical step."

"I lack experience. I have no money, no idea how to finance it."

"But you can cook. You've been a party planner; you know how to organize complicated events. You manage social gatherings with ease."

"Well, if that's all it takes . . ."

"Having the desire and the skill is ninety percent of it, in my experience. The rest is follow-through."

Tom sweeps stray cookie crumbs into a pile, brushes them into his cupped palm, and deposits them back on the plate. This is a man who likes to control his environment. I think of the neglected wife, his self-described monomania, the autocratic arrogance that draws acolytes to his workshop.

And then I think: This man knows what he wants; he takes chances, changes careers, acts impulsively and decisively, clearly enjoys his life. He is unlike anyone I've ever met.

"So who are these interns of yours?" I ask. "Are they—groupies?"

He smiles. "They call themselves apprentices."

"Did Katrin start out as an apprentice?"

"No. She's a Realtor. She sold me my space."

"She seems nice."

He gives me a skeptical look. "That's charitable, considering that she gave your boyfriend a flaying. I've been on the receiving end of that, and let me tell you, it's not pretty."

"I'm sure he deserved it. And—" I hesitate. "He really isn't my boyfriend."

"Oh?"

"I did come here for him. But he's not the reason I stayed."

"I see. So you've decided."

"What?"

"You're staying."

"Did I say that?"

"Seemed like it."

For a moment I reflect on this. "I don't know what I'm doing. I have this class to teach. I don't have any plans to leave right now."

"That's usually how it works," he says.

"How what works?"

"How people stay."

"Is that how it was for you?"

"No, not really. I made a conscious decision to move here, and my intention has always been to stay. I want to be part of it—part of the island. I can see raising a family here. Growing old here. Having my ashes tossed off Cadillac someday."

"Wow. I can't imagine being that sure of anything."

"I'm a lot older than you."

"You mean wiser, right?"

"Nah," he says, looking over at me. "You might be wiser. But I've got that fuddy-duddy thing of wanting to put down roots. It's pretty simple, isn't it? You turn forty—"

"You're forty?"

"Oh, damn," he says. "Gave myself away."

"I wouldn't have guessed a day over thirty-nine," I say.

CHAPTER 21

"Tonight we're going to concentrate on *il primo piatto,* the first course," I tell the group. "We'll be making *stracciatella alla Romana,* spinach and egg soup; clams and mussels *fra diavola*; eggplant *rollatini;* and asparagus wrapped in prosciutto di Parma." We are gathered in Rebecca's stunning kitchen in Egret Bay, with its picture window onto the darkening bay, standing around her butcher-block island.

To make soup stock, I explain, you begin with the parts of a chicken you can't or won't use, the parts you would otherwise discard: backs, necks, skin, wings, innards. Buy whole chickens, and when you cut them up, save and freeze these parts. When you are ready to make stock, simply thaw and place them in a large heavy pot with a lid. Add any sturdy vegetables you have lying around—carrots, onion, garlic, celery—and a bay leaf or two. Sprinkle generously with sea salt and peppercorns, add water to cover, and then bring to a boil and simmer for several hours or longer—all day, if you can. Strain well with a fine sieve. Let cool, skim the fat off the top, and strain. Strain again.

Use this stock as a base for *zuppa di legume,* a broth of beans, peas, and chickpeas, or *minestra,* a thick soup with escarole, cannellini beans, and sliced pepperoni. Or make pasta *fagioli:* Sauté garlic in olive oil in a Dutch oven until soft. Add white beans and tubatini, cooked al dente, or resistant to the bite. Add the stock and bring to a boil, then simmer. Stir in a scoop of fresh marinara for flavor.

When I make stock, I tell them, the smell that fills the house conjures up images in my mind, deeper than memory, sifted from my grandmother's stories of her village in Italy.

"Oh goody," Flynn says. "I love granny stories."

I describe the women in the kitchen and the men coming home at noon, their lunch simmering on the stove, sitting down to eat the soup with whatever else was in the pantry: salty sardines and onions, cheese, bread, wine. I imagine it all: the cobblestones on the square, the cold brackish sea, the wild rosemary in the meadow. I picture Nonna in the kitchen with her own grandmother, pulling out the heavy pan, setting aside chicken parts, chopping vegetables on the warped wooden board she still uses, its grain worn and scarred with knife grooves. I can smell the broth, the sea, the scent of her own long hair, swaying to her waist.

Like a TV chef, I actually thought ahead and prepared a pot of chicken soup for today. "This soup, *stracciatella,* is one of Nonna's favorites," I say. "It's very simple, only four main ingredients: chicken stock, fresh spinach, eggs, and grated Pecorino Romano cheese."

When Eileen asks for exact measurements, I am prepared. I have printed a recipe:

Stracciatella alla Romana

8 cups chicken broth, preferably homemade
6 ounces fresh spinach, cut into strips
4 eggs, plus 2 tablespoons water

½ cup grated Pecorino Romano cheese
Salt and pepper

Boil the stock and add spinach, cooking until wilted, about 3 minutes. In a separate bowl, beat the eggs with the water; add grated cheese. Whisk the egg mixture briskly into the boiling broth, and add salt and pepper to taste, then serve.

I ladle the soup into small, blue-and-white Chinese bowls that Rebecca has stacked on the counter, and dinner begins. Tasting it, I remember that day several months ago in Nonna's kitchen when she wasn't feeling well and wanted only this soup. It reminds me of her—comforting and yet intense, not to everyone's liking. It seems fitting that of any food she might have craved, this is the one.

As if to illustrate this thought, Flynn pushes his bowl away.

"I don't know," he says with a grimace. "Something about that slimy spinach."

"It's not slimy, you philistine," Lance says. "It's silky. This soup reminds me of egg drop, but more intense."

"You're just saying that because of the bowls," Flynn says.

"It *is* interesting how different cultures do versions of the same dish," says Tom. "I'm thinking of matzo ball soup or chicken and dumplings in the south."

"I just think everything is connected," says Rebecca. "Each civilization has its own interpretation of universal themes. We share the same emotions, right? Aren't all cultures, despite the variations, linked by a shared core of humanity?"

For a moment everyone is silent. Rebecca has startled us, accustomed as we have become to her reticence.

"Personally, I tend to be less 'we are the world' and more 'life is random,'" Flynn says. "But hey, it's nice to believe in patterns. We have to order the world somehow."

"You're such a pagan," Lance says. "I agree with Rebecca."

"This magic soup is affecting your brains!" says Flynn.

"Actually," Tom says hesitantly, "I think you're conflating two disparate ideas. Whether various cultures share like characteristics—which on some level seems indisputable—and whether you believe that life is random, not predetermined by fate or religious deity, are two completely different questions."

"What did he just say?" Flynn asks, raising his arm in a gesture of bafflement.

"He's saying you're full of shit," says Lance.

"Not at all," Tom says.

"The point is," Flynn says, "whatever all *that* was, I'm just saying I'm a realist. A pragmatist."

"I'd say narcissist," says Lance, "but that's a whole other story."

Tom glances over, gives me a covert wink, and I feel a quiver of pleasure.

"Oh!" Eileen says, pouring herself a second glass of wine. "Let's hear it."

Lance laughs, his hearty guffaw breaking the tension. "I'd need to start drinking again."

Shaking his head, Flynn says, "Maybe it's time for all of us to switch to bottled water."

I assign tasks for the remainder of the menu: the rolled stuffed eggplant, asparagus wrapped in sliver-thin prosciutto di Parma, spicy clams and mussels. We all get to work, scrubbing mussels, cutting eggplant horizontally into quarter-inch-thick slices, trimming and blanching asparagus. Rebecca's kitchen is perfect for this, with two sinks and two undercounter pull-out garbage pails. We move easily around the large black granite island without jostling each other; the recessed lighting under the cherry cabinets, the industrial-size range hood, and the brushed-steel appliances make the whole enterprise seem somehow more professional.

Rebecca's son, Josh, bored with his rented G-rated movie, perches on a stool at the island. I cut him a crumbly slice of Parmigiana and he takes a tentative bite, looks at it, takes another. "Salty," he says.

"This cheese took five years to mature," I tell him. "That's why it's so pungent."

"I was a baby five years ago," Josh says.

"And think how much more pungent you are now than you were then," Tom says. For the first time this evening, he is standing beside me.

"What does 'pungent' mean?" Josh asks.

"Strong," Tom says. He smiles at me, showing those white teeth. "Hi."

I feel myself flush. "Hi."

"This worked out, didn't it?"

"Thanks to you," I say. "Almost everything here came from the market."

"What market?" Josh asks.

"We went to a farmers' market in Blue Hill yesterday," Tom says.

"I know that place," Josh says.

"Hey, is that your art on the refrigerator?" Tom asks.

We look over. The picture, an evident self-portrait, is crayon and watercolor. In it, a green-faced boy with a riot of purple hair and an uneven grin raises his stick arms in the air. Orange clouds hover over his head.

"I did that last year. I'm better now," Josh says.

"Not bad," Tom says. "Do you take lessons?"

"I made that at school. I mostly just draw at home."

"You should come by my barn in Deep Spring Harbor," Tom says. "There are always kids around, painting and drawing."

Josh nods. "Cool."

"I want to come," I interject.

"So come," Tom says.

A moment passes between us, a held gaze.

Perhaps sensing Tom's shift of focus, Josh hops off his stool. Eileen touches my arm, asking, "How many eggs in the ricotta filling? Do you have a recipe for the *rollatini*?" I turn to answer, feeling Tom's eyes lingering on my back a moment more.

"This is an everyday marinara," I say. "The staple of many Italian dishes and the base of the *fra diavola* sauce we're making for the shellfish. Anyone know what '*fra diavola*' means?"

"'*Diavola*' is devil, right?" Flynn says. "I think Lance called me that once.'"

"No doubt," Lance says.

I hand around my approximation of Nonna's magic:

Basil Marinara

6 to 8 garlic cloves, peeled
½ cup olive oil (half extra virgin, half regular)
3 (28-ounce) cans whole tomatoes, crushed by hand
½ cup fresh basil leaves
Salt and pepper

Sauté whole garlic cloves slowly in olive oil over medium heat until golden brown or even caramelized (the longer the better). Then add tomatoes, mashing them as they cook into sauce before adding fresh basil in strips, a stream of oil, salt and pepper to taste, and perhaps a sprinkle of sugar to blunt the acidity of the tomatoes. Place the pot on low, on a back burner, and simmer as long as time allows.

This sauce, like most Italian cooking, is better on the second day. I relate Nonna's method for reheating: Heat it until the oil rises to the top, then stir it back in and serve.

For *fra diavola* you crush a generous pinch of red pepper flakes with your fingers, sprinkle it into the marinara, and taste. The amount of spice is up to you.

Next, we steam clams and mussels in seawater, wine, a little garlic, and a splash of oil. When they've opened, we dish them into bowls and ladle the sauce over the top. Then we take our bowls and migrate to the knotty pine farmhouse table laden with our prepared dishes: rolled eggplant stuffed with *impestata,* or dried ricotta, egg, and cheese, covered in marinara and baked in the oven; asparagus wrapped in prosciutto di Parma, sautéed with a lemon-butter sauce; a simple salad of mixed greens.

Through the picture window, the bay is dark. Darkness came fast, the sky draining from charcoal to black in a flash. A heavy crust of snow, illuminated by the lights on the porch, hangs on the tree branches outside the window. Across the water, small, isolated lights shine in a few other homes, dotting the shore like party lanterns. Most houses on this bay are closed for the season, Rebecca explains, the owners back in residence in Boston or New York or Washington. Some, like migratory birds, fly to Florida at the first sign of frost.

In this moment, I feel perfectly happy. Here I am, opening a mussel shell like a spring-loaded trap, taking out the plump golden, black-rimmed creature inside, running it through the sauce, tasting its elastic brine with the kick of red pepper. There's no place I'd rather be right now than in this kitchen with these people, eating this feast, looking out at the frosted trees framed by the window to the satin blackness beyond.

CHAPTER 22

"When are you coming home for Christmas?"

Lindsay's voice is indistinct. I'm driving through a weak-signal area, a brief stretch of road between Dory Cove and Spruce Harbor.

Perfect timing.

"You're breaking up, Linz," I shout into the phone, which is on Speaker, in my lap as I drive. "I'll call you back!"

"Are you at that goddamn part of the road again? Why even bother to call me when you know—"

Silence.

I snap the phone shut.

Though I wanted to talk to Lindsay, I've been avoiding this particular conversation. People come and go from the shop all day long chattering about shopping lists and finding the perfect tree and packing up to visit relatives in faraway places, but I've been in a blissfully holiday-free bubble. I don't know if I want to celebrate Christmas this year, in any form. What I do know is that I'm not ready to go home.

The weak-signal area is actually located along the shore-loop road of Dory Cove, on the way to Mollusk Point—the long scenic drive to Spruce Harbor, the route I prefer. At a wide, flat expanse of rocky beach I pull off to the side, as I do every day, so Sam can get some exercise before I take him to the shop, where he'll laze near the baseboard heater for the rest of the morning.

Sam leaps from the car and trots toward the water, tail in air, ears perked, jubilant as always at the roar of the waves, the white caps fifty feet out, the searing cold surf. "Not too far, Sam!" I call, as if he understands English. I've heard tales of people swept out to sea near these rocks, children turning delightedly toward parents—*Look! Look at me!*—and disappearing in an instant, knocked off by a wave and sucked in by the undertow.

Leaning against the car, zipped in my parka, the hood's faux fur brushing my cheek, I gaze at the view. A pebbled beach extends to boulders visible only when the tide is low, as it is today. The austere shapes of the rocks are softened by their colors, charcoal and sand and green-brown. Though the air is frigid, the sun makes a valiant effort to warm these rocks, this place, my face. The coast is not cold in the way that people think, or even in the way I imagined before I came. The coldness is threaded with warmth, tempered by moments of grace.

I see Sam down at the end of the beach. "C'mon, Sam! Let's go!"

He stops, lifts his nose in the air, cocks his ear, and bounds back to me.

The library is quiet. When I approach the front desk, Eileen's face lights up. "I can't tell you how much I needed something like that cooking class," she says. "I haven't been here long enough to make real friends." When I ask her where she's from, she replies, "A town up north. But I had to leave. There wasn't anything there for me anymore."

"Oh." I pause, unsure of how much to ask. I'm coming to discover that on this island so many of us are from somewhere else, and everyone has a story. I don't know how much Eileen wants to tell me, or even how much I want to know.

I hand her the Wodehouse novel. She is disappointed that I didn't love it. "I wanted to, but he's so—English. And so male," I say. "I want to read something I can relate to. Any other ideas?"

She nods thoughtfully and leads me down a narrow row of stacks. "Maybe memoir," she muses. "How about—" She runs her fingertips along the glossy Mylar spines, hesitating on *The Liars' Club, Anywhere But Here, The Glass Castle*—all books I've read; I shake my head—until she stops on a spine I don't recognize. She pulls it out. *Crazy in the Kitchen*, by Louise DeSalvo. "I think you'll like this," she says. "The Italian grandmother, the food. Try it."

She presses the book in my hand and I open it at random. My eye falls on a sentence—*I begin my education in the pleasures of the kitchen, in the pleasures of the flesh.* I take the book back to the coffee shop and read all afternoon with a voracious hunger.

"Excuse me, do you work here?" Flynn inquires.

I look up. "I think you have me confused with someone else."

"Well, stranger, would you mind checking to see if the muffins are done?"

Mine, the dilemma of all the descendants of immigrants. To want to belong, yet to know that you do not. "That's presumptuous of you," I say, closing my book with great reluctance.

The menu, I've found, must derive from the shopping trip. Tom calls to ask if I want to visit the Blue Hill market again. The vegans demand organic vegetables, he says, making them sound like an angry tribe.

This time the front seat is free of clutter. Riding in Tom's car on the plush heated seat, with the tinted skylight and iPod dock,

I realize what a clunker I drive. My car announces each bump, each pothole; when it rains, the wipers push water lazily back and forth across the windshield in an opaque scrim. Cold seeps along the windows; the chassis vibrates if I go above fifty miles an hour. One speaker is blown. In this car, with its multiple air bags and vacuum-sealed panes, I feel protected, snug, invulnerable to the vagaries of the chilly world outside my window.

At the farmers' market I find butternut and acorn squash, onions, garlic, beets, and goat cheese. A menu begins to take shape. Even though Flynn will grouse, I want to make risotto again, this time with seafood—because I know how, and I think people will learn something new, even those who have made risotto before. Our first course: roasted squash soup and a salad of marinated beets and goat cheese.

Some of the growers recognize me from last time. "Next week I'll have fennel," a ruddy farmer in a flannel shirt, from Cherryfield Farms, tells me.

"I'll be here," I say.

By the time we finish, the merchants are packing up. Tom has an armload of bags, and I'm loaded down with squash. We stagger to the car, heave the bags in the trunk.

"Do you want to stop at that place in Ellsworth and order some contraband animal protein?" I ask.

"I'd love to, but . . ." Tom looks pained. "I think Katrin has something planned."

"Oh, right."

It's awkward between us now, the air thick with unease. I had put the girlfriend out of my mind, forgotten she existed. And maybe for a moment, I tell myself, he had, too.

With my cleaver I stab the slippery butternut, the tortoise-shelled acorn squash, in several places before splitting them in half. Alone in my house, I am cautious. I imagine slicing through the webbing between thumb and forefinger, cutting a tendon, bleeding to death (can you bleed to death from a cut hand?) on the kitchen floor. An item in last week's *Islander* told about an elderly woman who, attempting to dispose of her trash, slipped and broke her hip, and was found the next morning frozen to death, twenty feet from her back door.

I'm not old, and my hips aren't brittle. But I do live alone down a dark road in a dark harbor.

The cooking class gathers around the squash and onions and garlic, roasted last night in my oven with olive oil and sea salt. These puckered vegetables fill a tray on Rebecca's gleaming island.

"This is the easiest soup in the world, and it allows for infinite variations," I tell them. "First, you roast hardy vegetables— pumpkins, squash, carrots, potatoes, beets—with onions and garlic in the oven at three hundred degrees until soft, about an hour and a half. Allow them to cool, then scoop out the seeds, if any," I say, scooping out the seeds in demonstration. "Spoon the vegetables into a food processor in batches with chicken stock and some herbs—in this case, tarragon. Add salt and pepper to taste. Heat on the stove, then add a splash of cream."

"Do you have a recipe?" Eileen asks.

"That was the recipe."

So much of this kind of cooking, I tell them, is about learning to trust yourself, developing an intuitive understanding of how flavors and textures work together. But first you must learn the crucial building blocks: stock, marinara, vinaigrette. If you learn how to make vinaigrette, for example, if you understand the simple science of emulsification, you can use that knowledge for every kind of dressing and marinade.

Josh wanders in and out, tastes the bright orange soup, nibbles a piece of cheese. He brings in a ball of string, and Tom shows him how to cut a length, tie a knot, and pin it to a board to begin a macramé bracelet.

We make the beet salad by steaming the beets until soft, about thirty minutes, plunging into cold water, and removing the skins. After cutting the beets into small cubes, we toss them with a vinaigrette of orange juice, vinegar, olive oil, and shallots, adding crumbles of goat cheese and green onion, for color and taste and crunch, at the end.

Finally, we're ready to make the risotto. It can be tricky, I emphasize; the proportions must be just right. I take live lobsters, shrimp, and scallops out of the fridge, and we prepare a broth with bay leaves, carrots, and onions in which to boil the lobsters. Later we'll use the broth as liquid for the risotto.

Anticipating Eileen's request, I hand around a recipe I've written out:

Risotto with Seafood

2 bay leaves

1 carrot, chopped

2 small onions: 1 chopped, 1 minced

3 (1-pound) lobsters

⅓ cup olive oil

3 tablespoons tomato paste

2 cups Arborio rice

1½ cups white wine (dry)

2 tablespoons butter

2 pounds medium shrimp, peeled

1 pound scallops

Fill pot with water sufficient to cover 3 lobsters. Add bay leaves, carrot, chopped onion. Bring to a boil, add lobsters, and cook 10 minutes. Reserve water the lobsters were cooked in. Cool lobsters and remove meat.

Cook minced onion in olive oil until translucent; add tomato paste until blended. Then add rice. Slowly add white wine and an equal amount of lobster water. Continue stirring and adding liquid as rice cooks, 20 minutes or so.

Melt butter in. Add shrimp; cook until pink. Remove shrimp and add scallops; sear until golden. Add shrimp and lobster to the risotto pan. Fold in. Season to taste.

The meal ready, the adults gather around the table. Josh sits ensconced in the window seat working on his bracelet, outside the circle but warmed by its glow. Looking at him, I think how safe he must feel—the smells of food in the house, his mother nearby. Each week he draws closer, stays longer. I watch him sitting quietly in the window seat, leaning his shoulder against the side of the bookshelf, his back to the huge black pane.

The meal is winding down. I bring out a plate of *taralli*, a southern Italian spicy cookie made by shaping a dough of flour, eggs, seasonings, and olive oil into circles, boiling, then baking them a crispy golden brown. I made them yesterday, knowing that we wouldn't have time tonight. I ask the group to identify the unusual combination of tastes, and with each bite the flavors emerge: black pepper, fennel, cinnamon.

Having finished the macramé bracelet, Josh wanders over to

the table, gets Tom to tie the bracelet off, snip the ends, and fasten it around his wrist. While Tom is tying, Josh sniffs a *taralli* and takes a bite. His grimace tells us he isn't having any of it. After fishing three Oreos out of the glass cookie jar on the counter, he disappears into the den, back to his movie.

Flynn has brought decaf espresso—"Isn't that an oxymoron?" Tom asks, and Flynn drawls, "You callin' me a moron?"

"Or an ox," Lance says dryly—and makes it in an old-fashioned French press.

We sit around the table eating the crunchy biscuits, sipping espresso out of Rebecca's bone china. She produces a bottle of port and pours it—deep red, blood viscous—into small crystal goblets, and passes them around.

Flynn downs the port like a shot of tequila, and Lance rolls his eyes.

"I have an idea," Flynn announces. "Let's play a game."

"Please, no," Lance groans.

"Don't be a knocker, Lance," Flynn says.

"What's a knocker?" Eileen asks.

"A knocker is someone who knocks you down for no good reason," Flynn says.

"Another of Flynn's delightful Australianisms," says Lance.

"Knock, knock," says Flynn. "So here's the game. Each of us has to tell something about ourselves that nobody else knows."

The silence is deafening. Then Rebecca offers, "That nobody knows, or that nobody here knows?"

"That nobody here knows," Flynn says decisively, as if it's a game he has played many times before. "We'll just hear from a few people each time. Two this week, two next week, and so on."

"You're scaring us. This is way too premeditated," Lance says.

"I've played it before," Flynn says. "Don't be a drag, Lance. It's fun."

"So, why don't you start, then, Flynn? Tell us something we don't know about you," Rebecca says.

"Okay, I will." He holds up his empty port glass. "Why are these little babies so tiny?"

Rebecca fills Flynn's glass.

"Sip, don't gulp," Lance stage-whispers.

"What nobody knows about me," Flynn says, "is that I'm going to help Angela launch a restaurant."

"What?" I say, setting down my glass.

"What?" Tom says.

Flynn nods. "You heard me."

"What are you talking about?" I splutter.

"I think it's time," he says. "The coffee shop is no longer a challenge. We need to take on something new."

"That's crazy," I say. "I don't know the first thing about running a restaurant."

"Nor do I," says Flynn. "That's where the challenge comes in."

Rebecca turns toward me in surprise. "I didn't know you'd decided to stay."

"I haven't!"

"Yes, she has," Flynn assures her.

"No, I haven't."

"Let's move on," Flynn says. "We'll come back to it, Angie. Lots of time to ponder. Just know that you can count me in."

"I need to point something out," Lance says. "Telling us that you might help Angela launch a restaurant she wasn't even thinking about is hardly revealing a lifelong secret."

"Are you accusing me of cheating?"

Lance shrugs.

"I *invented* this game."

"I'm just saying."

Flynn sighs dramatically. "All right, fine," he says. "Here's a secret. I don't know how to swim."

"What? Really?" Lance seems genuinely astonished. "Are you making this up?"

Flynn shakes his head.

"How can that be? What about . . . the time we jumped off that picnic boat in Somes Sound?"

"Life jacket."

"What about all those times at Echo Lake?"

"Lounging. Tanning. Wading."

"The vacation in St. Bart's?"

"Boogie board. Remember?" Flynn says.

"Yeeesss." Lance nods slowly.

"Happy now?" Flynn says.

"I'm not sure," Lance says, "but I guess that qualifies."

"All right then," Flynn says. "Since you were so officious with me, why don't you go next?"

Lance smiles. "I actually do have a deep, dark secret."

"You used to be a woman," Flynn says. "No—I would have figured that out."

"Close," Lance says. "I used to be a Chippendales dancer."

A murmur goes around the table.

"Were not," Flynn gasps.

"Was, too," says Lance. "When I was a student at Northwestern, in Chicago, I needed cash. So I went to a tanning salon, pumped some iron, got blond streaks in my hair, and next thing I knew, ten-dollar bills were being stuffed in my G-string."

"I can't believe you didn't tell me," Flynn murmurs.

"Well, at first I didn't want to freak you out, and then it seemed like too much ammunition," Lance says.

"That's our relationship in a nutshell, isn't it?" Flynn says.

"Well, for what it's worth, Lance, I think it's *awesome*."

"The older I get, the more I do, too." Lance sighs. "Ah, glory days."

Early the next morning, I throw my orange parka over my pajamas and walk to the Dory Cove dock, Sam sniffing along behind me. It's damp outside, the kind of damp that turns chest colds into pneumonia. Even the wood on my porch is sodden. This is tricky weather for dressing; it's easy to feel too hot or too cold, so you have to wear layers.

The tide is low, so I venture down to the shore and perch on a flat rock. Far out, white boats bob in the steely bay. Last night's snow looks as light as foam on the shore. Sam runs up and down the banks, leaving a crazy Braille of dark prints. The cold twists up my legs like a vine, and I pull my coat tighter around me. I wonder if this place, with its rocky hills and surrounding ocean, is anything like Ireland—the pallid sky, the inhospitable shore. In one of my last conversations with my mother, I asked, "Where are we from, exactly?" (knowing she'd be flattered by the plural "we,"—Irish, not Italian—and pleased that I wanted to know about her people, our shared history).

"Your grandmother was raised in a sod hut near Roscommon, in the middle of the country," she told me. "Your grandfather grew up on the streets of Dublin. Quite a ladies' man."

When I was growing up, my father sometimes joked about my mother's Irish background, saying that she was descended from a wavering line of drunks and potato eaters. For her part, my mother expressed little interest in going back to her homeland. Her parents—both first-generation immigrants—had died when she was young; for her, the ties of family were severed when she lost them.

"Why have you never gone there?" I asked.

"I don't know," she said. "I think I picked up on my parents' shame about where they came from. The poverty and the alcohol and all that. It was too close."

"Do you think you'll change your mind?"

"Maybe," she said. "Maybe one day you'll go with me." But she died before either of us was ready to take that trip.

It is only six A.M., but already I can see lobstermen in the distance, throwing out traps. I think of my hardy forebears, Irish and Italian, who lived in the elements and rooted pleasure out of the simplest of things. I remember what Lindsay said about my mother and me, each of us seeking a place to call home. Maybe we both were following the immigrant's path, in quest of adventure but drawn toward the intuitively familiar. I suspect that my mother loved the Pacific Northwest for many of the reasons I am beginning to feel at home in this place—its snaggle-tooth shoreline, the lemony warmth of the sun, lush evergreens against grays and browns. Even the damp. Maybe she found her Ireland out west, and maybe, just maybe, I have found mine here, on this island off the coast of Maine.

CHAPTER 23

"So you can't swim, huh?"

"Please. I made that up. Threw the dogs a bone."

"Yeah, right."

Flynn and I are kneeling on the floor, unpacking a foam-peanut-filled crate of coffee cups with the Daily Grind logo printed on the sides, which he ordered off the Internet.

Only . . .

"Flynn, did you see this?" I hold up a mug.

"Bonzer, aren't they?"

"Look closer."

"What am I looking at?" It takes a moment to compute. "'The Doily Grind.' Oh, shit."

"The Doily Grind." I start to giggle, and before I know it I am laughing so hard that I clutch my stomach and fall over. "The—Doily—Grind!"

"Jesus, it's not funny. This cost me a hundred bucks."

"Oh, come on," I gasp. "It is funny." Trying to collect myself, I sit up. "I'm sure you can get your money back."

He pulls another mug out of the box and looks at it, clearly vexed. Then he paws through the polystyrene packing peanuts, flinging them this way and that, to find the receipt. "It's a typo," he says, clutching the invoice.

"Yours or theirs?"

"Fuck all, it's probably mine."

I can't help it, I start giggling again. "Look, you can still sell them. They're collectors' items!"

"I'm taking this box down to the harbor and smashing every one."

"That sounds cathartic," I say. "But how about this—Nonna's a big crocheter. I'll get her to make some doilies. And you can sell them. A coffee—and doily—shop. The Doily Grind."

He looks at me edgily. "What is a doily, anyway?"

"It's a little decorative—I don't know—mat. Fun word, isn't it? But hard to say. Doily. Doily. Try it five times fast."

I can tell he's beginning to relent. "Doily, doily, doily, doily, doy-lee . . . ," he says, and the combination of his Australian accent and my already near-hysteria overwhelms us both. We howl with laughter, gasping ideas—We'll put doilies under coffee cups! Feature a doily a day! Start a newsletter—*The Doily News*!

The bell tinkles and Lance walks in.

"*The Daily Doily!*" Flynn shouts, holding up a mug for Lance to see.

"What the hell is going on?" Lance asks, kicking a path through the peanuts. "This place is a mess."

"Says the exotic dancer." Flynn struggles to his feet. "Lance, you will never be able to pull that holier-than-thou crap on me again. I've got your number."

"And baby can't swim," Lance says. "Maybe we'll have to get you one of those floaty swimsuits with foam in the sides. I think I saw them at Target in Bangor."

"He says he was lying about that," I tell Lance, sweeping up the foam peanuts with my arm. Electrostatically charged, they hop and scatter.

"Yeah, right."

"That's what *I* said!"

"Well, just for the record, I was lying, too," Lance says.

Flynn puts up his hands, as if pushing the thought away. "You'd better not have been. And even if you were, I now have an indelible image in my mind of you in a sparkly G-string, dancing on a table. You'll never take that away."

"And Lord knows I wouldn't want to," Lance says dryly.

"Want a mug?" I ask, handing one to Lance. "You're in luck; we're having a sale—only five dollars with purchase."

"That's the spirit," Flynn says.

Lance looks at the mug and does a double take. A grin spreads across his face.

"With us now?" I ask.

"Oh, yes indeed," he says.

"I get it—a 'White Christmas' theme," Flynn says. "White Bolognese, Tuscan white-bean puree, fennel and Parmigiana salad, custard gelato."

I hadn't thought of that, but the menu *is* awfully white.

It's the fifth night of Hanukkah, and Rebecca's crystal menorah sparkles festively in the center of the table. We've all brought presents for Josh, which Rebecca says should be spread out over the remaining days but which we all insist he open now.

Lance and Flynn have gone in together on the entire *A Series of Unfortunate Events*. Lance warns that the books may be a little old for Josh, but Flynn insists it's never too early to develop a morbid sense of humor. Tom has brought a small oil painting by a local artist, a stylized view of sunset over evergreens, all purples and oranges and greens. Eileen gives Josh a leather-bound 1863 edition of Bulfinch's *Age of Chivalry or Legends of King Arthur*, with gilt edges and marbled endpapers, which she tells us she stumbled on at a library sale. My gift is the most vulgar—three video games I found at Wal-Mart: Harry Potter's Quidditch Match, Jack and Daxter, and Spyro the purple dragon. Sometimes, I figure, vulgar is just what a boy needs.

"How lucky are you?" Rebecca asks him. "Not an educational one in the bunch."

"I can take them back," I tell her, but Rebecca says, "As long as I didn't buy them, I feel no guilt! And obviously Josh is thrilled."

Josh, sitting amid the detritus of wrapping paper and gift bags and wadded-up sheets of tissue, gives me a thumbs-up. "Thanks, guys!" he says, disappearing with the first Lemony Snicket book and all three video games.

"Perhaps it's time to set limits," Rebecca says ruefully.

Flynn nods. "Absolutely. Just not tonight."

We get to work on dinner. Over the past few weeks, we've figured out how to maneuver around each other in the kitchen; we're getting to be old pros. White Bolognese, one of my favorite comfort foods, seems the right choice. Nonna learned it from the priest in Matera when she was working as her aunt's assistant, and has made it ever since. She often makes a pot on cold winter nights; even my stepmother admits to craving it (despite the red meat and dash of cream). Most Bolognese sauces contain tomatoes—this one does not. It is richer, its flavors more complex. Perfect for December.

As with many Italian dishes, I tell the group, you begin with the *soffrrito*—onions sautéed in olive oil with garlic, cooked until soft and golden—and the *insaporire*—parsley, carrots, celery. I sometimes add wild mushrooms, chopped fine. Then comes the ground meat. You may use ground beef, but it is much better with pork sausage. Add white wine and beef stock, and simmer, tossing in salt and pepper to taste. When the sauce reduces, after ten or fifteen minutes, you pour in a stream of milk until the color is golden brown. The priest Nonna worked for preferred the dish with nutmeg, but we usually leave it out.

Rigatoni, wide-ridged, tube-shaped noodles, makes a good complement. The ridges allow the pasta to hold more sauce; the wide holes capture pieces of meat and vegetables. After cooking the rigatoni al dente, or firm to the bite, drain it, reserving a small amount of the starchy water. Then ladle the sauce onto the pasta, stirring to blend it through. Ladle the Bolognese in scoops until the rigatoni is coated.

The fennel salad is simple. I slice the bulbs into thin sheets and add a generous amount of Parmigiano-Reggiano shaved in slivers. Lemon juice and extra-virgin olive oil whisked into a vinaigrette, along with freshly ground pepper, complete the dish.

Steaming bowls of rigatoni Bolognese in hand, we move to the table, along with the remaining hunk of Parmigiano and the fennel salad. Conversation is easy and relaxed—recent shared experiences, island gossip. When there's a lull, we talk about the food.

In time, Tom and I clear the emptied plates. He is in charge of the gelato, so I get out small bowls while he inspects the stainless-steel interior of Rebecca's ice-cream maker. We haven't spoken alone since our trip to Blue Hill last week. Clearly he's been avoiding me: He hasn't come into the shop, didn't call me to go to the farmers' market. I went alone in my old Honda.

I had allowed myself to think that maybe there was something between us. But of course there isn't; he has a girlfriend. Some men are just that way—solicitous, attentive, with an intimacy that borders, perhaps, on the inappropriate. Tom's small flirtations probably seem harmless to him, and come across as more than he intends. Or maybe he knows what he's doing.

Maybe he likes having the power to charm and entice, even if he can't or won't admit it.

Whatever it is, I won't put myself in that position again. All evening I've sensed Tom's gaze, but I refuse to look him in the eye.

I smile brightly. "Is it ready?"

"I think so." He dips a spoon into the creamy custard, holds it out for me to taste.

Pointedly, I take the spoon. "Thanks." And take a bite. A bite I barely taste. "Good."

"Glad you like it."

We return to the table with the gelato and bowls. Tom serves while I pass.

"So, I've been thinking," Eileen says softly—so softly that I'm the only one, standing next to her, who can hear.

"Yes?" I say.

"About that game. The one Flynn started. I have—something to share."

Conversation around the table subsides. We all turn in her direction. Eileen is twisting her napkin, and looks ill at ease. "I don't want to shock you," she says.

"Nothing can shock me after finding out that Lance is a stripper," Flynn says.

"*Was* a stripper," Lance says.

"Whatever."

"I wouldn't be so sure." Eileen gives us a tense smile and looks down. "Almost no one knows about this, and I'd appreciate it if you wouldn't mind keeping it quiet." She takes a deep breath. "The reason I showed up on this island a year ago is that I'd just gotten out of prison, and I needed a place where nobody knew who I was."

Moments pass while this news sinks in. The mild-mannered,

gray-braided, bespectacled librarian sitting here in a purple floral dress, a convict? I try to visualize Eileen in orange regulation prison gear, and I can't see it.

"What—?" Rebecca begins, then stops abruptly, the question hanging in the air.

"You want to know what I did." Eileen swallows hard and blinks behind her glasses. "I killed my husband. It was manslaughter. He used to beat me. He came at me one time too many, and the last time I had a knife."

Stunned silence hangs in the air.

"Holy dooley," Flynn breathes.

"How long were you in prison?" Tom asks.

"My sentence was twenty years, but I got out in seven. Good behavior, and also new laws about spousal abuse. Some persistent law students were on my case."

"Do you have children?" Rebecca asks.

Eileen nods. "Two. They were teenagers at the time. My son, Jesse, refuses to speak to me. Sue will talk to me, but she's still embarrassed, so I have to meet her at fast-food places on the highway where we don't know anyone."

Rebecca reaches across the table and clasps Eileen's hand. "I'm so sorry," she says. "That must be terrible."

"Well, it is," Eileen says. "But, you know, I'm grateful to have a job and an apartment, and to live in a place where I can just *be*. And to work with books. I find that words help. But it's been hard, not having anybody I could talk to about my life. It's felt so lonely. I wasn't sure about this, but it's a relief to talk about it now."

Lance pours red wine into our glasses, seltzer into his, then raises his glass in the air. "To Eileen."

"To Eileen," we repeat. We sip in silence. Eileen is wiping her eyes, and Tom has his arm around her shoulders. I can sense that, like me, people have questions, but this is not the time to ask. There's something about the nature of this group, the ritual gathering, which allows for a slow unfolding. We know that, one way or another, there will be a time and place for more.

"Well, if Eileen is going to be that brave, I guess I can, too," Rebecca says finally.

"Lord, you haven't killed somebody, have you?" Flynn asks.

We all laugh a little.

Rebecca puts up a finger—*wait*—and goes to the hallway, cocking her head. "Josh is still doing PlayStation," she says, coming back to the table. She smiles at me. Then she eases into her chair with a heavy sigh. "I'm just going to say it. We moved here because my husband was killed in the World Trade Center attacks. He was in the north tower; he worked for Bear Stearns. We lived in Gramercy Park, and Josh had just turned two." She shifts in her chair, tucks her leg under her. "I don't really talk about it because—that's part of why I came here, to get away from having to talk about it."

"Blimey," Flynn says. "You don't have to do this, Rebecca."

"No, I want to. I do." She takes a deep breath. "It was, as you know, September. I was taking him in his stroller to nursery school, a few blocks from our apartment, when suddenly there was this sound. Like nothing I'd ever heard before. A—boom, up in the sky. I looked up . . ." Her voice trails off.

"Jesus," Tom says. Eileen reaches for Rebecca's hand.

"It was such a sunny day," she says. "Ever since then, I've been a little nervous about beautiful days. I saw the smoke rise into this clear blue sky, and it didn't make sense. You know?" Rebecca's eyes are dry; her voice is quiet and steady. But her hands, I notice, tremble.

"They never found his body," she continues. "He was just—

gone. Over the next few months I tried to keep going, for Josh, if nothing else. Every normal day we got through felt like a small victory. I wanted to remain in New York, to prove that life would go on, that I wasn't scared. But something inside me had shifted. I had always been fearless and open, and I became fearful and self-protective. I was always looking around, startled by sudden noise. Those attacks had come from out of nowhere, and they could come from out of nowhere again.

"After a few months, I decided to leave. For my sanity, and for Josh's—so I could be a good mother to Josh. We had this place, so we came."

The room is quiet. Finally Lance says, "I can't imagine how devastating . . ." He stops, shakes his head.

"It was," she says pensively. "And it was even harder for me because that morning, before John left for work, we had an argument. It wasn't anything major; I wanted him to go to a silly meet-the-teacher thing at Josh's preschool, and John said he had a meeting with a client he couldn't get out of—but the last words I said to him were, 'If you can't put your son first once in a while, there's something seriously wrong.' And then—he was gone."

She pauses a moment, as if unsure whether to say more. "I still replay those words. But the truth is, we were going through a difficult time, and I don't want to—sentimentalize our relationship in hindsight. Things weren't perfect between us. I sometimes wonder if—if we'd have stayed together had he lived. That's something I'll never know.

"At any rate, I'm sure I wouldn't be here, now, on my own like this, with Josh. But I'm glad I'm here. John loved this place—he built this house; we planned every square foot of it together. He wanted us to use it. He would be so happy that we're here.

I think of all the things he loved about this island—the hiking, the water, the trees. And I love it all the more because he loved it so much."

She shakes her head, as if to say she's ready to move on. I can tell that she feels exposed, probably having revealed more than she intended.

I remember 9/11. I was on the subway when the first plane hit; as soon as I got to work, I was told to go home. Lindsay and I spent the next twelve hours together walking around my Upper West Side neighborhood and watching TV in my apartment. Three people from our hometown died in the towers, two acquaintances from college, a business-school friend of my brother's. For months afterward any reminder of the attacks— an American flag outside a fire station on Fifty-ninth Street, the rows and rows of faces of the dead in the *Times*—moved me to tears.

Rebecca turns to Tom, sitting beside her, and nudges him. "I think you're next."

"Oh, shit," Tom says, startled, and we all laugh. "I think I should wait until next time."

"But this is it," I say. "There isn't a next time."

"Well, maybe there should be," Flynn says.

"Or maybe—we could just keep meeting. Not call it a class," says Rebecca. "There are a few things I know how to make. There's a great recipe called Chicken Marbella in the *Silver Palate Cookbook* that I always made for friends in New York."

"I remember that," Tom says. "Chicken and prunes, right?"

"Maybe we could all bring what we have," Eileen says. "You know—stone soup."

Taking a bite of biscotti, a sip of wine, I am reminded of the rituals of worship, of strangers gathered in reflection. No one in my family goes to church any longer except Nonna, who makes her way several times a week to the eight-thirty mass at the Church of St. Agnes. Its massive carved wooden doors and stained-glass windows, peopled with sharp-featured saints and angels floating toward heaven, remind her, she says, of Italy. The church is a refuge from all that is confusing and overwhelming about America—the Latin words the same as they were in her village, the rituals and songs familiar. I think of Nonna walking slowly to the altar rail for Communion, kneeling to accept the body and the blood of Christ, with outstretched hands, eyes closed, head bent in prayer. *Thanks be to God.* I think of confession, the words of penance and solace.

Something akin to that feeling, a feeling I've never had anywhere else, is what I'm experiencing now.

Perhaps it is simply this: the bread, the wine; the Hanukkah candles; community and ritual. A sharing of experience, of stories, the facts of each person's life distinct and yet inseparable from the whole. Each one might be a saga told around a campfire or chanted in an epic poem, seemingly improbable, colored by emotion and hindsight, and yet utterly believable. These are the chronicles of legend, the tales we tell over and over, the stories that remind us we are not alone.

CHAPTER 24

My cell phone, ringing urgently on its charger, jars me from sleep. I reach a hand from under the covers and grope for it. The clock says 5:47 A.M. The air in my room is so chilly that I can see my breath.

"Angela, your grandmother is—not well."

At the sound of my father's voice, I am wide awake. I sit up, pull my comforter cover around me. "What?"

"We're at the hospital."

"Oh God. What happened?"

"They think she had a stroke. She fell out of bed early this morning, around two thirty. I heard her cry out and found her lying on the floor; she was incoherent, didn't even know where she was. I called 911 and an ambulance came. Sharon and I followed in the car."

A rushed trip through a maze of streets, the fluorescent blur of the emergency room, the trouble finding a vein in Nonna's arm, doctors conferring in a corner, the transfer to intensive care. Nonna mumbling in Italian; then praying. Sharon had thought to bring Nonna's rosary. On the other end of the phone, my father's voice is so shaky I can barely make out what he's saying. It occurs to me that he must feel very alone. I can guess what Sharon is saying under her breath: *Eighty-eight years is a long time to live.* But Nonna is my father's only mother, his one remaining parent. He does not want her to die.

He tells me that he doesn't know what will happen next; he doesn't want to tell me what to do. I should come home if I want, but Sharon and Paul are standing by and Nonna seems stable now.

Of course he knows I'll come.

After taking a shower and throwing some clothes in a bag, I drive to the coffee shop. It's seven fifteen, and customers cluster at the counter. Flynn moves back and forth between the cash register and the espresso machine. When he sees me he says, "Morning, sleepyhead. Nice of you to show up."

"I'm sorry. My grandmother had a stroke," I blurt out. "I need to go home."

"Oh, blimey," he says, holding his hand up, asking the customers to wait. "Nonna?"

I nod.

"She's in the hospital?"

"Yeah."

"Go, then. Go."

"I'm going."

"Want me to keep the dog for you?"

"Thanks—I guess I'll take Sam. I don't want him to think I'm abandoning him already."

As I'm leaving, Flynn calls, "Make Nonna some *stracciatella.* Show her what you've learned."

Four hours later, with Sam splayed across the backseat, lulled to sleep by the loud hum of the old motor, I drive over the green bridge that joins Maine to New Hampshire. It is December 21, nearly three months since I was last in this spot.

At the crest of the bridge, I feel a cleaving, an almost physical sensation in my chest. Maine is past now; I have left it behind. What if I never return? What if these months were no more than a brief interlude, a respite, a regrouping? Maybe someday I'll describe this as a journey I needed to take, the otherness of the experience revealing the importance of the things I really value. I'll remember it with fondness, through the gauzy lens of partial recollection. The unheated shack, the characters I met—even Rich Saunders. "When I was in Maine," I'll say; I'll refer to "that time when my life was falling apart and I escaped to Maine." In time the entire experience will become illusory, a dream state.

One time long ago, when I needed to get away, I went to Maine.

Nonna is sitting up in bed when I get to the hospital, awake but dazed. When I put my hand on hers, she looks at me with disinterest. Then she says, "They are giving me drugs."

My father says, "They are not giving her drugs. Just a sedative to calm her down. She's been berating the nurses all morning. They don't understand what she's saying, but believe me, they get the idea."

She does seem out of it, but I don't know how much of that is a result of the stroke. A ministroke, my father said, but she looks very different from the last time I saw her. Her skin is waxy yellow and deeply creased, her mouth a violet slash. Her arms, naked as plucked chicken skin, poke out of the loose blue hospital gown. She clutches the sheet with bony talons.

"She doesn't like it here much. Do you, Annalisa?" Sharon says in a loud, artificially chipper voice.

Nonna fixes a beady eye on her. *"Cafona,"* she mutters under her breath. It is a harsh word, meaning ignorant or low class, and though I know there's no love lost between them, Nonna's use of the word shocks me.

I try to imagine how it must feel to be treated like a relic, a bother, reliant on the condescending kindness of the strong-willed wife of your weak-willed son. What an indignity to be dependent in this way, so old that death seems inevitable, natural; everyone is waiting for you to breathe your last. How has it come to this—to a hospital room in northern New Jersey, to such an abbreviated family that the burden of caring for you rests on the narrow shoulders of this one man?

She should have had half a dozen children, my grandmother, daughters to take care of her.

And my father—what is he thinking? Does he harbor old resentments toward her for placing her aspirations squarely on his shoulders? If only he had a sibling to share the burden! He did his part; he took his mother in, though his new wife wrinkled her nose when she woke in the morning, sniffed, "Is that—cabbage?" and pulled her robe around her in disgust. And who could really blame her? Go on a lunch date; end up living with someone else's mother. What kind of deal is that?

But surely my father also remembers what it was like when he was small, clutching his mother's hand as they crossed the street to visit the fish market, the iridescent shimmer of sardines swimming in tubs of water. How his mother would look over his shoulder as he studied English from his first-grade primer, at the kitchen table, learning to read the words at the same time he did. How he would stand beside her at the counter as she wielded the pastry bag, filling the cannelloni shells, cooling on the counter, with creamy ricotta. At the narrow neighborhood market, she let him press the tomatoes to test ripeness, taste a leaf of peppery arugula. His father would come home from work and inhale deeply in the front hall, trying to guess what was for dinner, making a game of it. And how could my father forget the look on his mother's face when he graduated from high school and then Rutgers, when he began to make a living, not with his hands but with his head?

And then there are things I suppose he doesn't want to think about—how he has been embarrassed by, exasperated with, this obstinate woman, how his background seemed to him unrefined. Having weeded those traits out of his own personality, he goes about his daily life unburdened by cultural identity. But when he sleeps at night, when he dreams, I wonder if he dreams about the two languages of his childhood, the wistful longings of his immigrant parents, the earth and sky of a village in Italy he knows only through stories his mother has told.

"How is she?" Paul asks when I reach him on his cell phone. "I wanted to leave work early to come out there, but I couldn't get away."

"Umm," I say. "Well, she's alive. Maybe you can make it tomorrow."

"Ahhh—actually, tomorrow's no good. I could try on the weekend—but Kim is running the Kwanzaa-Hanukkah-Christmas pageant at the preschool, and I promised I'd be in charge of the basket raffle. I still haven't gotten donations from a bunch of merchants in town, which reminds me—"

He sounds tense and harried, and I want to empathize, but instead I snap, "Jesus Christ, Paul! We're talking about *Nonna*. She had a *stroke*. I'm sure you're unbelievably busy, but this *really actually* matters."

"Look, Angela," he says stiffly. "You have no fucking idea what my life is like. While you've been flaking off to Maine, I've been riding Metro North every day and taking care of my family. And checking in on Dad and Nonna, I might add."

"Okay, Paul." I don't want to get into this with him. "Nonna's in the hospital."

I hear him suck on his teeth, an old habit from childhood. "All right, fine," he says. "I'll try to cancel my afternoon tomorrow."

"Do what you want," I say.

The house is empty. The kitchen is spotless. Without Nonna, the place feels sterile, like a long-term residency hotel. In my stepmother's dressing room, I toss my bag in a corner. Dad and Sharon have gone out to "grab a bite" at a diner on Route 3 that I loved as a child but which has since been transformed into a chrome-and-glass monstrosity. I begged off and came back here on my own. I survey the room, still wallpapered in the garish floral print I chose in ninth grade. Draped across the couch and hanging on a coatrack are dresses and skirt suits shrouded in dry cleaner's plastic. My old twin blanket, one I used in college, hangs folded over the back of a chair, just where I left it when I accordioned the sofa bed the day I left for Maine. On a small bookcase sits an assortment of my dog-eared paperbacks from high school and college—*The Catcher in the Rye, Chemistry 251, Lady Chatterley's Lover, The Madwoman in the Attic.*

My blanket, my books, my wallpaper. Artifacts from a distant era.

Moving aside the whispery dry cleaner's bags, I sit on the couch. Bounce a bit. I can feel the springs through the cheap cushions. I run my hand along the wool blanket, stroke the worn satin band with my finger. Though tired, I am not ready for sleep. I don't really want to be in this house alone. Picking up the phone by the couch—Pepto-Bismol pink, another vestige of my teen years—I dial Lindsay's number.

"It's you? What are you doing home?" she says when she picks up, recognizing the number. "I thought it was your dad."

"Nonna's had a stroke," I say. "She's in the hospital."

"Ohh," she says. "I'm so sorry. How is she?"

"They don't know yet." Sitting there on the small couch, twirling the phone cord between my fingers, pink and curly as a pig's tail, I feel my eyes fill with tears. I didn't cry on the drive through six states, didn't cry at the hospital, but now, hearing Lindsay's voice, I feel myself being pulled to a place I've tried to avoid. This odd, fractured family—the center keeps shifting. When my grandmother dies, who will hold it all together? My mother is dead; my stepmother doesn't care to learn or even understand our family's ways. My brother and I barely speak. Where is the sense of continuity? In their village in Italy, my grandparents had parents and brothers and sisters, aunts and uncles, cousins and second cousins. *La famiglia.*

I say as much to Lindsay, and she says, "You know you're romanticizing the whole Italian-village thing. If it was so great over there, why was everybody so eager to leave?"

At the hospital the next day, my father and I set up camp, ignoring visiting hours. Sharon comes and goes. Late in the morning, Paul makes an appearance, arriving at Nonna's bedside without taking off his overcoat. His three-button suit looks well-groomed, stylish. I, on the other hand, am dressed in paint-spattered jeans and a Rutgers sweatshirt I found in the closet, and have dark circles under my eyes.

His lips brush my cheek. "Hey, Angela," he says casually, as if he saw me last week. He nods toward Nonna. "She's looking well."

As it happens, she is not looking well. She is sleeping so lightly that I can see her eyes flickering with movement under her closed lids. Her breath is a soft wheeze, her jaw slack. What Paul means is, *What were you so hysterical about? She's not dying.*

"You think so?" I ask. *Don't minimize this to make yourself feel better.*

My father comes into the room, and Paul nods in greeting. "What's the prognosis, Dad?" he asks. *Let the men handle the medical facts.*

My father dutifully reports the details. Nonna has had a transient ischemic attack, also known as TIA, or—he dumbed it down for me—ministroke. The blood supply to her brain was briefly interrupted; she has some facial paralysis, which the doctors hope is temporary. A TIA is a warning sign that a person is at risk for a more serious and debilitating stroke. The sooner Nonna can get out of bed and walk around, the better. "We just have to see how it goes," he says.

"Sorry I couldn't get here sooner. Work is—"

My father shakes his head, cutting him off. "Don't even think about it. Glad you're here." It's his mission in life to let Paul off the hook. He doesn't want him to feel guilty about anything. Dad thinks that if he doesn't put pressure on Paul to be a real part of the family, he will be more inclined to do so—a kind of reverse psychology that, as far as I'm concerned, is destined to fail.

Paul knows all of this, and as a result he's making an effort to ingratiate himself for the short time he's here. No point in being rude, and being pleasant will ease his conscience.

For the first time all day, my dad is animated. He is excited to talk to Paul, flattered by the attention. He flushes with pride. My son, the hotshot consultant! Now making small talk about the traffic on Route 80, now sharing a confidential tidbit about the inner dealings of a bankrupt company, now asking Dad's opinion on titanium golf clubs. My father is amazed to have a son like this.

The two of them settle into chairs on either side of the big window, three feet from Nonna's bed. My father leans toward

Paul eagerly. My brother, sitting back, crosses his leg over his knee crossbow-style, waggles his foot.

On the other side of Nonna's bed, I sit watching her breathe. She is sleeping again; her chest heaving with each shallow breath, like a sick child's. I have a sudden, panicked fear that she is stealing away in her sleep, that without our noticing she will be gone.

The contrast of Nonna's visible decline with the antiseptic brightness of the hospital room is jarring. She doesn't belong here. She hates bright lights, is bewildered by newness. She finds comfort in old clothes, darning and redarning socks, mending holes in her aprons until the fabric can't hold the stitches. When my stepmother, in a frenzy of spring cleaning several years ago, filled several garbage bags with old clothing she found in bureaus throughout the house, Nonna pawed through them, confiscating wool sweaters that she later unraveled, saving the yarn for her own knitting projects: afghans and throws, sometimes a sweater. When she finishes a throw, she drapes it over the living room couch. When my stepmother comes home from work, she removes the throw and puts it in a drawer.

Nonna saves scraps in the refrigerator to combine with other scraps, endless small containers of leftovers. How it exasperates Sharon to open a drawer in the kitchen only to find it jammed with Nonna's odds and ends: pieces of string, twist ties, rubber bands from the newspaper, yarn, outdated grocery-store coupons, free key chains bearing car-wash logos stamped in garish gold print. Ziploc bags, several times washed and dried, pooched like jellyfish over wooden spoons in the jar on the counter. *Waste not, want not.* The concept of disposability is anathema to Nonna. Yet here she is, in a place where everything is disposable. Including her.

She stirs and moans, and my brother leaps to his feet and reaches for her hand. My father closes his mouth midsentence and rises silently. Of course Paul isn't here merely to chat; he came to see Nonna. It's a little disappointing, all the same.

Paul stands, hands on hips, shirtsleeves rolled up like an attending physician. He looks at Nonna intently. Glances at the clock beside her bed. I read his mind: It would be great if she'd wake up long enough to register his presence, long enough for him to say a few words. Otherwise, damn it, he'll have to do this all over again in a day or two.

"So you're still in Maine, huh?" he says. It takes me a moment to realize he's talking to me, since he's still facing the bed.

"Yep."

"Must be cold up there."

"Yep."

"Tell you the truth, I'm shocked that sailor guy didn't turn out to be a sleaze. I'd've put money on it. But hey. Good for you."

I just nod. No point in confirming his expectations.

Nonna turns her head from side to side, moaning. *"L'acqua."* Paul and I knock into each other reaching for the plastic pitcher on her cluttered bedside table. "I've got it," he says, and pours her a cup, holding it gently to her mouth. She sips greedily, reaching her lips toward the water like a horse seeking a treat. Paul recoils a little but holds the cup steady.

Nonna's eyes flutter open. They roam the room, unfocused, before settling on Paul's face. "Eh?" she says.

"Hey, Nonna," Paul says in a hearty radio announcer's voice. "It's me, Paul."

"I know who you are," she says.

"How'r ya feelin'?" His words contract with false cheer.

"Eh." She looks at him blankly. Then she says, "You should be at work."

We all laugh, because we know that Paul is thinking the same thing. My father approaches the bed, straightens the covers, smooths the sheet. "That's how special you are, *mia madre*," he says. "Paul took time from his busy day to come and see you."

She peers up at Paul. "You can go back to work. *Sto bene.*" I'm okay.

It isn't until this sentence that I actually see that one side of her face is immobile.

Paul pats her hand. "You're a fighter, Nonna. That's for sure."

I wonder what she thinks of this, of being treated like a child by her grandson.

"Not fighting. Just breathing," she says.

"A strong woman," says my father.

Nonna doesn't answer. We stand around awkwardly for a while before, inevitably, Paul glances at his Hermès watch and pantomimes a gasp. Look at the time!

After Paul says his good-byes, I walk him to the elevator. He'll check in with me tomorrow to see how it's going, he says. We talk about Christmas, three days from now, and agree to play it by ear. Nonna could still be in the hospital. I mention the possibility of getting together with Kim and the kids, but their schedule is complicated, what with the holiday festival and play dates and indoor soccer games. We make noises about staying in better touch, but we both know we're only making a gesture.

CHAPTER 25

Two days later, Nonna is home. The paralysis on the left side of her face is less noticeable; she moves gingerly but without a limp. As soon as we get in the front door, she says she's ready for a rest. Refusing offers of help, she leans heavily on the banister as she makes her way to the second floor. She seems chastened by her time in the hospital, newly aware of the precariousness of her place in this world.

Christmas, with its rigid rituals, enforced family time, and re-flexive, programmed cheer, looms. "Can't we pretend we're Jewish this year and order Chinese?" Sharon jokes, but my father isn't amused. "How hard is it to cook a ham?" he says. "You take it out of the fridge; you stick it in the oven." I think Sharon is only beginning to realize the double edge of Nonna's legacy: Her presence in their home has made it easy for Sharon to avoid the kitchen, but it has also stoked my father's desire for home cook-ing. Unless he steps up and learns how to make a few dishes himself, Sharon will have to either make it clear that she won't do it, or face the stove.

"I'll make Christmas dinner," I volunteer. "But no ham, all right? Let's do Nonna's favorites." I put together a menu of dishes I know Nonna likes: potato-crusted sole, seared scallops and es-carole with orecchiette, veal piccata, baked ziti.

"Fava beans and chicory!" my father requests happily. He gets on the phone and calls Paul, reinviting him and his family. Sharon calls her elderly father in Queens, and I call Lindsay to ask if she wants to join us at six o'clock on Christmas Day.

"I can't wait," she says. "You'll finally meet Peter!"

I hadn't thought to invite Mr. Hot4U, but the more the merrier—isn't that what they say?

I review the menu with Nonna, who is sitting up in her bed draped like a Sherpa with three or four of her colorful afghans. A bit dubious, she suggests I trim the list. I think she's afraid I won't pull it off. Perhaps she's also concerned that her role is being usurped and she won't have anything to do.

"It's all in the timing," she frets. "You must be thinking at every second about what is on the stove and what needs to go in the oven."

"I know, Nonna, I know," I say, and pat her hand. "You'll be my consultant. From bed."

She slips her hand out from under mine. She will not be appeased. She gives me instructions about where to get the freshest fish, which butcher to approach at the grocery store about the veal, how to grate and store the raw potato for the crust so it won't brown. "You need help," she says, swinging her legs over the side of the bed. It takes all my wiles to restrain her. "This is my job, Nonna. Think of me as your protégé. You have to let me blunder through."

Christmas morning I wake early to the sound of rain tapping on the windows. How can it be warm enough for rain? On the front lawn the snow is melting into soupy piles, revealing ugly patches of rutted earth. Later the rain will likely freeze, making roads and sidewalks slick and treacherous.

I head downstairs to get started on dinner and find Nonna standing at the counter in her bathrobe, draping a damp towel over a mound of dough. Sam, at her feet, stretched out on the linoleum, raises his head and thumps his tail.

I pat his head. "Nonna, what are you doing?"

"I'm making the *ciabatta*," she says. "Too much for you to do on your own."

"No, it's not. And you're supposed to be resting!"

She flaps her hand. "For me, this is resting."

I know there's little point in arguing. "Merry Christmas," I say, kissing her on the head. "But I want you to go slow."

"*Buon Natale.* I made coffee for you."

Before anyone else is up, I give Nonna her present: a book of photographs of the village of Matera. I found a link for it online, at a website dedicated to Basilicata. After unwrapping it and gazing at the glossy cover—a haunting picture of Matera's maze of white stone dwellings—Nonna clasps the oversize volume to her chest. Thumbing slowly through the pages, she handles the book like a precious artifact, an illuminated manuscript. Here is a wall painting from a church built into the mountain face, here a winding street with ivy and geraniums spilling from balconies, here a group of young women walking, laughing, one pushing a stroller. Nonna examines the photographs closely, as though she is looking for someone, anyone, familiar, but she doesn't speak a word.

As she closes the book, I see that her eyes are full of tears. "I will treasure it," she says simply, and clasps my hands. "I have something, too." She disappears into the dining room and returns with a paper grocery sack in outstretched hands. I reach inside and pull out a scarf—no, a throw blanket. Clearly Nonna has made it, but this one is utterly unlike her others. Nonna's throws are usually sensible wool blends, in pastel or primary colors. Mine is a dazzling riot of heathered strands—a royal-hued weave of reds and purples, with interlaced threads of gold.

"Nonna," I gasp, pulling the throw around my shoulders. "It's gorgeous. And so soft! Is it mohair?"

"Angora, mostly," she says, caressing the throw like a kitten she is reluctantly giving away, "with some lamb's wool for shape. I told the girl at the yarn shop—she's about your age—that I wanted to make a special present for my granddaughter, and she showed me this yarn. I chose the colors. The blend is Tuscany. I liked the name."

I lift my cloaked arms and engulf her, pulling her in. "I'll use it every day."

"You won't hide it in a drawer?" she asks slyly.

I smile. "I won't hide it in a drawer."

She fingers the throw. "Maybe someday you'll learn to knit."

"Will you teach me?"

Nudging me in the ribs, she says, "Haven't I taught you enough?"

Nonna refuses to leave the kitchen. She sits ensconced at the table, chopping garlic, blending ricotta with eggs and cheese for the baked ziti, forming homemade orecchiette, little ear-shaped pasta, between her palm and thumb. I have given up trying to persuade her to join the others in the living room; I suspect she'd rather wash a heap of dirty dishes than listen to small talk. I catch bits of chatter: Paul's wife, Kim, fusses over two-year-old Brianna's curls, admonishes four-year-old Ryan to stop bothering the dog. My father consults Paul about the stock market. Sharon pops in every few minutes to offer assistance, but we understand she's only being polite.

At five thirty the doorbell rings and I dry my hands and hurry out to the hall. Lindsay spills in with an armful of presents, trailing the boyfriend, a wisp of a man with brown hair and glasses. I can only trust that he's the Clark Kent alter ego of the passionate Hot4U.

She gives me a hug, then stands back and clutches his hand. "Angela, Peter. Finally, you two meet."

Mr. Hot shakes my hand and smiles shyly. "I've heard a lot about you. Lindsay really misses you."

"I miss Lindsay, too," I say, putting my arm around her middle. "Did you know you're the reason I left? After meeting you, she was so jazzed about online dating she convinced me to try. That's how I ended up going to Maine."

"You shouldn't have told her about the 'extend search' option," he tells Lindsay.

"She discovered that all on her own," Lindsay says.

Scarves, hats, mittens. Thermal underwear. A theme is apparent in the gifts I receive this year. Lindsay gives me black Emus, laced sheepskin boots with a fluffy lamb's wool lining that, she tells me, will be warm in Maine and stylish in New York—"so they'll still be useful when you come to your senses."

"They're perfect," I tell her. "Did you get a pair for yourself?" She nods.

"You'll have to bring them when you visit."

"You really think I'll need them in August?" she says.

Unfortunately, Nonna is more skilled than I at making potato-crusted sole. My first fillet is gummy and undercooked; the second is dry. Ignoring my protests, Nonna gets up from chatting with Lindsay at the table and inspects the butter (too hot), then smoothly works her way through the steps of coating and re-coating the fish as I watch at her elbow. With a flick of her wrist, Nonna dips the fish in flour and egg, leaving just enough moisture for the shredded potato to adhere. As she works, Nonna instructs. "You see," she says softly, "the lightness. Always the lightness. Just so. The balance of dry and wet, cool and hot. You improve only with practice; you make this dish again and again. How many times, in my lifetime, have I made this?"

Mr. Hot is on all fours on the living room floor with a jump rope between his teeth. Ryan and Brianna have sized him up, in the shrewd way that children do, and determined that he is perfect horsey material.

"Go, go, *go!*" Brianna squeals, kicking his flanks with her heels and pulling on the rope.

Paul leans against the door frame between the kitchen and living room, an open wine bottle in one hand and a stem glass in the other. "Looks like Lindsay won't have any trouble with that one. He's already broken," he says under his breath.

"Hush."

"I should hire him as a nanny."

"Paul," I warn him. "Enough."

"So," he says, filling his glass from the bottle and surveying the kitchen. "Who taught you to cook?"

"Why do you have to be such a bastard?"

"Hey, watch it. Nonna's sitting right here," he says, cutting his eyes over at her.

"*Non sia un tal asino,*" she says without looking up from the orecchiette.

Paul looks at me questioningly. He learned little Italian from our father, and was gone by the time Nonna moved in.

"'Don't be such an ass,'" I translate.

We both burst out laughing.

"Going into the office later?" I ask him.

He shifts uncomfortably. "How'd you guess?"

"Thomas Pink shirt, okay," I say. "It's kind of festive. But I can't imagine you'd wear those five-hundred-dollar shoes to Nutley otherwise, even for Christmas."

"I'll only check in for an hour or two after this shindig is over. The international markets don't care if it's Christmas, you know."

"I'm sure Santa feels the same way about the international markets," I say.

Watching me sprinkle mozzarella on the half-baked ziti and slide it back in the oven, he takes a long sip of wine. "You're a funny girl," he says. "I should take the time to get to know you better."

This is classic Paul-speak—a biting aside with a nugget of genuine feeling buried deep within.

"At this point, why bother?" I say.

Paul looks at me for a long moment. Then he says, "You're not with that sailor guy anymore, are you?"

"No, I'm not."

"Why didn't you tell me?"

I don't know whether it's the stuffy kitchen or the pressure of having all these dishes in the oven at once or whether I'm just deeply angry at Paul's generally dismissive attitude, but I am suddenly incapable of banter. "Why? Because I knew you'd ridicule me. As usual. And frankly, I wasn't up for it."

"Hey," he says, and there's a different note in his voice. "I never really mean it, you know."

"Come on."

"I don't." He sets down his wineglass.

I brush the grated cheese off the cutting board and into the sink. "Yes. You do mean it. You think I should be settled down. You can't understand why I'm not. You think that going to Maine was the most idiotic thing anybody could ever do."

"Augh." He puts the heels of his palms over his eyes. "You want to know, really, what I think?"

"No."

He looks to see if I'm kidding. I refuse him the satisfaction of a response.

"I think I'm an ass."

Nonna, sitting at the table, purses her lips in a smile.

"Good," I say. "We agree."

"I guess we do," he says.

"All right," I relent. "What do you mean?"

He twirls the wine in his glass, tilts it up and swallows. "You and I are very different people. And sometimes—okay, most of the time—I just want you to be . . . normal, like me. Like everyone else. I don't know why I do, because frankly, half the time . . . Look, I don't wake up in the morning questioning my life. But if I did . . . " His voice trails off.

"If you did—?"

"Let me finish," he snaps. Even when contrite, Paul needs to be in control. "But it does seem to me that if I hadn't made the choices I've made, if I didn't live the life I live, I'd probably be—lost. But you're not, are you?"

I think about this for a moment. "No. I don't think I am."

"Ange," he says, swaying toward me, "I may not ever say this again, so listen closely."

Against my will, I lean in.

"I actually think you're pretty cool," he whispers.

"Are you drunk?"

"What if I am?"

I look at the empty bottle, his near empty glass, and shrug. "I'll take it anyway."

Just then our father comes in, and Paul holds up the bottle. "We need more wine, Dad. We're celebrating!"

Dad retrieves a bottle of merlot from the pantry. "So what are we celebrating?" He looks dizzy with joy, and I can guess the reasons—his children home, his mother alive, his favorite dish, *fave e cicoria*, simmering on the stove.

"Angela and I have forged a truce," Paul says.

Dad finds the wine opener in the dish drainer. "Oh?"

"Actually, we're just celebrating being here with you, Dad," I say.

He pops the cork. Reaching up in the cabinet, he finds wineglasses and pours for the three of us. Then he remembers Nonna, still sitting at the table, now cutting escarole, and gets another glass.

She shakes her head. "Not for me. My medication."

"Oh, that's right," he says. He fills the wineglass with seltzer and hands it to her. "You need to be part of this toast anyway, *Madre*," he says. "*La famiglia*." We clink our glasses all around.

"Far-flung as it may be," Paul says.

CHAPTER 26

Sitting at the Christmas table, we clasp hands as Ryan and Brianna sing at the top of their lungs:

> *For health and strength and daily food*
> *we give thee thanks, Oh Lord.*
> *For health and strength and daily food*
> *we give thee thanks, Oh Lord.*
> *For health and strength,*
> *For health and strength . . .*

Turns out it's a round, and we're expected to participate. Coming in at different times, starting and stopping as the whim strikes, we sound like a chorus of the mentally challenged.

"Give thee thanks, Oh Lord," Mr. Hot intones in a nasal tenor, hurrying the tune along as he realizes he's the only one still singing.

"That's not Catholic," my father mutters when it's over.

"Sounds Quaker," Lindsay remarks.

"We're raising the children multidenominational," Kim explains. "We don't want them to feel oppressed by religious dogma."

"Dogma?" My father grunts. "Oppressed?"

"La famiglia!" Paul says, unsteadily raising his glass. Sitting

beside him, I notice that he has kicked off his fancy shoes. A stain like a gunshot wound blots his chest, probably the marinara I caught him slurping out of the pot a few minutes ago. We all clink glasses. "Bring us some figgy pudding," he adds. "Or at least baked ziti. God bless us, everyone!"

Somewhere in the background, I hear a high-pitched trill. Back in Maine, in honor of Thanksgiving, Flynn had changed my cell phone ring, and now I see people around the table straining to identify the jaunty melody. "Turkey in the Straw." I dash off to find the phone, tracing it to my cavernous handbag on a hook in the back hall. Frantically I paw past wallet, camera, keys, and mini-umbrella, and find it buried at the bottom, coated in crumbs.

Clutching the phone in both hands, I squint at the little window.

Unavailable.

"Hello?"

"Angela? It's Tom. I didn't think you were going to pick up."

Tom, from that faraway, possibly imagined place, calling me here? It takes a moment to process. "Hi. I—we were just sitting down to dinner."

"I'm sorry. I can call back."

"No, no, it's fine," I say. "Things were getting a little out of hand in there anyway."

He laughs. "Well, I won't keep you. I just wanted to say Merry Christmas. I've missed you. I mean, everyone's missed you. I mean—well, I've missed you, actually. To hell with the rest of them."

"Oh." We both laugh.

"Anyway," he says. "How's your grandmother? I should've asked right away. I'm not very good at this."

"At what?"

"I don't know. Talking."

We laugh again.

"Well, thanks for asking. Nonna had a stroke—a small stroke—but she's doing better. She's home with us now, running the whole show, of course." I tell him about my vain attempts to keep her in bed and her insistence on managing every detail of Christmas dinner, and he tells me about the vegan buffet featuring the "mock ham" the Zen master is preparing for him and the other acolytes. (He doesn't say "acolytes.")

"What's mock ham?" I ask.

"I'm not exactly sure. Something to do with tofu skins, from what I understand."

"Oh. Yummy."

He laughs. "Let's just say I wish I were eating with you instead. An Italian feast. Splendid. And I'd like to meet Nonna."

"So how's Katrin?" I ask pointedly.

"Oh, she's fine," he says. "Busy. You know." He clears his throat. "Honestly, I'm not sure. We're not seeing each other anymore."

"Really?"

"Yeah. It was just sort of—time for it to end."

"Oh." I don't know what to say.

"It's all right. It actually is. Things haven't been right between us for a long time. I wanted to say something earlier, but I just—I couldn't. I needed to see it through in a way that wasn't—hurtful or disrespectful. Does that make sense?"

"No. Yes," I say.

He laughs.

I smile.

"Hey," he says, "stuff has happened since you left. Did you know that Flynn and Lance are back together?"

"No!"

"Oh yeah. The Christmas spirit, I guess. You gotta get back here to see it. And anyway, we have so much to do."

"So much to do? What do you mean?"

"Look, I don't want to get ahead of myself," he says. "But this restaurant idea—I want to help. I might as well do something productive with those dot-com spoils, right? And I can't think of anything more worthwhile at the moment than getting this idea off the ground."

"Are you serious?"

"I think it will be fun."

"Are you . . . Santa?" I ask.

He laughs again. "If Christ was Jewish, I guess Santa can be, too."

"I'm—speechless," I tell him. "I don't know what to say."

"You should know that I have an ulterior motive. I'm hoping it'll give me a chance to spend more time with you," he says. "So don't say anything. Just hurry back."

I hang up the phone and stand still for a moment, thinking it through. What I feel is unfamiliar; I don't know how to interpret it. I do know I've never felt this way before. Hearing Tom's voice on the phone was like hearing a forgotten song from childhood, the melody, long thought lost, suddenly flooding back.

At the table, Lindsay says, "Finally. Who was that?" Everyone looks at me, forks poised in midair.

"Oh—somebody from Maine," I say, sitting down.

Lindsay furrows her brow, trying to decode what this means, then raises her palms in a shrug. She taps her glass with her spoon and stands up. "Peter and I have news," she says, clearing her throat and looking over at Mr. Hot. Every visible inch of his skin reddens. "Last night we stayed at my parents' house—in separate bedrooms, of course, Mr. Russo—and this morning when I woke up there was a knock on my door. It was Peter, with a beautiful little Tiffany box."

In real time, Mr. Hot pulls an aqua box out of his pocket.

"Oh my God!" Kim says.

"And he asked me to marry him!"

Squeals and murmurs all around.

"The ring is too big; we need to have it sized," Mr. Hot says. "That's why Lindsay isn't wearing it yet."

"Let's see it," Sharon demands.

Mr. Hot opens the box, revealing a bona fide diamond engagement ring, neither too big nor too small. Having never turned my attention to this particular custom, I know little about what I'm gazing at, except that it sparkles brilliantly in the candlelight.

"The stone is a princess-cut, 1.03-carat, grade H, VVS2-quality in an 18-carat white gold band," Peter explains, taking the ring out of the box. Lindsay extends her hand as if commanding him to dance. He slips the ring on her finger, and we all cheer.

"I now pronounce you man and rhymes-with-the-rest-of-your-LIFE," Paul says.

"Okay, that's enough," Kim says, moving the wine bottle down the table. "I'm cutting you off."

"Be sure, buddy," Paul says, wagging his finger at Mr. Hot. "Be very sure."

I hug Lindsay, who is now crying. "See? Soul mates do exist," she whispers in my ear. "It will work out for you—I know it will. Don't give up hope."

I sit back down and look around. My father and Sharon are negotiating whether he should have a second helping of ziti; my brother and Kim are debating how many broccoli spears their kids have to eat before they can leave the table; my best friend and her fiancé are gazing, punch-drunk, at the ring wobbling on her finger. Carefully, Nonna rises from her place at the table to scrape one mostly empty serving dish into another, making room for more.

She catches my eye and smiles. "Well, you did it, *la mia cara.* You pulled it off."

"We did it, Nonna, didn't we?" I say.

Two days later, after my father and Sharon leave for work, I go down to the kitchen to make coffee and find Nonna chopping onions.

"Early for onions, isn't it?" I ask, scooping coffee into the paper filter.

"Veal meatballs for your father," she announces. "A special request."

I fill the carafe with water and pour it into the coffeemaker. "He should know better than to make special requests," I grumble. "You need to take it easy."

"What else am I going to do? Lie in bed? *Grazie non.*"

I watch her mix ground veal and pork and beef in a bowl, adding bread crumbs, parsley, rosemary, chopped onions from the cutting board. "So how are you feeling?" I ask.

Nonna seems a little low now that the whirlwind of Christmas has passed. Before we left the hospital, the doctor took my father and me aside and explained that it's common for people who've had strokes to be depressed, and that we should be attentive to this possibility.

Nonna whisks two eggs together in a bowl and stirs them into the meat. "*Tutto bene,*" she says.

"Really all right?"

"All right." She shrugs.

Not wanting to push, I hesitate. "You know, they say it's not unusual to feel a bit down after you've had a stroke."

"I don't feel 'down,' exactly." She plucks a gob of the meat mixture from a shallow metal mixing bowl, rolls it between her palms, and drops it on wax paper on a baking sheet. Her hands, I notice, are quavering. "I'm just . . . thinking."

I move the dishes to the sink, turn on the water, and squirt in some soap.

"I tell you, Angela," she says. "The older I get, the more I think about home."

"Home?"

"When I was young, my village was the whole world. I knew nothing else," she says. "Now that I'm old, I am drawn back to that place. But there is no way to get there." She pauses. "I miss my cousins. The white caves. I remember it all like I was just there."

Nonna has never been back to the land of her birth. When she left, a twenty-year-old newlywed, she said good-bye to her mother and father, cousins and nieces and nephews, her closest friends, a language and culture and history that were in her blood.

"Do you want to go home for a visit, like we talked about a few days ago?" I ask. "I would go with you, Nonna."

"Eh. It's too late."

I turn off the water. "When you get better and stronger—"

"I can never go back," she says.

Her vehemence takes me aback. "Why?"

"Ah, Angela, there are . . ." Her voice trails off. "For me it wasn't always easy to be good. I was . . . Things happened."

I try to contain my surprise. At the sink, I wash the cutting board and set it in the drying rack. I pour a cup of coffee, add milk from the fridge. Then I watch for a few minutes as she plucks and rolls and drops. "What kinds of things, Nonna?" I ask finally.

She shakes her head no, but I can tell that she wants to talk. "Things I never told a soul," she says.

The hairs on my arms rise a little.

She scrapes the meat mixture out of the bowl, enough for one final meatball, forms and drops it on the wax paper. "You will tell nobody. *Nessuno.*"

I dry my hands on a dish towel and sit at the table. "Of course."

"Promise."

"I promise."

She carries the bowl to the sink and drops it in the soapy water, washes her hands and dries them on the damp striped dish towel, then turns to face me. "There was a priest who came to our village from Rome."

"I know," I say. "You cooked for him."

She nods. "I was helping my aunt. But my aunt was busy, working for other people. More and more she left me alone with him." Nonna turns and drapes the dish towel over the edge of the counter to dry. "Well, things happened," she says slowly, looking away. "I was sixteen. He was older. We developed a friendship. He was a gentle soul. Pious and devout. But with a sense of humor, too. And *intelligente.* I had never met anyone like him. He gave me books to read. Led me to make dishes from other regions that I had never heard of."

"The white Bolognese."

"Yes, the white Bolognese," she nods. "But most of all . . . he was the first person who ever saw me. Who thought I was special. It was—*eccitante.* You know?"

I dig in my mind for the word. "Thrilling."

"Thrilling," she says. "Yes, it was thrilling. I wanted to be with him, spend all my time with him. I dreamed that we might somehow have a future together. I suppose—I was in love with him. And then . . ." She pauses.

"And then . . ."

"I am pregnant." She looks at me, studying my face. "And my dreams crumble."

"Oh, Nonna," I say.

"The day I tell him, he says that he can never see me again. He tells me never to come back."

I reach for her hand.

"I understand. It is impossible. But I have never felt such pain," she says, clutching her chest. "I cry for a week. And then—*il signore e buono,*" the Lord is good, "I lose the baby."

For a moment both of us are silent. Then I ask, "Did you tell anyone? Your mother?"

"Never. *Ringraziato a dio.* Thank god," she whispers. "The shame would kill her. My family knew something was wrong, very wrong, with me, but they thought it was a mood, or a girlish dream."

As she speaks, I picture Nonna, for the first time, as a sixteen-year-old.

Rising, she opens the cabinet above the counter, and takes out the *olio,* half olive and half canola. She pours it unsteadily in a large skillet and turns on the blue flame. When the oil is hot, she drops in the meatballs, each a sizzle. Standing at the stove with the long-handled flat spatula, she rolls the balls over as they brown, talking with her back to me.

"I thought my life was over. And into my misery came a man with strong opinions. A kind man. *Il tuo nonno.* Your grandfather. I don't know what he saw in me. Well . . . his own mother had been sick when he was a boy, and he knew how to take care of a woman. When he told me of his wish to leave Matera, and asked me to marry him, I accepted. Nothing was left for me there."

As each meatball cooks, Nonna lifts it onto a plate covered with a paper towel. The window above the counter fogs with the heat.

"Did you . . . ," I venture. I'm not sure if I should ask, but I want to know. "Did you love him?"

She struggles with both hands to lift a large pot from below the counter to the sink, and I hurry to help. I set the pot in the sink, and she faces me. "I am being honest? Then I did not love him. But love had gotten me nowhere. I didn't want to be in love. I wanted to be—content."

"Did he ever know about any of this?"

"Angela, *la mia cara,* no one knows. No one but you."

"Why? Why have you never told anyone?"

"It was long ago. It had nothing to do with what came after. Telling would only have caused hurt. And, you see, there was no proof; what happened might as well have been my imagination. It existed only inside me, and maybe inside the man I loved. I don't know—I'll never know."

"But . . . you think of him."

"I think of him," she says. "I can't deny it. How old am I, eighty-eight years? And that man—*il mio dio,* a priest—was the love of my life. A cruel trick life can play, eh?"

"Well," I say striving for lightness, "I'm glad you came to America. I wouldn't be here if you hadn't."

"No," she says matter-of-factly, "you wouldn't. Nor would I. I would be in Italy, probably poor as dirt and worked to the bone. But you know, despite it all, I miss that life. My family. I miss the sun on my back in the market square." Nonna fills the pot with water and tosses in a handful of salt. She ignites the large burner and sets the water to boil. "I didn't follow my heart, Angela. I followed my head. And when it comes down to it, the longing in the heart lingers. Do you want to know the truth?"

I nod, though I'm not sure I do.

"I wish I had not left. I did what I thought would save me from heartache, but in many ways it kept me from living." She motions with her hand. "This stove here, this window. This is my world. It did not have to be, but I made it so. And now— *maledizione il Dio,* I regret it."

"You don't mean that, Nonna," I protest, but as I utter these words, they sound hollow and desultory. Of course she means it. She is weary and sick; she has had a stroke and might have died. I find it deeply unsettling that she should view the past sixty years with such regret, that for her entire adult life she has carried this secret of a man she loved who could not love her back, of a priest who took advantage of a young girl and changed the course of her life. But I also understand why Nonna laments what she left behind—her family and friends, the love affair that has lingered and expanded in memory, in secrecy, for all these years, the place that, to this day, she calls home.

CHAPTER 27

"Are you crazy? You can't drive to Maine on New Year's Eve!" my father says when I tell him my plans.

"It's not really New Year's *Eve*," I say. "I'll be home before dark."

"So it's home now?"

I smile and give him a hug. "Thanks for putting up with me."

"I have a choice?" he says, but I feel his arm tight around my shoulder.

In the morning, Sam refuses to budge from the front passenger seat of the Honda, fearful that I will leave him behind. He sat at my feet as I packed my duffel, followed me into the garage as I went through the boxes I had taped up nearly three months ago, and now sits anxiously as I fill the backseat with clothes and books, photo albums and candlesticks.

One last time, I return to the kitchen. As I pour a cup of coffee, Nonna disappears into another room, then emerges holding what looks like a very large pelt—the rabbit-fur coat my grandfather gave her those many years ago.

"I want you to have this," she says. "I have no use for it now. And the weather in Maine is very cold, is it not?"

I have never aspired to a fur coat. But I think of what this coat means to Nonna, how she wore it as a symbol of all she'd left behind. Inside the coat, the embroidered label sewn into the satin lining says: "Handmade in Italy."

Nonna holds up the coat with both hands, and I slip it on, one sleeve and then the other. Its bulky weight surprises me.

I grasp her hand. "Thank you."

"Prego," she says.

Pulling the coat around me, I feel protected, brave. "Nonna, I've been thinking. The other day you said something like . . . you feel that your world is no bigger than this kitchen."

She flaps her hand. "That was—a moment."

"I know. I know. But . . ." I don't know what I'm trying to say, only that I want to give something to Nonna, who has given so much to me. "You know how you tell me that I have 'the gift'? *Il regalo?*"

She nods.

"Nonna, you gave me that gift."

"No. You made your own path, *la mia cara.*"

"But—I'm finally beginning to figure out what I want to do with my life because of what you taught me. Did you know—did I tell you—that I plan to open a restaurant someday, in Maine?" I surprise myself as I hear the words come out. "I want to call it 'Matera.' And serve the food you showed me how to make."

"In Maine?" she echoes.

I have not been sure of this, was not even thinking seriously about it, but as I talk, my certainty grows. "In Maine."

"I may have to come."

"You will come."

She adjusts the coat on my shoulders. "I'm glad that I could teach you something. And that it matters to you," she says, stroking the coat like a pet. "Maybe we will someday go to Italy. If I live a little longer. You would like that?"

As I say good-bye I feel her cheek against mine, the rabbity quickness of her breath. For a moment she holds my face in her cool hands, and when I raise my hands to cover hers, she squeezes them and closes her eyes.

All the way up the East Coast, through New York and Connecticut and Massachusetts, I am caught in slow traffic. My father was right: Driving to Maine on New Year's Eve wasn't such a bright idea. Close to Worcester I hit rush hour near I-495, but by the time I get to New Hampshire, the traffic has thinned. Sam, secure in the knowledge that he has not been abandoned, sleeps on the passenger seat most of the way.

Crossing the now familiar green bridge that links New Hampshire to Maine, I feel not a cleaving but a joining, my disparate selves linking up. Three months ago, I was drawn to Maine by a fantasy, unconnected to real life. On this return journey, I am bringing my past along—my grandmother's blessing, a throw blanket of many colors, the rabbit-fur coat.

I wonder if Nonna and I will ever get to Italy. In some ways I feel that she has taken me there already—but even as this thought flits through my mind I am aware that it is sentimental, and not exactly true. I don't really feel that I've been to Italy, only that I finally understand what it meant for her to leave it behind.

Up ahead on the right, a green-and-white road sign proclaims WELCOME TO MAINE—THE WAY LIFE SHOULD BE. I missed it the first time I drove past. As I think about it now, it's a strange thing to say about a place. Is it a smug admonition to people who don't live in this state about what they're missing? A marketer's vision of a land of lobsters and blueberries that never has, and never will, exist? Regardless, the slogan is clearly aimed at tourists, since for people who live in this state, Maine is just the way life is.

I think of the tattered picture tacked to my long-ago bulletin board, the man of my fantasies on Blueberry Cove Lane, the mirage of a perfect life that brought me to Maine in the first place. Fairy tales end happily ever after because children crave certainty and resolution; they need to know how things turn out. But if my experiences in the past three months have shown me anything, it's that I am comfortable living with more questions than answers. My own story will always be a work in progress.

When I reach Mount Desert Island, it will still be winter. I will still be living in a shack. I will make muffins and soups for the shop, I may teach more cooking classes, and perhaps I will think seriously about that restaurant. Truthfully, I may not belong in that small harbor town. It is everything I am not: spare, spiritual, contemplative, quiet. But the island, within its boundaries, offers a kind of freedom that I have come to appreciate. I look forward to making fires in the woodstove and watching the embers burn, cooking and reading books and taking hikes, growing hardy rugosa roses in my backyard. Perhaps these things, after all, are enough, the ingredients of a life well lived.

Perhaps. And yet—I want to find out how I feel about this man who urges me to hurry back, who tells me that he wants to help make my dreams come true. Might he be my soul mate? I'm still not sure that such a thing exists. What I do know is that I don't want to end up feeling like Nonna, that my life has been a series of circumscribed choices, each cutting off other options; that my memories are tinged with regret. Nonna made one mistake that irrevocably altered her life; I have made dozens. But I live in a different time, and I can start over. I can be open to change, to chance—to the possibility of happiness.

I am far from the island, still, and the sky is dark. I need to stop for gas. Snow sits thickly on the black pine trees that line the road, which is covered in a light dusting, freshly plowed. It's starting to snow again, and driving is slow. But I'm not worried. Sooner or later I'll get there, and make a fire, and feed my dog, and take up right where I left off, in the blessed middle of nowhere.

RECISES

The following recipes comprise a selection of the soups, salads, appetizers, main courses, and desserts that appear in the pages of this book. The recipes are eclectic, ranging from Nonna's trove of favorites—from Basilicata, from her time with the Roman priest, and from the Italian American enclave of Nutley, New Jersey—to Angela's experience baking for the coffee shop and devising cooking-class menus. The dishes that already appear in recipe form in the novel (some quite loosely) are listed with page numbers.

If you have thoughts or questions or would like another recipe from this novel that I haven't included here, you can contact me through my website, www.christinabakerkline.com.

Fra Diavola Marinara, 197

Pasta with White Bolognese, 214

Fennel and Parmesan Salad with Lemon, 215

Marinated Beets and Goat Cheese, 204

Pasta e Fagioli

2 garlic cloves, minced

2 tablespoons extra-virgin olive oil

2 (14-ounce) cans stewed tomatoes with Italian seasoning, or a scoop of marinara

6 cups chicken broth

2½ cups cannellini beans, drained and rinsed

¾ to 1 pound tubatini pasta, depending on how thick you want the soup

3 tablespoons fresh basil, shredded

Freshly grated Parmesan cheese

Sauté the minced garlic in the olive oil until golden. Add the tomatoes with their liquid, breaking up with a fork. Add the chicken broth and simmer for 30 minutes or longer. Add the beans, pasta, 2 tablespoons basil, and Parmesan, and bring to a boil, stirring frequently. Cook until the pasta is al dente, or firm to the bite. Serve with grated Parmesan and basil on top. This soup is even better the next day!

Veal Meatballs

1 pound ground veal
¼ cup bread crumbs
1 egg, beaten
½ cup grated Parmesan cheese
1 tablespoon fresh parsley, minced
1 teaspoon salt
Freshly ground pepper

Combine all the ingredients and refrigerate for several hours, to combine the flavors. Then roll into 1-inch balls. Either fry in olive oil (not extra-virgin) or bake at 375° F for 15 minutes. Serve with marinara and pasta, or add to soup.

Chicken Marsala

4 skinless, boneless chicken breasts
¼ cup unbleached all-purpose flour, for coating
½ teaspoon salt
¼ teaspoon pepper
1 teaspoon dried oregano
2 tablespoons butter
4 tablespoons olive oil
4 garlic cloves, thinly sliced
2 cups sliced mushrooms
¾ cup Marsala wine
½ cup chicken broth
¼ cup heavy cream (optional)

Pound the chicken breasts until they are ¼ inch thick. Combine the flour, salt, pepper, and oregano in a shallow bowl or resealable bag. Coat the chicken pieces in the flour mixture.

In a large pan, melt the butter in the oil. Add the garlic and chicken pieces; lightly brown and turn over. Add the mushrooms, wine, and chicken broth. Cover the pan and simmer for 10 minutes, turning once. If a creamier sauce is desired, stir in the heavy cream.

Potato-Crusted Sole

2 white potatoes, peeled and grated
1 teaspoon lemon juice
2 eggs, beaten
1 tablespoon fresh parsley, minced
¼ cup grated Pecorino Romano cheese
Freshly ground pepper
1 cup flour
6 (6-ounce) sole filets
Salt
4 tablespoons sweet butter

Toss the grated potatoes in boiling water, and add the lemon juice (to avoid discoloration). Boil 3 minutes or until soft, then drain and set aside. Combine the eggs, parsley, cheese, and pepper in a shallow bowl. Place the flour in another bowl. Dredge each piece of sole in flour, then dunk in the egg mixture until coated, then coat in flour again. This will form a gluey paste over the sole. Pat the shredded, cooked potato over the sole. Add salt and pepper. Sauté the sole on high heat quickly in butter, turning once. Then finish in a very hot oven—450° F—for 5 minutes.

Simple Baked Ziti

16 ounces ricotta cheese

2 eggs, beaten

1 tablespoon fresh parsley, minced

½ cup grated Pecorino Romano cheese

1 pound ziti, cooked al dente

2 to 3 cups basil marinara (see recipe)

2 to 3 cups grated mozzarella cheese

Preheat the oven to 350° F. Grease a 9 x 13-inch baking dish.

Combine the ricotta, eggs, parsley, and Pecorino Romano. Add ziti and mix well. Fold in marinara. Pour half of ziti mixture into baking dish; sprinkle with mozzarella. Add rest of ziti. Bake for 30 minutes or until bubbly, then remove from oven and sprinkle remaining mozzarella on top. Return to oven until cheese is melted, 10 minutes or so.

Torta al Limone (Lemon Tart)

For the dough

1¼ cups unbleached all-purpose flour

¼ cup granulated sugar

⅛ teaspoon salt

½ cup sweet butter, chilled and cut into slices

1 egg yolk, beaten

2 to 3 tablespoons milk

For the filling

2 cups whole milk

⅔ cup fresh lemon juice

Zest of 1 lemon, minced

4 eggs

½ cup granulated sugar

To make the dough: Combine the flour, sugar, salt, and butter with your fingers or with an electric mixer until the mixture resembles coarse meal. Combine the egg yolk and milk; add to the flour mixture and shape into a ball of dough. Refrigerate for 1 hour. Meanwhile, preheat oven to 375° F and butter and flour an 8-inch pie pan. After an hour, roll out the dough on a lightly floured surface. Line the pie pan with the dough and cut off any excess. Prick the bottom with a fork and bake for 25 minutes or until lightly golden brown. Cool.

To make the filling: Combine the milk, lemon juice, and lemon zest in a pot and cook on medium heat until almost boiling. Meanwhile, whisk the eggs and sugar until creamy. Pour the warm milk slowly into the egg mixture, whisking the entire time, then pour the entire mixture back into the pot. Cook over medium heat until thick, whisking often. Spoon the filling into the pie crust and refrigerate. Serve chilled.

Oatmeal Chocolate-Chip Cookies

1 cup sweet butter

1 cup granulated sugar

1 cup brown sugar

2 eggs

1 teaspoon vanilla extract

2 cups unbleached all-purpose flour

1 teaspoon baking soda
½ teaspoon baking powder
½ teaspoon salt
2 cups oatmeal
1 cup chocolate chips

Preheat the oven to 350° F. Grease 2 cookie sheets.

Cream the butter and sugars until creamy. Add the eggs one at a time, beating well after each addition. Mix in the vanilla. Sift together the flour, baking soda, baking powder, and salt and add to the creamed mixture. Stir in the oatmeal until crumbly. Fold in the chocolate chips. Drop spoonfuls of the dough onto cookie sheets. Bake for 10 minutes, until the edges are firm and the centers are soft. Cool on a wire rack.

Nonna's Banana Bread

½ cup sweet butter
1 cup granulated sugar
2 eggs
1½ cups unbleached all-purpose flour
1 teaspoon baking soda
1 cup mashed bananas
½ cup sour cream
1 teaspoon vanilla
1 cup walnuts, chopped (optional)

Preheat the oven to 350° F. Grease a 9 x 5-inch loaf pan.

Beat the butter and sugar until creamy. Add the eggs one at a time, beating well after each addition. Sift together the flour and baking soda and add to the creamed mixture. Stir in the bananas, sour cream, and vanilla. Add the nuts, if desired. Bake for 1 hour or until a cake tester comes out clean. Cool on a wire rack.

Lemony Pound Cake

1½ cups sweet butter
2 cups granulated sugar
5 eggs
3 cups unbleached all-purpose flour
1 teaspoon baking powder
½ teaspoon salt
1 cup milk
1½ tablespoons lemon juice
¾ teaspoon vanilla

Preheat the oven to 300° F. Grease a Bundt pan with butter; sprinkle with flour to coat. Shake out excess.

Beat the butter and sugar until creamy. Add the eggs one at a time, beating well after each addition. Sift together the flour, baking powder, and salt and add to the creamed mixture, alternating with the milk. Add the lemon juice and vanilla. Bake for 1¼ hours or until a cake tester comes out clean. Cool on a wire rack.

Maine Blueberry Muffins

1 cup sweet butter
1 cup granulated sugar
1 cup milk
1 egg
2 cups unbleached all-purpose flour, plus 1 tablespoon for
  the blueberries
3 teaspoons baking powder
½ teaspoon salt
1 teaspoon cinnamon
½ teaspoon lemon zest
1 cup blueberries

Preheat the oven to 400° F. Line a muffin tin with paper liners.

Beat the butter and sugar until creamy. Add the milk and egg. Sift together the flour, baking powder, and salt and add to the creamed mixture, mixing until moist. Add the cinnamon and lemon zest. Toss blueberries with 1 tablespoon flour, and fold them into the batter. Bake for 20 minutes or until springy to touch.

ACKNOWLEDGMENTS

I want to thank Cynthia Baker, Anne Burt, Alice Elliott Dark, Judy Goldman, Meredith Maran, Pamela Redmond Satran, and John Veague, all of whom read parts of the book in process. My parents, Bill and Tina Baker, who live on Mount Desert Island, read each page and provided astute counsel. Thanks also to Catherine Baker, Clara Baker, Jerry Bauer, Patricia Chao, Liza Cohn, Maureen Connolly, Jillian DiGiacomo, Allison Gilbert, Reva Jaffe-Walter, Carole Kline, Benilde Little, Virginia Middlemiss, Frida Persson, and Karen Sacks. The Geraldine R. Dodge Foundation and the Virginia Center for the Creative Arts provided me with all that a woman writer needs—a room of my own and some grant money to go with it.

Kenny Mahon, chef and owner of the fine Italian-American restaurant American Bistro, in Nutley, New Jersey, allowed me to shadow him in the kitchen on a number of occasions, ask dozens of questions, and take notes as he worked his magic. The authentic Italian restaurant Osteria Giotto in Montclair also provided inspiration. My Italian-American muses and fellow writers, Louise DeSalvo and Laura Schenone, gave advice at every step. A number of books guided my research. In particular: *Lidia's Italian-American Kitchen*, by Lidia Matticchio Bastianich; *La Cucina di Lidia: Recipes and Memories from Italy's Adriatic Coast*, by Lidia Bastianich and Jay Jacobs; *Crazy in the Kitchen: Food, Feuds, and Forgiveness in an Italian American Family*, by Louise DeSalvo; *Hungering for America: Italian, Irish and Jewish Foodways in the Age of Migration*, by Hasia R. Diner; *In Nonna's Kitchen: Recipes and Traditions from Italy's Grandmothers*, by Carol Field; *Essentials of Classic Italian Dishes*, by Marcella Hazan; *Were You Always an Italian? Ancestors and Other Icons of Italian America*, by Maria Laurino; *Italy for the Gourmet Traveler*, by Fred Plotkin; and *A Thousand Years over a Hot Stove*, by Laura Schenone.

I wrote this book with my own grandmothers in mind, Ethel Baker and Christina Looper, both strong and opinionated women and, not incidentally, wonderful cooks. I was also inspired by my mother, a fabulous cook in her own right, who set me loose in the kitchen at an early age, tolerating my disasters and celebrating my occasional successes.

Many thanks to my brilliant and gracious editor, Katherine Nintzel, who read the manuscript more times than anyone should; my agent, Beth Vesel, who shepherded this book through several incarnations; my husband, David Kline, who—as always—provided support and encouragement of every kind; and, finally, my three boys, Hayden, Will, and Eli, who endured my occasional absences and more-than-occasional absentmindedness with good humor and grace.